I0729396

The Nova Quadrant

Brian W. Peterson

Dedication

To Dr. Michael Collins. Without his expertise, my brain would still be scrambled from my history of concussions.

I can never thank him enough for how much my life has improved after he fixed my broken brain.

Prologue

In a remote arm of the Milky Way galaxy, far removed from other sentient creatures, a cluster of star systems sustained more than two dozen planets teeming with life. Six-hundred light-years long, 200 light-years wide, and 200 light-years in depth, over the generations the oasis of life became identifiable by imaginary dividing lines based on location. Populations had grown on individual planets in each star system, with systems unifying to varying degrees until four distinct quadrants emerged.

These quadrants experienced internal and external strife, as would be expected with myriad differences between the inhabitants; they nurtured relationships, brokered treaties, and maintained alliances, as would be expected from civilized societies.

A simple numbering system identified the quadrants. Perhaps descriptive identifiers would have been created had each quadrant maintained its own unified system of government. Instead, the largest united entity resided in Quadrant One, with five star systems out of nine living under one authority.

A new kind of turmoil developed. Scientists discovered an alarming situation in a star beyond Quadrant Four called Kirkzen; collapse was inevitable—sooner rather than later. The rate of collapse pointed to a troubling end within five Heislerian years (400 days to a year) at the latest; perhaps within months, according to other scientists. The resulting explosion and flood of radiation was predicted to render Quadrant 4 uninhabitable.

With a touch of irony, the star did not support life, although two of its planets were mined for natural resources. Nevertheless, the star resided close enough to Quadrant Four to threaten all life in that quadrant.

With fourteen inhabited planets threatened, billions of intelligent, civilized creatures fled to the other quadrants. Others waited for the initial rush to end—at their own peril. Residents in the other three quadrants reacted as any sociologist would have predicted: some opened their arms, their homes, and their cities. Others did not wish to accept disparate cultures, preferring to keep them light-years away. Still others understood the devastating impact created by the emergency migration and fretted over potential political and economic instability.

The politics in the other three quadrants meant nothing to one group of Quadrant Four inhabitants: those who chose to remain. Some stayed out of a sense of duty—law enforcement and other infrastructural workers decided to maintain civilization for as long as possible. Others saw opportunities to get rich by claiming what was left behind by those who fled or pilfering natural resources. Still others simply followed nihilistic or suicidal yearnings and faced death.

A certain psychological profile emerged among the Remainers, as they were dubbed. Lawlessness, indifference, and nihilism ruled. Small outlaw fiefdoms appeared. Life held little value. Anarchy overwhelmed civility; death and destruction became the norm. Economic and technological advancements ceased. Bands of outlaws dominated individuals and cities, and they fought each other in hopes of gaining even more wealth.

In the midst of the chaos, one band of outlaws, known as the "UU Gang," began to reconsider their illicit actions and cynical view of life; but, to leave the quadrant would mean certain incarceration elsewhere. They would have to pay for their crimes—as prisoners in other quadrants, or with their lives in the section of the Milky Way which had become known as...

The Nova Quadrant

Chapter One

The first explosion rocked the deep, almost unending cave, shaking walls and floor alike. The opening salvo of the battle signaled the other bandits to leap into action as it also opened an alternate pathway for invasion and hurried escape. With their signature attack launch—explosives piercing ear drums, debris littering the air, and a cacophony of weapons of war thereafter—the UU Gang hurled themselves forward into the fight.

The diamond mine officials and their well-trained guards fought to repel the attack—militarized theft and other forms of lawlessness were ways of life since the day the Mass Exodus began. Despite preparations and outnumbering the attackers by a three-to-one ratio, the first wave of guards found little success against the militant plunderers.

Beyond the deserted cities and towns, far from the ruins of neighborhoods and businesses, Remainers inhabited small outposts throughout the planet Zhilo. Some encampments housed the guards and miners at the various diamond and silver mines while mobile camps helped bands of criminals to operate until the land was bare of its natural riches.

Even a short distance from Mine Number 41, the peaceful weather conditions and gorgeous sunset saw nothing of the terrible and bloody battle. The blueish red sky gave way to a lively orange as the yellow star Ma'eek slid below the horizon. Wild animals made their way from their caves, holes in the ground, trees, and shallow pools of water to emerge for the night's hunt.

As explosions ripped through the cavernous mine, sunset and wild animals held no value to the combatants.

"Kreeg! Over here!" the leader of the UU Gang called out in his own battle to be heard over the sounds of war. "Kreeg!"

Humanoids all, the gang cared little about the identities of their victims. While all intelligent creatures in the quadrants indeed were humanoid, retired Colonel Untas Ursulanus, known as "UU," would have led his bunch of bandits against any type of creature provided riches of some sort were on the other side.

A blue laser blast whistled by UU's ear. Rather than take cover, he announced to himself, "Drebehran Laser," referring to the type of weapon which would have decapitated him had the shot found its mark. The realization hit that he should avoid getting shot, so he made a belated move to avoid his foe's next laser blast. He turned to a cohort and commanded, "Whatever you do, don't fire that Rojani Hyper Grenade!" He paused to shake his head. "The ceilings in this place are lower than we were led to believe."

The bandit nodded to his boss, then turned to find another position several meters away as he repeated UU's announcement over his wrist communicator.

The gang did not sport consistent uniforms; rather, each dressed in his own battle attire. The former military officers in their group usually wore army pants, desired for the numerous pockets which helped each individual carry more ammo. For nighttime exploits, the group made a habit of wearing black or other dark colors.

"Colonel!" came a shout in UU's earpiece, known as a "dover." "We've lost Golb and he had the restraints!" The harried voice belonged to Anthun, an old military buddy of UU's, although his stock was falling in UU's eyes.

"Lost him?" UU needed additional information.

"Dead!" came Anthun's response.

"Relax, Anthun. Just kill the guards if you have to. If you capture them, tie them up and let's get this done." UU spoke into his wristband communicator.

"Yes, sir." Before he turned off his microphone, Anthun gave the order. "Kill the guards!" UU heard the pronouncement.

Irrespective of the noise and confusion, the words rang in UU's mind. "I said, 'if you have to,'" he muttered. The leader responsible for this operation understood if he allowed an Andalian to make decisions, everyone would be killed—including those within a five-kilometer radius, "just to protect secrecy" Anthun always said.

What felt like a temblor shook the cave. Debris cluttered the air and dimmed the effectiveness of their tactical lights. Three members of the gang felt their bodies launch into the air as life left them—dead when they hit the floor of the mine—as the concussion from the Rojani Hyper Grenade unleashed its power. UU climbed to his feet in time to see the Drebehran lasers go to work. Three guards opened fire with simultaneous three-round bursts. Before the stunned bandits could respond, two more of the group lay dead.

"Three guards! Three!" UU shouted as he opened fire, unsure whether the gangster to whom he shouted had survived the initial barrage. UU dropped one guard with his weapon of choice: his Zhiloan laser. The green and yellow blasts attracted the attention of the other two before UU felt the need to again take cover. Up again, another of UU's rounds struck true; only one guard remained. Shots from behind the guard lit up the cave as UU's troops returned to provide assistance. The now-exposed guard fell to crossfire from Anthun, several meters away. The counterattack by the three guards reached its end.

"Got him!" Anthun yelled, the pride in his battle-worthiness evident.

The radio burst with shouts and laser fire. It was Geeba, but UU could not understand her over the confusion of the ferocious firefight.

"Come again, Geeba!" UU shouted into his wrist, but to no avail.

In a small portion of the underground labyrinth, 50 meters away from the main action in a cavernous storage area, UU debated breaking from his own plan and joining that fight. He had assigned himself to the perimeter fights he knew would boil up. Before he could make his decision, he could see Geeba and Yane running at him, brown cloth bags in hand, followed by six more bandits also clutching large bags.

"Retreat!" UU shouted, although his force had shrunk by more than he realized.

The call to retreat signaled readiness to launch the next stage of the foray—the exit through some heretofore unknown conflagration, channeled by guards into specific directions to finish off the marauding band. Instead, they were greeted by silence. Only the sounds of members of the gang trailing behind, from the direction of the diamond storage area, filled the cave. The blackened walls provided an almost ghoulish feel—as though ghosts or demons would leap on them, out of the darkness, at any moment.

The silence led them to feel emboldened to speed up their departure.

"Wait!" UU tried not to shout as he barked the order. "We're going too fast. Do not get strung out." His attention was averted by a loud, pained groan in the back of the fleeing bandits' informal formation. With a motion of his head, UU signaled for Anthun to take the lead.

UU found Mookie half-dragging, half-carrying Rytkjmk, a smallish member of a tribe from the planet Heisler. Heisler, the jewel of Quadrant 4, prided itself for its adoration of all things aristocratic and lust for all things lavish. Rytkjmk never met such lofty expectations; now he faced the prospect of bleeding out in a dank diamond mine.

UU grabbed under Rytkjmk's free arm and lightened Mookie's load, allowing the three to move far faster than the two could have.

The colonel preferred to lead from the front, but on this particular mission, the bandits suspected the guards—like many guards at other mines on various planets—would employ a pincer move to trap the attackers during their retreat then annihilate them over the course of the evening. Instead, no such counterattack materialized, and the bandits did not have to deploy their own plans for another nihilistic life and death struggle which dominated the local planets.

Anthun and Kreeg leaped out into the night, lasers at the ready. Nothing. No defenses; no resistance of any kind. What had been the quiet surface of the planet found itself filled with the distant roar of fleeing aircraft. The mine employees, by no means professional fighters, refused to fight and disappeared with their ships into the night sky, the closest craft nearly a kilometer away as UU's gang reached fresh air. Within seconds, the fleeing ships were barely visible to the group.

The last to reach the surface was the trio of UU, Mookie, and Rytkjmk. UU and Mookie exchanged glances as they saw their friend approach, causing Mookie to call out, "Kimberlina!" The tall female with pinkish skin covered by light scales rushed out of the craft and took UU's position aiding their injured comrade.

"Is he gonna make it?" Mookie asked.

"I have no way of knowing," Kimberlina responded, her face displaying her skepticism.

UU stopped and took a mental inventory of the situation. That one troop carrier would have sufficed was readily apparent to the gang leader. He watched the first air vehicle speed away, low to the ground, then he climbed into the second troop carrier as a leader of a gang considerably smaller than when the night began.

Chapter Two

At their encampment on Zhilo, UU surveyed the number of his gang members who had survived the brutal battle. Both transport craft were products of the war materiel capital in the quadrants: the planet Rojan. Not a creature in the quadrants could build finer military equipment; the Rojanis possessed a penchant for outstanding military design and manufacturing brilliance.

In the darkness, outside the one large light set up for their post-raid meeting, sat 18 separate spacecraft belonging to all the members, living and dead. Once the loot was divided appropriately, they would go their separate ways for a time predetermined by UU. They would go to their favorite stashes—usually in a ruined city or nifty country hideaway—and await the next raid.

"I count twelve," UU barked to cover his pain. Under his leadership, he now led an organization just one quarter the size of its zenith. "Same as I counted when we left. I was hoping I missed some."

While some of the members considered in secret that a smaller group meant a greater percentage of the spoils, most knew fewer combatants meant smaller targets. They were not criminals for entertainment—they intended to gain as much for themselves as possible before the explosion of Kirkzen took everything, including their very lives if they failed to get out of the quadrant in time. The loss hit them hard; a group of twelve was smaller than they wished to be.

UU, a native of a city on the opposite side of the planet from which he found himself, stood with shoulders and head drooped toward his chest. The over-sized Zhiloan stood "two-meters-twenty" tall—two meters, twenty centimeters. His long arms and legs allowed for lengthy, thick muscles. With a large neck, large head, and hands which could crush an enemy's skull, his size, dark eyes, and light blue skin intimidated most creatures, including other blue-skinned Zhiloans.

Zhiloans came in several colors, but his light blue reflected a pure royal heritage, although royalty had faded from the society over ten generations prior. His thick torso and calves added to the aura of strength, which he indeed possessed.

Now, Colonel Ursulanus felt one meter tall. In the military, on several campaigns, he never lost more than a couple of members at a time. Today he had just lost one third of his gang from their number just five Heislerian hours prior. His melancholy demeanor and softened voice caused his team to take notice.

"Are you telling me we're a gang of twelve now?" UU asked to anyone within earshot.

An equally large creature by the name of Krokreeg Grust—"Kreeg" to his friends and cohorts—approached him with deference. The Eemlurian had only gotten to know his leader over the past Heislerian year and was considered fortunate to have been in the inner circle. The same height as UU, he was, as Yane frequently stated, "the largest Eemlurian I've ever seen."

"Colonel," Kreeg began. The softness in his voice conveyed he shared in the pain. "I could read off everyone we lost but it's not going to serve anyone." He paused to gauge whether UU was listening. "We need to divvy up the loot and get moving."

UU moved his large head with a slow, deliberate motion. He stared into Kreeg's bright green eyes and said nothing. He only nodded.

"Yane!" Kreeg shouted to his friend and fellow bandit. "I need your help dividing up the loot." The explosives expert wished only to tidy up the job and get off the planet.

Giryanix limped over to Kreeg. The native of the Quadrant 2 planet Mang, the warrior who went by the nickname of Yane had taken a piece of rock in his right leg— the result of a Ceratofs Rocket Grenade explosion near him early in the fight. At one-meter-sixty tall, he claimed the title as shortest member of the band. With hands and feet a bit larger proportionally compared to others, his race was known for their intelligence.

"You better get that looked at, Yane," Kreeg said in a mocking tone. "You don't need to be walking like an old Nonoan female at our next job."

Yane shook his head and snatched a bag of diamonds from Kreeg. "You are ever the caring one, Kreeg."

The Eemlurian let out a loud, annoying laugh, which Yane had come to appreciate for its sincerity. The laugh signaled Kreeg's enjoyment of the banter.

"Where's Blik and Geeba?!" UU snapped.

"They're over here, boss," Kreeg allowed the residue of his laugh to disappear. "They're fine."

UU's brief depression found a distraction when reacquainted with the severely injured warrior, Rytkjmk. Geeba, a tall, slender Corsan held up the injured creature who was equal to her size. Rytkjmk, native of Heisler, looked even smaller, his body hunched as he fought off pain.

The Corsan was a favorite of UU's. The soft-spoken female possessed the fire of an erupting volcano when annoyed. Sweet, reserved, and almost dainty, Geeba became nothing short of a monster when angered.

The male she assisted, Rytkjmk, with light brown skin and jet black hair, trickled red blood onto the ground wherever he limped. "Untas," Geeba began, the only member of the gang who addressed the colonel by his first name, "We've got to get him medical attention soon. Kimberlina's done all she can."

Still distracted by the situation, UU only nodded.

With anyone else, Geeba would have pushed back, hard. With UU, she knew he would come around in minutes.

Though speaking to someone else, Anthun's husky voice carried to the entire group. "The colonel's not going through another feeling of guilt for being an outlaw, is he?"

"Not now," Blik snapped. Both Andalians, they stood only two centimeters shorter than UU and Kreeg, and they had wide-bodied, muscular frames to match. They also possessed a wider mean streak than anyone in the group. Andalians were bulky, hairy beasts known for their lack of social graces. A crude, often vicious species which took pleasure in fighting and killing, Andalians cared more about the thrill of victory—and the thrill of killing to gain victory—than such meaningless pursuits as art, dignity, or approval from other races. Other species joked Andalians were the backward cousins one did not wish "decent" creatures to know about. In fact, the planet Andalian revolved around its sun Arre, the most distant star in Quadrant 4; they were indeed a remote, isolated species until light-speed travel had been achieved.

"I get tired of the second-guessing and belly-aching," Anthun sneered. "We're outlaws and we know it. And we can't turn back, anyway."

Enraged, UU raced toward the complainer. "Any more mockery from you and I'll ship you off this planet in a—"

Kreeg cut him short, stepping into his boss' path at just the right moment. "Easy, UU. Easy."

A dull growl flowed from UU's throat. His blue skin radiated a darker hue.

Anthun looked away, then at UU's feet. The latter understood the former's demeanor.

After taking a deep breath, UU calmed himself. "Okay, Anthun. You're in charge for 10 seconds." UU again breathed in to fully fill his lungs. "What would you do?"

"I'd quit talking about going straight," Anthun snapped.

UU shook his head. "That's not a plan, my friend. That's not a plan."

Kreeg felt confident enough to walk away. His mission was to help Yane divide the loot so they could leave.

The others pulled in closer. Under an artificial light set up by Kimberlina, standing in the middle of nowhere, the outlaws discussed their future. Off to the side, seated in the dirt, Yane and Kreeg attempted to make quick work of the spoils.

"Colonel," a medium-sized Rojani male known as Chabdab spoke up. "What we do and where we go is up to you. I'll follow."

UU nodded his appreciation.

"I'm with you, Colonel," Alana agreed, her black hair partially shielding her eyes. "But if I had to vote, I'd want to remain an outlaw."

"It looks like we females are unanimous," Geeba smiled as she spoke. "I'm with you, boss, and so is Kimberlina."

Blbbbimukx, or "Bill," as they called him because no one appreciated the native language of Ozkzokoj, had his own ideas. "I say we break out of the quadrant and set up business in Quadrant 3." Bill's lightly-populated home world, which seemed to suffer from a paucity of vowels in their native language, could be found in Quadrant 2. Misanthropic by nature, Bill's species was prone to engage in intellectual rather than physical pursuits. Quiet individuals, not prone to command or resist, Bill stood out as an exception. Though not vocal, he took pleasure in being, as he saw himself, a "rebel." Dark creatures with light spots dominating their bodies, Ozkzokojites were easy to spot.

"We'd never make it," Anthun protested. "They have the borders electronically locked down."

"We're not leaving now," UU admonished Bill before turning to Anthun. "But we will get out before Kirkzen goes supernova."

A silence fell over the group, disturbed only by the measuring of jewels and tallying the results as communicated from Yane to Kreeg.

"Look," UU began, missing the irony that he stared at the ground as he spoke. "We were the 'Band of 44,' and now look at us." He paused to survey the group as he walked around them, leaving his comrades inside an imaginary circle. "You know what happened to those who split off. They split again, then got themselves wiped out two and three at a time."

Again a pause to allow his words, past and future, to sink in. "They were smaller groups and hit smaller targets. But they maintained the same risk—every time we attack it's a huge risk."

Anthun frowned; he recognized how UU was about to appeal to his fellow outlaws.

"We're never going to attain power. Never." UU felt his energy level rise as he shifted into a philosophical mode. "All we have is our greed. That's it." He continued his slow circling of the group. "We cannot avoid the politics of the quadrants—we can't. So instead of worrying about an overlord who's been trying to control us and take a cut of our loot, let's clear our names and get out of here."

"It makes sense," Blik offered. His deep voice, which chose to remain silent in most instances, added weight to UU's case.

"If we become hired killers or enforcers," UU continued. "We'll have to deal with those same politics. We'll get sucked into regional and local scuffles—I don't want that."

"So, what do you propose?" Anthun asked, his skepticism evident.

"I've been thinking about that very question." UU's strong voice rose as his energy climbed to its normal, pre-depressed, level. "If we help authorities, we can regain our reputations and be allowed to escape this place."

"What makes you think that?" Bill inquired as he tried to not sound as though he were allied with Anthun.

"I've been talking to friends of mine in the military, in the other quadrants," UU answered. "They have discussed the matter in military circles. I think it's time we discuss this in civilian law enforcement circles."

UU's audience responded in a range from wide-eyed to mouths agape to nods of approval.

Kreeg walked the few meters to the group and nodded at the boss. The division of riches was complete.

"How many planets are we wanted on?" Kimberlina asked.

"All of them," Kreeg quipped.

When the laughter subsided, Kreeg pulled a hand-sized computer from a pocket. After a few seconds of scrolling and button pushing, he began the list. "Asimon, Corsar, Gigorl, Fank."

"All right, all right," Kimberlina laughed. "I get it."

"We just lost one-third of the group we started with today." UU's words drifted into the night as he contemplated the seriousness of the situation and thought of those they had lost. "All six had been with us since the 'Gang of 44' days." UU again paused. "Golb. Ranx." UU paused between each name. "Sheila. Roffl. Tibora. Sa'a."

An unplanned moment of silence settled over the group before UU continued. "Being wanted everywhere increases the odds we'll be caught and killed—and sooner than later."

"We really are wanted everywhere, aren't we?" Anthun asked, although his voice displayed amusement over concern.

"We are. Sanlandan," Kreeg picked up where he left off. "Ceratofs, Nanotomrayfeous, Heis—"

"What?!" Bill interrupted. "What do the Nonoans have on us?"

"We stole those 'personal foot crafts,' or whatever they were called, and sold them all on the black market," Kreeg answered.

"Oh! Yeah. I forgot about that," Bill nodded as his memory kicked in. "Those fat bastards. They couldn't even chase us themselves." The group laughed as Bill continued. "They had to hire thugs to chase us."

"That's the Nonoans for you," Geeba chipped in.

"Uh, Colonel!" Yane possessed an urgency in his voice which caught everyone's attention. "Company." He pointed straight up, toward the zenith of the night sky.

A single light divided into two, then four, then eight. Still silent from the ground, the attacking force possessed the element of surprise.

"Let's get out of here!" UU shouted. "Be at the Eemlurie base in three Heislerian days!"

Blik, Geeba, Kreeg and Yane grabbed the bags of diamonds and departed with all of the loot. The others gave no thought to what they were leaving behind—arrest and possible death awaited anyone foolish enough to worry about physical possessions.

Chapter Three

The capital city of Eese had been the jewel of the planet Zhilo. With over 25 million souls inhabiting the river city, great care had been taken to ensure beautiful parks, clean air and water, and low poverty levels. Other Zhiloan cities were not as fortunate, with the focus on the capital city preeminent in the minds of governance.

The coordinated air traffic—invisible highways determined by electronic parameters—had once run with a smooth alacrity, with every craft in sync with all others. Below, the din above served as background noise as their lives benefited from the work of the machines.

Now, the city sat unoccupied with little exception.

One oddity of the "known universe," as the quadrant residents referred to their star systems, was the lack of artificial intelligence. The technology had existed for generations, but laws limited its usage.

Militaries were allowed to employ artificial intelligence within well-defined limits. The only reason it had not been eliminated completely was due to the widespread fear of alien invasion. The quadrants were fertile for many types of species, and they imagined other such fertile sectors of the galaxy existed. Aliens with the technology to reach them surely possessed the technology to destroy them. Even though populations in the quadrants collectively understood military or civilian coups could gain access to artificial intelligence, the fear of invasion weighed heavily.

The militaries, all having departed from Quadrant 4, utilized drones and random robotic technologies. Functioning, speaking robots were banned throughout the quadrants, as were anything with more than one leg or wheel, with the idea being a two- or four-legged robot could arrest the movement or control the environment of sentient creatures if programmed to do so. With that in mind, "dumb bots," as they came to be known—electronic vehicles and equipment—were allowed and used in daily life.

After the military vacated the quadrant, little robotic technology remained.

The days of military security and civilized society were long gone. Within the brief time frame of discovering the imminent supernova to confirmation of pending disaster, citizens of the capital city managed to exit early. In most cities on the planet, as with other Quadrant 4 planets, thousands stayed behind for their own reasons. In Eese, the Remainers could be counted in the hundreds.

The few Remainers of Eese forced stragglers to become slaves—working to acquire loot and difficult-to-find items for their masters. Disobedience came with a price: immediate and merciless death. The planet which considered itself the bastion of civility, like the rest of the quadrant, had descended into wanton lawlessness.

From an urban paradise to a modern jungle dominated by unbathed, smelly opportunists—at least for a season, for soon death would catch up to them in a flash of light, heat, and neutrinos—the city evoked fear rather than glory. Beautiful parks gone, layers of filth coated every object, every surface.

With a knowledge of the city likely not in the possession of his pursuers, UU raced his Drebehran Personal Craft two meters above the ground. Capable of light speed for short distances, the colonel lacked sufficient fuel to get far; and, he understood his pursuers likely came from a mothership outside of the atmosphere. To fly into space now likely would lead to immediate destruction.

He felt a ray of hope for his group when he looked over first his left, then his right shoulders and saw his compatriots being pursued—they had the same idea as he did; maybe they would survive.

While the others dodged laser cannon fire from their pursuers, UU realized he was to be captured, not killed. On multiple occasions, his pursuers had clear shots at him but declined to fire. That fact told him the identity of those who hounded him.

Before finishing thoughts about his fate, UU made two quick turns above the city streets and dropped to a meter above the ground as the pavement whizzed underneath his craft. His electronic tracking device told him two craft monitored his route from above, at 500 meters, denying him the possibility of using the buildings as cover. Due to the lack of artificial light, UU could not turn off his lights for concealment—within seconds he would surely crash.

Recognizing his surroundings, he recalled the huge Eese Planetary Museum, a tremendous building which had housed voluminous pieces of artwork commemorating the millennia of Zhiloan growth and advancements. As a child, his family would take an annual journey to ensure UU and his siblings were dipped in enough culture to at least appreciate the value of art.

UU slowed his craft. The ground level pursuers had either broken off or simply laid back, able to regain contact with UU's ship thanks to the higher-altitude chasers.

He looked up to see, as he expected, the glass entryway did not survive the ensuing mayhem, post-evacuation. With his flashlight and Zhiloan laser in hand, UU leaped from his craft as it settled to a stop. The colonel did not doubt enemy presence and moved with zeal as he abandoned the craft and raced up stairs. The plan was to hide out—out-wait his pursuers. As long as he could find food, with the most likely candidates small native critters or the invasive Ceratofs rat, he could stay hidden for weeks. He could check his craft for tracking devices then rejoin his gang. That was the plan as he ran up a flight of wide, decorative stairs and reached the shattered museum entryway.

As he entered the expansive structure, two pursuing craft landed nearby, with occupants ready to chase down UU. He knew they would employ heat seeking devices to follow his heat signature, but he also knew the labyrinth of hallways and tunnels included enough concrete to help confound their electronic signals.

The absolute darkness should have unnerved him, but UU possessed neither time nor concern to notice. Past a room which formerly housed paintings considered valuable—from bucolic countryside settings to ancient nudes—the walls and display cases presently held nothing but air. What curators did not rescue found its way to the black market; although, the museums of Zhilo boasted a high success rate of absconding with most of the artwork to secure museums in the other quadrants.

As UU entered a room which used to hold sculptures, he tripped over an unseen chunk of what had been an ancient portrayal of a male embracing a female. The din of bust scraping across tile floor, followed by the crashing sound of it striking the wall, served as an audible beacon to his pursuers. At the first sight of stairs, he dashed downward, deeper into the belly of the spacious museum.

The colonel understood his predicament. By entering a building, he risked being trapped. On the other hand, he realized that he could not be burned out—the building occupied a full city block with a scarcity of flammable materials. He continued down a second set of stairs and to the Hall of the Ancients: a narrow maze which had held paintings depicting Zhiloan progress. These hallways served as the destination he sought. He was not aware of a heat seeking device which could operate when surrounded by one-meter-thick concrete walls.

After making several turns and zigzags down the winding, confusing hallways, UU paused to catch his breath; he had been on the run since the first cry of invaders and he needed to pause, lower his heart rate, and think. He noted the presence of a door-less entry in front of him. He clicked off his flashlight as he slid his back down a wall and landed on the floor in a state of exhaustion.

Each week, it seemed, brought greater challenges for his gang. Every day arrived with something new and dangerous on the horizon. If not law enforcement, then small-time outlaws. If not the small-timers, then it was the big-timers. If not them, then a property owner who returned to claim goods left behind without realizing that, like a carcass in the forest, every last morsel had been picked clean within the first few Heislerian months. Many of the "Returners," as the Remainers jokingly called them, did not live to escape the quadrant a second time.

Before focusing on the pursuers, thoughts darted from his boyhood visits to these very hallways to what he would do if allowed to live freely in another quadrant. His adrenaline dropped low enough to tempt slumber, although he fought the urge with a leap to his feet.

Just as he reached his feet, he heard a noise. The sound was too close for his liking. He took two steps, felt the walls, comfortable that he had reached the threshold of the mysterious entry, and clicked on his flashlight. In front of him lay another set of concrete stairs; he rushed down them.

Voices closed in on his location as he turned a corner and stopped, shock gripping his entire frame. In front of him on all sides except the stairway behind him, stood walls— thick, concrete, impenetrable walls. He dropped his head as he again turned off his flashlight and approached the far wall in defeat. Judging by the growing decibels of the voices, he was about to be captured.

As he reached the wall, he slapped it in anger. His disgust turned to shock and fear.

The slap of his hand against the concrete wall activated—maybe detonated—something. A brilliant white flash soaked his tired blue flesh. In half a second, he felt a sensation of being moved—not moving as though dragged or pushed, but almost carried, floating on a magic carpet—across an undefined space. He lacked a sensation of imbalance. He simply moved. Somehow.

The quick flash of light caused him to close his eyes involuntarily. When he opened them again, he did not hear anything, but he could see a small amount of light in front of him, as though in another room, up ahead. But there should be no "up ahead." He still faced in the direction of the wall, which had disappeared. He turned behind him to see a stone wall just a meter away.

He walked ahead, as though by instinct, even though he feared his pursuers would be waiting. He followed the faint light. Up a set of stairs wider than what he remembered descending, he reached a small dungeon with an ancient incandescent light hanging from the ceiling. This was not the path he had taken. This was not a part of the museum he recalled seeing. This was not possible, he reasoned.

A low, muffled sound of music reached him. He walked a short distance before seeing another set of stairs—this one with a greater amount of light at the top. With nighttime enveloping Eese and power not available anywhere on the planet except mining facilities, he lost his concern and proceeded; besides, he no longer heard the voices of pursuers.

At the top of the stairs, he peered into the well-lit room and saw a female of an unknown species, her back to him. He could discern neither species nor actions—she seemed to simply stand in place.

A male voice broadcast by way of a communications box resting on a table near the female. Multiple paintings graced easels and painting accessories littered a table. That he had found an artist's shop he did not doubt, but the artwork was not recognizable.

"Don't go anywhere," the voice from the box announced with vigor. "We'll be right back with another sixty-minute block of your favorite classic rock bands. You're listening to western Kansas' favorite rock, 96.9, K-F-I-X, Hays. K-F-I-X Rocks!"

Chapter Four

The female reached over to the box and moved a switch. The speaking ceased. She hummed a tune UU failed to recognize, then turned her attention to the small canvas in front of her. She reached for a paint brush but stopped with a sudden jerk when she heard an unfamiliar sound behind her. She turned to look and spotted the large blue monster. Her brief scream jolted UU as he took a step backward, toward the stairs.

To UU, the female looked unfamiliar—to a certain degree, she looked like a Heislerian or Rojani female, but she seemed soft, frail. The female was built similar to most others he had seen, yet her skin and hair lacked the harsh, thick qualities of creatures in his home world. Her bone structure appeared slight. He also noticed that, beyond her, a window allowed sunlight into the walkout basement. Somehow, beyond his understanding, he had left Zhilo.

The five-feet-seven, 30-year-old brunette, with mildly attractive features and brown hair not quite reaching her shoulders, reached behind her with both hands and clutched the edge of her work table. For the first few seconds, words eluded her. Her light-blue eyes flashed fear; her body trembled. After a deep breath, she steadied herself.

"I like cosplay, but I don't think you need to do it in my house."

"What kind of creature are you?" UU asked, baffled by her appearance.

"Are you headed to Planet Comicon? That's not until next weekend, you know."

"Is that where I am? Is this," he hesitated, looking at her with an intent stare. He took note her voice was a similar pitch to that of females in his world. "Is this the planet Comicon?"

Her sigh signaled annoyance; her demeanor displayed a higher level of comfort for her own safety. "You know, I have plenty of employees not far away. They'll protect me."

"Protect you from what?"

"Oh boy." She looked around for a moment   as though she could find answers in any of the many inanimate objects which surrounded her. She looked at the shelves of boxes which contained family photo albums and other memorabilia. She glanced at an exercise mat not far from her, complete with a small set of weights. "Are you from Colorado?"

"Where?"

"What do you want, mister?"

"Just tell me where I am."

"You're in my basement. On my farm. In Kansas."

"Is this the planet Comicon? I've never heard of it."

Another sigh preceded her response. "This is still the same planet you woke up on this morning: Earth."

"No, I woke up on Zhilo."

"*Shilo*? What, are you into Neil Diamond or something?"

UU's demeanor changed. Bewilderment gave way to anger and suspicion. "How did you know I was in the diamond mines? Are you with the authorities?" He pulled from his belt the Zhiloan laser he carried at all times.

"That looks pretty cool. Does it make noises when you pull the trigger? Those are the best."

UU glanced behind him, as though expecting someone to charge up the stairway toward him.

"You didn't bring your little friends with you, did you?!" The woman's demeanor changed to match the colonel's. "Because I'm about tired of this charade."

Bafflement returned to UU's face and brain. "So, is this Erf or Comicon?"

"Earth! Earth, dammit! Stop this game!" She paused to collect her emotions. "I mean, you have great makeup and I'm sure it took you all morning to get that blue painted on evenly, but I still don't know what you're doing in my basement! Tell me!"

Nothing and no one intimidated UU, but now a fear of upsetting an innocent being as frail as this, apparently not associated with outlaw gangs which ruled the quadrant, caused him to soften his tone. "Are we still in the museum?"

"Put your gun back in your belt." Julie's soft brown hair danced just shy of her shoulders as she gave the order.

UU looked at his hand then obeyed the command. Because he had never before laid eyes on an earthling, he had no way of knowing Julie appeared frumpy and geeky to her own kind. He also could not possess the knowledge of how determined she was when the situation called for unwavering toughness.

"I've got something to show you." She turned her back to him for just enough time to pull an object out of a drawer. UU could not see the twinkle in her faint blue eyes which now reflected her cunning and a heavy dose of fear. When she turned back around, .357 magnum in hand, he was gone. Fear gripped her as she ducked for cover. After all of three seconds in hiding, underneath her table, she spoke aloud, as though there were two of her. "What are you doing? You have a gun; he has a toy."

With self-confidence restored, she rose from her hideout and again saw the intruder, this time several paces closer. A calmness pervaded her thin frame as she pulled the hammer back with her thumb. She did not speak.

Before she could blink, a glow surrounded the colonel's entire body. The blue tint to the faint light which surrounded him served to make him more difficult to see.

"Lower your weapon. If you're not with the authorities or rival gangs, then I'm not here to hurt you."

"Who are you? *What* are you?!" She stressed "what" as her eyes widened with a slow realization that this man—this beast—might not be from Earth after all.

He closed three of the four steps of distance between them as he tried to ease the tension in the air, but the advance achieved the opposite effect. His "personal shields," as they were called, let out a low hum. "Your weapon is useless against my shields. I am not here to hurt you unless you wish to hurt me." Standing over seven-feet-two-inches, he towered above the short earthling.

"One more step, mister, and it's gonna take a shovel and a plastic bag to get you outta here!" Her eyes narrowed. She fought the effects of an increased heart rate.

He stepped forward again as he pleaded his case. "I'm from the planet Zhilo. I was—"

The deafening blast from the Ruger revolver crashed throughout the basement, amplified by the concrete walls and wood ceiling joists. As the explosion of the gunpowder assaulted her ear drums, she blinked hard, in shock, at what her eyes reported to her brain: the intruder was not only still standing, he did not flinch. She stumbled back two steps and leaned against a table.

"That's a loud weapon!" UU remarked, although his level of surprise failed to rise to that of his apparent adversary.

"You—you should be—you should be dead." Her voice barely reached above a whisper as her words struggled to travel past the end of her slightly-curled nose. "You should be dead," she repeated, nerves frayed. She considered whether the words had failed to create sound; the ringing in her ears muffled her auditory abilities. Mouth open, she stared at the bizarre-looking giant.

UU stepped forward. As he dissipated the force field which surrounded him, he grabbed the gun from her with a gentle motion, the faint blue light now gone. "I know you're scared. I understand. I'd be scared of me, too."

Gun in hand, UU examined the weapon as he provided commentary. "You shot a rock at me. What kind of weapon is this? It's loud and shoots rocks." He opened the cylinder and allowed the four remaining rounds to fall to the floor. He tossed the gun onto her work table, careful not to hit the half-completed painting of a meadow backed by a small forest.

The woman fell into her chair, staring past her unwelcome guest. "That should've blown a hole in you and come out the other side the size of a softball." The force of her words from just moments ago had faded into a weak stupor of nearly indiscernible babble. "I don't understand. What are you? Where are you from? How did you get here? Why are you here?"

He grabbed the seated woman by the shoulders. "Where am I? What planet is this?"

Instead of answering, she reached up and touched the skin on his forearm. Her eyes and head lifted upward, toward his face. When their eyes locked, hers grew to look like blue saucers. "It's true. It's really true."

That a sudden realization hit her was apparent to UU. "Are you recovered yet, female?" UU's tone was meant to be gentler than his words would have been to any earthling.

"The family lore is true!" She stood, forcing UU to take an involuntary step back, and looked upward, into UU's eyes again.

UU remained silent as he observed the change in her.

"You're back," she said with amazement dripping off her words.

"I've never been here before."

"No. No, I mean, aliens are back." When UU failed to respond, she continued. "There are family stories that aliens—or ghosts; it depends on who's telling the story—would occasionally come out of our basement. I remember when I was a little girl, me and my brothers would go down there, scared to death but wanting to see what was down there."

In a reflexive move, UU glanced behind him, toward the stairs, then back to his inadvertent host.

"My family has owned this house for over a hundred years," she explained. "But no one has ever refurbished the second or lower basements. They were afraid to." A deep incredulity covered every word she spoke, almost smothering them before they reached UU's ears. "Supposedly, my great-grandfather first encountered an alien," she continued, just above a whisper. "He told my grandfather they were like explorers, not warriors."

UU rotated his head in thought, considering her words. He squinted as though he could physically create in the basement what occupied his mind.

"When they appeared to my grandfather, they were friendly, but they said their world was collapsing." Her eyes drifted over UU's shoulder as she interlocked the mental puzzle pieces.

"The Shersheen," UU nodded. "The planet Shershin was responsible for the development of many civilizations throughout the galaxy. Of course, I don't know what galaxy I'm in right now."

The young woman snapped out of her trance for a moment before continuing, this time with greater vocal strength. "Over the years, the stories got altered by family members, and some people said it was ghosts and others said it was different kinds of spirits." She looked at him again. "People outside the family heard about it and it caused people to think the Pitts family was all crazy."

For the first time since his arrival, the intruder relaxed. He understood the trauma he had caused.

"I'm Julie Pitts," the young woman offered as she stuck out her hand.

"I'm Colonel Untas Ursulanus," he smiled as he grabbed her hand, familiar with the custom.

"Was your family named after Ursa Major?" Julie asked, referring to the constellation.

"No, all my family through the generations attained the rank of at least colonel."

She froze as she attempted to suppress a laugh. Instead, a smile overcame her beleaguered face. "How do you know English?"

"Who's that?"

"It's what you're speaking. English."

"No. Sorry. I'm speaking Shersheen."

She smiled again. "Okay," she said with a slow, curious cadence.

He pulled from his ear an electronic device which she recognized as a hearing aid. "If you weren't speaking Shersheen, my native language, I would hear your words through this translator. But I'm not." He placed the device back inside his ear. "I'm understanding you in both ears."

"Okay, but we call it English."

"That's a funny word. Engrish."

"English."

"English," UU repeated.

"What is Sheeshing?" Julie asked.

"Shersheen. They were ancient creatures who spread their knowledge throughout the galaxy."

"What galaxy are you from?"

"Crik. I assume we're still in the Crik galaxy here. I've never heard of anyone leaving the galaxy and living to tell the tale."

"'Living to tell the tale.' That's something we say on Earth."

A thought penetrated UU's mind and his facial expression telegraphed its arrival. "Do you have pyramids on this planet?"

"You mean like, ancient pyramids?"

"Well, they're ancient for us. I don't know about you."

"Yes. We do," Julie smiled, her heart rate now nearing normal. "They were built thousands of years ago by the Egyptians. And we have some built by the Mayans."

"Are those creatures from your planet or other planets?"

"My planet. Although some have always said they had help from aliens."

"They did," UU nodded with confidence. "Since you're speaking the same language as me, I know the Shersheen were here at some point. Their technology surpassed everyone else's."

Without warning, Julie grabbed the large alien by the hand and pulled him across the basement to a couch; she sat on a nearby chair. Both items of furniture were covered with cloth upholstery. She did not bother to turn on the 42-inch television. From her seated perch, she motioned with her hand for him to sit, which he obliged.

Before they could continue their conversation, a thought struck Julie; she leaped from her chair, held out a finger, and said, "Hold on. I'll be right back," then ran to her work area and grabbed her laptop.

UU pulled his computer out of a pocket in his pants leg. He looked at the screen to see everything was blank: no readouts of any kind, including date or time.

She returned with laptop in hand as she sat in her chair. "I wanna know where you're from. Give me a minute." She accessed the internet as she asked for more information about him. "Tell me how you got here. No one's ever known why aliens come out of our basement. Of course, most people don't believe it's true."

UU looked toward the stairs, then back to Julie. "I was being chased by thugs from a rival gang. They were trying to capture me."

"Why?" Julie sounded alarmed.

"Because my gang is independent of them. They want all the outlaws working for them."

"Why are you an outlaw? Do you kill people?"

"People? You keep using that word. What does that mean?"

"Other creatures."

"Yes."

Julie looked up from her computer screen. "Yes what?"

"Yes, I kill other creatures."

She put her head down but kept her eyes up, watching UU. She paused long enough to consider her words before releasing them. "Why do you kill other creatures?"

"They deserve it." He read her face before asking, "Is that bad to you?"

"Well, yeah. On Earth, it's wrong to kill people except in war or self-defense."

"Oh. I see. Well, in the quadrants it's wrong there, too. Except in my quadrant there is no law and some deserve to die. So, I kill them." He added as an afterthought, "Only when I have to, of course."

"I'd be more comfortable if you weren't a criminal."

With a slow, deliberate movement, the colonel lowered his head. Thoughts rolled through his mind of his deceased wife and son; his stellar military record; his friends in law enforcement; his time in Quadrant 2 putting down a rebellion because, in part, the anarchic rebels destroyed and looted everything in sight, necessitating the military's lethal force. The Quadrant 3 Wars. His family life, which no longer existed. His military record had been wiped out in the minds of the military and civilian public. His friends still liked him but could not trust him. In some ways, he was only a mirage of himself.

She continued to eye him with concern. Movement on her screen caught her eye and she changed the subject. "Oh!"

she exclaimed as she looked at the monitor. "Here." She jumped from her chair and plopped next to him on the couch, then thrust the laptop his way. "Here's an interactive representation of the galaxy—at least what we believe it looks like." She then asked in an exuberant tone, "Show me where you live."

Once he saw how she manipulated the cursor on the screen, he moved the 3D display of the galaxy multiple times before announcing, "I don't think I can find it. This is just a mass of stars." He looked at her with a quizzical expression. "Have you Earthers been all around the galaxy?"

"No," she said, almost embarrassed at her people's limitations. "This is just a representation."

"I see. So, it's a mass of stars for the purpose of displaying the shape of your galaxy."

"I guess," she responded, unsure of the accuracy of his words.

She grabbed the laptop from him and returned to her chair. "Tell me about where you live."

UU spent the next fifteen minutes telling her about the four quadrants, the collapsing star Kirkzen, and the resulting chaos. He went into great detail about red-giant stars. A star in that stage often faced the destiny of supernova when it collapsed. In the case of Kirkzen, the next stage would see it become a neutron star, according to quadrant scientists. For generations, underground mining had occurred in the far-off system, which lay 20 light-years beyond the imaginary boundary of Quadrant 4, with such mining now dormant due to the impending doom.

Julie also learned only the planet Andalian would suffer physical damage from the supernova, although the entire quadrant would be devoid of life due to intense radiation which would flood the area. Parts of Quadrant 3 had been evacuated due to expected long-term effects of the harmful radiation.

That education was followed by her spending twenty minutes informing him of life on Earth and why he could not be seen by earthlings. At one point, she considered the fun she could have if she took him to the upcoming comicon in Kansas City, 270 miles to the east. She considered all that could go wrong—after all, forty-five minutes prior, he had assumed he was *on* Planet Comicon. She thought better of the idea and decided to convince him to not leave her house.

As she neared completion of her explanation of life on Earth, he interrupted to ask an important question. "I have a wounded member of my team. Could I bring him here?"

"What would I do with him?" she asked, stunned by his request.

"He's wounded—shot in the leg by a laser. He would be safe here."

"Well, I don't have experience treating laser burns, but I do have a little homegrown nursing experience." A concern rose to the fore. "Does he look like you?"

"No. He looks closer to your species: pale skin; small facial features." He thought for a moment before continuing. "I have to warn you, though. He's Heislerian, and those brutes tend to be stubborn and arrogant—kind of a bad combination."

"And he's hurt?"

"Yes. I do believe he could blend in better than me—unless you have blue creatures here."

Julie laughed as she answered. "No. No one with blue skin here."

"Oh," UU answered, a bit deflated, as though he felt a sudden loneliness.

"Bring him here and I'll see what I can do."

"Okay. I just have to wait a while. I'm not sure the evil gangsters looking for me are gone yet. I don't know how time was altered by me coming here. I don't know whether it's moving at the same pace here."

"It wasn't law enforcement looking for you?" Julie asked with surprise. She knew what he had said earlier, but she wanted to test him.

"No. There's a crime boss trying to take over the entire quadrant."

"You're serious like a military guy. It's who you are, isn't it?"

The question took him by surprise and he was unsure how to respond. He had successfully walled off his feelings about leading an honest life, but multiple times in the conversation with the earthling, he found himself questioning who and what he was.

As the minutes and conversation passed, UU decided the time for his departure was at hand. The unlikely and disparate pair again shook hands, then the colonel disappeared down the stairs, into the Pitts family's second basement on his way to the room which lay deeper still. The brief interlude of peace and relaxation had reached its end for UU.

Chapter Five

Eemlurie was one of six planets which orbited the star Lucan, but the only one capable of sustaining life. The blue planet, dominated by its oceans, possessed rich soil in most areas except the polar regions and had been a major food source and provided extravagant fruit throughout all four quadrants. Lucan was out of the way compared to the layout of other star systems, 90 degrees from a tight grouping of Quadrant 4 stars, yet it was less than a light-year from Zhilo—a mere stone's throw for modern spacecraft.

Because farmland did not provide shelter for fugitives, post-Great-Exodus authorities rarely visited the planet. Farming had ceased; after the final harvest after the announcement of the supernova, crops were not replanted. Volunteers populated much of the planet, living among a mixture of Eemlurian fruit trees which dotted the surface. Food sources which had to be planted every year died off quickly, all but disappearing forever.

The planet's forests were small, cleared away thousands of generations ago to take advantage of the rich black soil. Without sentient beings intervening, signs littered the land that forests would expand. Not enough time had passed to confirm the suspicions, but in all likelihood, the forests would return, but over the course of decades—time which the forests would not be granted.

The UU Gang had spent considerable time between early raids setting up a force field and providing itself with a food source—at least a supplement; meat had not been a forte of the planet—for their favorite hideout yet.

The electronic force field deflected attempts from space to scan the surface and identify life forms. Readouts showed what appeared to be more farmland. A visual aerial inspection provided the same result. Even if followed to the planet, if a pursuer failed to witness the point of landing, it was improbable the bandits could be found.

After the disastrous raid near the Zhiloan diamond mine, which culminated in the gang dispersing throughout the quadrant as they fled for their lives, the mood of the gang bordered on depression.

"You what?!" Blik's tone revealed his amazement.

"Yeah," Mookie nodded as he explained. "Everyone took off along the surface, so I decided to leave the planet."

"That was risky!" Blik's response did not wane in intensity. "You're crazier than I realized!"

"He is Andalian," Kimberlina laughed.

"How did you not get blown out of the sky?" Blik asked.

"As soon as I cleared the atmosphere, I went to light speed." Mookie looked around at the others as though gauging reactions. Small for his species—he stood two meters tall—and mild-mannered in relative terms, he saw the facial expressions of his friends which reflected their surprise at his bravery—or stupidity.

"That's the craziest thing I've heard all day," Kimberlina shook her head.

"Didn't you just figure a mothership was waiting up there?" Blik did not seem willing to allow the subject to die.

"Yeah, but I programmed my ship as I was in the atmosphere," Mookie answered.

"Then you're a better pilot than I am," Blik chuckled. "You have one of those old Model 12's. That's some fast programming."

Through all of the recent adversity the UU Gang had endured, Anthun had not lost his title as the most cynical of the group. Reactions from various members of the gang grew increasingly hostile as their patience frayed.

"Well, we're going to have to figure out how we're going to move forward," Anthun said for the third time in the last ten Heislerian minutes. "We can't sit here forever. We know everyone in the quadrant is looking for us. If he were alive, he would have been here by now."

Kreeg was the first to act. "Hey, Anthun. Come with me, please. I want to show you this new explosive compound I'm working on."

"Why me?" Anthunulu Rok, the stereotypical Andalian in appearance and attitude, looked bewildered.

"Because if the compound becomes unstable, you should be the first to know."

Smirks and fights to suppress laughter dominated the group of eleven outlaws.

"That doesn't sound good," the cranky warrior responded with all seriousness.

"You're from Andalian, correct?" Kreeg asked.

"Yes."

"Well, everyone knows Andalians are annoying when they're unhappy." Kreeg flashed a cold smile of steel toward Anthun.

Anthun's expression reflected the unhappy look to which the team had become accustomed.

"Anthun, I promise. I will do my best to not blow you up. So, come on."

Anthun laughed—at long last, he understood the sharp edge of the joke. "No thank you."

"Anthun, I'm serious. Come with me."

"Why?"

"Because the entire group is going to kill you if they hear your voice any longer."

Smiles broke out among everyone, no matter how hard they tried to hide their amusement.

Anthun climbed to his feet with a reluctant groan. As he did so, a craft approached at high speed before making a sudden stop. Everyone scattered in order to find cover as they prepared to fire.

The Drebehran Personal Craft touched down with a soft thud next to other personal craft owned by the group's members. Everyone recognized the ship which belonged to their leader.

As he exited the craft knowing his team stood ready to annihilate him if he were an intruder, UU shouted, "Sorry I'm late. I didn't know the time or date until I got back in my craft."

No one on the team understood his comment, but all came out of tactical hiding to greet him.

•   •   •

"I've been thinking about a lot of things," UU explained as he looked at his group. The eleven sat on the ground before their leader around the fire made from wood Blik and Chabdab had gathered from a small clump of trees nearby.

The others waited with anticipation, except Anthun, who felt convinced his outlaw days were about to end.

"I've rethought everything, from where we park our craft when encamped, like now, to how we are going to get out of this quadrant alive." UU paused to look at the faces of everyone on his team. "After I got back to my craft, I hid out for a while, waiting to ensure no one was watching," he lied. "But when I was hiding out in Eese, I took plenty of time to think."

Usually enraptured by whatever he said, Geeba instead interrupted him. "Once out of the quadrant, are we going to remain together?"

46

UU shook his head. "I doubt it." He stood, which everyone understood to mean he was now going to perform his customary ritual of walking around the group in an imaginary circle as he spoke.

Geeba fell silent. The unspoken bond between her and UU was one of great affection. To the gang, Geeba was an excellent weapons expert—Kreeg's back-up—who possessed a sharp military mind. To UU, she was the lithe, graceful, beautiful Corsan with a perfect female figure in the eyes of any male in the quadrants. Her sweet demeanor when not speaking of military matters would have led UU to pursue her romantically if not for the circumstances. To UU, the time for considering companionship would come after they escaped the quadrant with their riches. To Geeba, to pass on an opportunity could prove foolish.

For a brief moment, a careful observer would have believed UU and Geeba were communicating through thoughts. He paused his walk around his fellow warriors and looked into Geeba's bright blue eyes. She returned the gaze and their locked eyes prohibited their throats from functioning—words ceased; he of the suppressed feelings and she of the mournful hope which would not die.

After a very long eight seconds, he ripped his eyes away from hers and continued his walk and speech. "I've found a place where we can take Rytkjmk and get him healed up." UU looked at his soldier and nodded.

"I went to a hospital on Heisler," Rytkjmk volunteered.

"That was a risky move," UU admonished.

"It was me," Kimberlina jumped in. "It was gruesome. At best, he was going to lose his leg. I had to risk it."

"I have a doctor friend back home. A surgeon," Rytkjmk added. "He fixed it all up in the hospital. He didn't let it be known how I was injured. He said it will be six months before I can walk normal." Everyone was in the habit of adding "Heislerian" to their time measurements; the planet's 400-day year, 10-month calendar, and 30-hour day served the basis for consistency throughout the quadrants. Only on each planet, with the lengths of days and years varying according to their planet's rotations and revolutions, were their own time frames used. To the others, hearing someone from Heisler not use the adjective "Heislerian" before making a time pronouncement amused them. "There was little chance of being turned in," Rytkjmk added.

UU nodded. "As a few of you know, I've been in frequent contact with current and ex-military friends of mine."

Anthun dropped his head. He knew what this meant.

"We believe our group has the ability to become successful bounty hunters by using our knowledge of Quadrant Four's underbelly." He paused for effect. "I've thought this through. If we become snipers or enforcers, we wind up beholden to local and regional politics. I know you all—none of you want that." Everyone remembered his similar admonitions on Zhilo.

UU ceased his pacing. "I've found an ideal place for a home base. We can keep using this one, too; but, we have to keep changing things or we'll get sloppy and get caught."

The colonel returned to a slow, deliberate walk, again making a circle around the group. "As bounty hunters, we'll work with law enforcement and help clean up the quadrant somewhat. Then, when we decide to go, some of the brass in the United Military will vouch for me, meaning they'll be vouching for you at the same time because I'll vouch for you."

"Colonel," Mookie spoke up. Andalians had the well-deserved reputation of being vile and vicious, but Mookie only attained the level of "mean." Much more refined and considerably more level-headed than most Andalians, he came across as calm and mild, particularly when juxtaposed with Anthun or Blik. "This all assumes we have time to reverse our reputations."

"I understand," UU reassured. "Even if we restore our names to some degree, if we have only a few good deeds to fall back on, then we'll still be able to use that to our advantage."

Mookie nodded. UU took it as agreement rather than contemplation.

"We also have to remember," UU continued. "The Premier." He paused for effect. "The Premier's outlaws could have killed me when they surprised us after the diamond raid on Zhilo, but they didn't. That means they want me alive."

"They were definitely trying to kill me," Anthun spoke up.

UU tried to determine whether Anthun's comment was favorable or not. "The whole idea is to capture me so they can use me. In fact, I'm sure they don't mind if we keep the gang together, but they want a large portion of our bounties."

"Forget that!" Kimberlina shouted. Others joined her in expressing their revulsion.

"I will never join the Premier," UU said, with emphasis provided by gesticulating arms releasing the sudden surge of adrenaline. "Here's my immediate plan." UU found an open spot on the ground and joined the group in front of the fire. "I'm going to take Rytkjmk to a new place where he can get some assistance. It's not medical, but it sounds like he has therapy to go through."

Rytkjmk appeared happy at the news.

"Kreeg, Yane, and Alana will meet with law enforcement in Ersch, at the main headquarters they've established there." UU then looked at Geeba. "Geeba, you're in charge of taking the rest of the group to Gunig to obtain more ammunition—and weapons, of course. Whatever you think we need. You can work with Blik on that before you go." Ersch, the capital of Drebehr, and Gunig, the epicenter of Drebehran weapons manufacturing, lay on opposite sides of the planet from each other.

"Colonel," Kreeg interjected, though with all deference he could muster. "Is there any reason why I'm not involved with the procurement of weapons?"

"You, Yane, and Alana are excellent negotiators. I want you dealing with the Board of Ten." UU paused as he glanced at Geeba. "She can handle the procurement."

"I was a lawyer before the chaos," Alana added, indirectly helping to explain why UU chose her for negotiations. She was well known on her home planet of Sanlandan, regarded highly in her profession. Aliana Andifius, better known by her nickname, belonged to an easily identifiable species. Their thick black hair, common in the quadrants, provided a sharp contrast with their skin: alternating streaks of orange and white adorning their bodies.

UU looked at Rytkjmk. "I'll take the crippled one with me, then we'll all meet up here in three Heislerian days."

UU stood as he finished speaking. "Kreeg, Alana, and Yane," he said. "I'll talk with you in a few minutes. I need to talk to Anthun first about our next hideout. Everyone," he raised his voice over the chatter which had erupted as they all stood. "We'll leave in the morning."

Anthun and UU walked toward the parked space vehicles as they spoke.

"Whatever he's telling him must be important," Kimberlina observed to Geeba. "He's not yelling at him."

"Untas still believes in him," Geeba answered. "I don't know why, but he does."

•   •   •

As the star Lucan climbed above the horizon, most of the group finished their preparations for their two-pronged excursion. UU had briefed both teams separately about parameters of the discussions with law enforcement and where to transport newly purchased weapons. All their craft were parked in a circle around the encampment, noses pointing outward—the idea being that if they had to leave in a hurry, the chances of crashing into each other were diminished, and the odds of finding the desired craft in a brief amount of time increased.

A few craft remained behind as they all headed out. For Rytkjmk, he lacked any idea of what would come next.

Chapter Six

"You again," Julie said with a smile as she walked into her house. UU and Rytkjmk stood in the entranceway to the kitchen, at the edge of her living room.

"I'm sorry," UU offered. "I felt like I was trespassing, but I need to see you."

"It's okay," she answered as she eyed Rytkjmk. She noted his deep set, black eyes and rough features which made him look like someone she did not want to meet at a gas station late at night. "Just know that I run a business, and I'm out of the house a lot." She paused to emphasize her next point. "And, it's best nobody else sees you." She motioned for the pair to sit on her couch, which caused UU to become aware of the lack of an introduction.

"Julie, this is Rytkjmk."

Just as she prepared to sit in a chair, she straightened up, took two steps forward, and reached out a hand to her new acquaintance. "Rick-ma-jik?"

"Rytkjmk," the new acquaintance corrected.

"Rick," she said as she nodded her head with authority. "Nice to meet you, Rick." She noted his sharp, almost pointed nose.

"I'm sorry," UU explained. "But we don't know how long it was since I was here last. We don't know how to judge time between our world and yours."

"You were here yesterday morning," she said as she sat in her chair, then motioned for her visitors to sit on the couch. "Which is why I was painting—it was the weekend. Today I'm working. I oversee the family wheat farm as well as the cattle farm."

"Cattle?" UU and "Rick" sat next to each other.

"Cows—a farm animal raised for eating and giving milk."

"So, you're a farmer then?" UU asked.

"I don't actually farm—we have a small company of employees who do everything. I oversee everything."

UU nodded his understanding. "Can I leave Rytkjmk here with you?"

Julie smiled as though the fact just hit her that her guests were aliens from another world. Julie looked over the Heislerian. He was humanoid, but his rough features and thick black hair looked out of place. Though unsure about his red headband, she decided, if dressed properly, he could pass as an ugly human.

"I think all he needs is to let his leg heal and get his strength back," UU continued.

"Well," Julie drew out the word as numerous thoughts crashed into each other inside her shell-shocked mind. "I, uh." She closed her mouth at the realization she was starting to stammer. "Yeah, I guess. But there has to be ground rules."

UU's facial expression emphasized his concern. "Such as?"

"Such as he's going to have to stay in the house a lot—unless he's with me, anyway."

"He can do that," UU nodded.

"I can?" Rick clearly did not like the thought of house arrest.

"You will." UU's tone conveyed an order.

Rick looked at his new host. "I will."

Julie let out a relieved smile, even though all three understood she still harbored doubts. "I broke my ankle several years ago," Julie told the pair. "I remember what I had to do for physical therapy. I'll get him back to normal—assuming everything's healing right."

"The doctor fixed everything," Rick responded.

"Great!" UU rose from the couch. "I have to get back to my world. We're bounty hunters now." He looked at Julie with a triumphant expression.

Julie smiled. "That's good to hear. But no clothes? No toiletries?"

Rick looked at UU for an explanation. The colonel gave his blank stare to Rick, then Julie.

"Never mind." She saw the confusion. "I'll take care of it."

"We know what clothes are," UU offered. "But don't you have your own toilet?"

"Never mind," she repeated. "I'll take care of him."

UU reached out for Julie's hand. "Thank you."

Julie flashed another smile as she shook his hand, then looked at Rick. "Well, Rick. It looks like I have to tell people you're my boyfriend."

Bewildered, Rick looked at UU, who was about to depart the room.

"Just trust her, whatever she says. I'll be back for you. We're going to need you. It's vital you get well soon."

"Yes, sir."

"Goodbye, Colonel," Julie called out as UU disappeared. She stood and looked down at the seated Rick. "We've got a lot to go over if you're going to stay on Earth," Julie said to her new guest. "Including, stop eating my potpourri."

Rick quickly put the remainder of the decorative pieces back into the bowl on the coffee table, then responded in a defensive tone. "It tastes good."

•　　•　　•

The meeting had reached a Drebehran hour in length, which was five minutes shy of a Heislerian hour, and at long last the threesome of Kreeg, Yane, and Alana felt they were making progress. The first fifteen minutes had turned into a comedy of explanations about UU's whereabouts, even though the answers had remained the same: "We don't know; he sent us here; and we're representing our entire gang." What appeared to be an exercise in futility at long last made headway when the negotiators changed tacks.

Abuss Onuss, the head of Quadrant 4 civilian law enforcement, convinced the two Zhiloans in the room to forget about UU's recent past. Their offer could mean an earlier exit from the quadrant for all law enforcement, allowing mass chaos to reign only in the final hours of these final days of life in this sector. Bingus Jam, the Zhiloan least likely to forgive UU for transgressions—real and imagined—agreed to listen to the threesome of thievery, but his hatred of UU failed to abate. Pracen, also from Zhilo, proved more moderate than either Bingus Jam or Abuss Onuss had expected.

The three leaders represented 30% of the Board of Ten, as the law enforcement council was known, and their power had been substantial when the term "Law and Order" held meaning. Bingus Jam and Pracen, both blue-skinned Zhiloans, resented that UU did not act in the same becoming manner as they did. Like them, UU descended from royalty and, in their minds, he should act like he was from a "higher cut of creature," as the Zhiloan phrase conveyed the haughty outlook. It was enough reason to mistrust the well-known and formerly-greatly-respected colonel.

"I like what you're doing," Abuss Onuss boomed, his voice in stark contrast to his small frame. His typical, larger-than-normal forehead gave him the appearance of a scientific experiment gone wrong. The bulge in a Drebehran forehead added only three centimeters to the diameter of the head, but it was enough to catch the eye of anyone unfamiliar with the species. His narrow eyes, a common trait among Drebehrans, gave him the look of an intense warrior, despite his natural tendencies. "We appreciate the magnanimous gesture—we really do—but you can understand our concerns."

Kreeg spoke up first. "You're focused—at least your two counterparts are focused," Kreeg swept his eyes at the other two officials seated across from him. "On Colonel Ursulanus." He paused for effect. "That's the wrong way to look at it. You should be focused on how much good we can do; how many outlaws we can bring you."

"I have a hard time believing UU will bring in anyone alive," Bingus Jam, the drollest of the two Zhiloans, commented. He laughed before proceeding. "Are you following my tone?"

"But Bingus Jam," Yane interjected, his smile broad. "You always laugh, and you're always skeptical. I recognize your tone." He stared with a rapt fascination at the grossly overweight beast who never failed to express his thoughts. "But this has been well-considered. This hasn't been easy on us," Yane continued. "We've discussed this for a long, long time." Yane's round Mangan face always gave him a look of innocence.

Bingus Jam turned to his more moderate—and modest—counterpart. "What do you think about their explanations, Pracen?"

The grizzled veteran of the Quadrant 3 Wars looked across at the officials he considered to be villains. Only on rare occasions did Pracen utter a sentence or ask a question not designed to advance his own ego or goals, or to signal his own superior intelligence; he was born to be a politician, wound up a soldier, but then found his way into his true calling by combining knowledge of the law with political desire. He looked Yane in the eyes before doing the same with Alana and Kreeg. "If I were UU I wouldn't have shown up here, either. On the other side of the scale, I don't think their offer is a waste of time."

"And why do you see it acceptable that UU not show his face to us?" Bingus Jam prodded.

"Because he would have been arrested. I commend him for not succumbing to his urges—I am certain he wanted to be here himself." Pracen's pronouncement matched what the three outlaws hoped the law enforcement officials would conclude—and the officials were indeed correct.

Bingus Jam knew he could not argue the point. Instead, he studied Kreeg for a moment. Eemlurians always managed to earn Bingus Jam's distrust by simply existing. Their pale red skin and bright green eyes, which possessed the rare quality of night vision, made the Zhiloan uncomfortable. Eemlurian size and personality characteristics were similar enough to Zhiloans that the two species gave the appearance they were distant cousins, although DNA proved otherwise. Bingus Jam shook his head as he continued to eye Kreeg. "I don't see how I can trust the friends of Colonel Ursulanus."

Kreeg groaned and frowned as Alana saw an opening. With her long, black hair unfettered, she looked like a Sanlandan princess from long ago eras of their planet's storied history. "You can trust us or distrust us—that is your choice. But know if you distrust us, your views of UU will become self-fulfilling. If you trust us, you will be challenged to change your beliefs. That is your real quandary, is it not?" The white-and-orange-streaks of skin on her face scrunched together as she smiled. "This is about you and your views being challenged."

Before Bingus Jam's scowl could allow words to escape, Pracen intervened. "It is a large task, but I favor the effort. I for one will give UU and his gang this opportunity at redemption."

"Seconded!" Abuss Onuss boomed.

As Bingus Jam squirmed in discomfort in his seat, to the delight of the three now-former criminals, he nodded his approval.

The group spent the next half hour drawing up an outline of expectations; the three outlaws closed in on accomplishing the purpose of their mission.

•   •   •

As part of their agreement, the threesome gave up information about a fellow outlaw—they called it a "peace offering." Before the day was out, law enforcement raided the hideout of another gang known by its leader: the Vilshoosh Gang. Vilshoosh possessed a rare ability to infuriate everyone with whom he came in contact. His gang stayed with him, and endured the verbal and physical punishment, because the Fankan was good at what he did—steal. *Was* good at. He and his gang never perpetrated another crime after being sold out by UU's ambassadors to law enforcement.

To law enforcement, they had struck an honorable deal with UU's thieves.

•　　•　　•

"Where's Kreeg?"

The question of the day, asked multiple times by several members of the gang, failed to meet with an answer. The last they knew, Yane and Alana repeated, Kreeg climbed into his own ship on Drebehr with the assumed intent of rejoining everyone on Eemlurie.

"Surely he has family on this planet," Mookie commented. Others responded with shrugs and expressions of "that makes sense."

The group meandered around the fire pit—all on their feet, the group walked out their nervous energy. Soon Eemlurian night would fall—the deep blackness due to the absence of city lights, the lack of a currently visible moon, and the remoteness from other stars all served as factors.

UU rarely worried in front of other creatures; and, when he found himself in the company of others, he hid his concerns with such idiosyncrasies as shredding small objects with his hands or tearing paper into tiny bits. Only a sharp eye noted the tiny pieces of yet-to-be-burned wood which piled up wherever their leader stopped. Geeba possessed such a sharp eye, particularly as it related to the male she admired the most, and approached him. "He's disappeared before, Boss," she offered. Her soft eyes sought to comfort UU.

Rather than give his response in words, he flashed a grateful yet pained look at her.

"We have to keep moving, Untas," her gentle voice admonished.

"We got rid of the Vilshoosh Gang," Alana yelled out. "We don't have to worry about them." Her intention succeeded: small conversations broke out, easing tensions for a few minutes, but UU felt the need to get the entire group in on the conversation.

"With that good faith move," UU said. "Law enforcement can feel a little better about trusting us. We need their trust."

Nods of agreement dominated the gang, except Anthun, who sat in silence, looking at the ground in front of him.

"We will wait here for the three days," UU explained to everyone. "No one else knows where we are. I have to package a present to some military friends," he continued, using an expression to communicate he had unfinished business. "Does anyone else need to leave the planet besides me?"

"I do," Anthun answered. "I have friends hiding out on Nanotomrayfeous. They say they have information about the Premier which could be helpful to us," he said, referring to the home of the laziest beings in the quadrants. "I need to see what they have for us."

"That's a challenge!" Yane quipped. "If you move too much you stand out."

"They say it's great because they don't have to do anything. The Nonoans accept they are going to die, so they're still enjoying their slothy lives."

The Nonoans were the least energetic, least independent creatures known to the inhabitants of the quadrants. Over time, they learned they did not have to do for themselves. The more other planets sent missionaries and aid workers, the less Nonoans did for themselves. Over dozens upon dozens of generations, the Nonoans grew fat, weak, and even lazier. They were so successful at indolence others expected them to do nothing. Missionaries and aid workers were subconsciously trained to not allow the Nonoans to act. If one of the foreign visitors saw a Nonoan outside to receive his own postal dispatches, a foreigner would race to him with a wheelchair, not wanting the poor beast to exert himself.

When the stellar emergency was announced, considerations for transporting the Nonoans were drawn up, but the terminally lethargic creatures feared their languid ways would not be tolerated if mingled with others. As a population, they decided to die an honorable death of staying true to their principles to the very end—besides, they reasoned, an incredible amount of effort would be required to board spacecraft and then move into new dwellings.

Hiding among the Nonoans required a certain brilliance. With all the foreign helpers on the planet, blending in would come easy. But if neither helping nor a fat Nonoan oneself, one would stand out.

UU and Anthun prepared to leave Eemlurie in their respective ships: as usual, UU did not communicate his destination to his band. They had to trust him.

Fifteen Heislerian hours late, the stolen Rojani silver fighter craft they all recognized as Kreeg's personal vehicle landed nearby, then rolled to join the parking formation previously demanded by UU.

The craft powered down; its shrill engines melted into a purr, then silence. Kreeg climbed from his ship and flashed a sheepish grin when confronted with looks of concern and confusion.

"Hello." He eyed everyone as UU approached. His comedic demeanor threatened to display itself, but he seemed to understand his timing would be off.

"Kreeg! What happened?" UU got to his point without delay.

"When we left Drebehr, I decided to take a different route—for safety, you know—and I kept spotting ships on my scope that concerned me."

"So, you just took a long route?" Thanks to Kreeg's delivery, UU doubted the story.

"Yeah. I made a couple of stops to hide out." Another idea hit him. "You have to remember, I'm flying a fighter craft. Creatures expect military or law enforcement. I had to be careful." He looked to the rest of the group. "What's to eat?"

UU shook his head. Happy he worried for nothing, Kreeg's story still did not resonate with the leader.

Geeba approached UU. "That was strange."

"So is Kreeg, I guess."

"Don't worry, Untas. You can trust him. Whatever he's hiding can't be important."

UU nodded and the pair joined the rest of the outlaws—allegedly former outlaws—in their conversations before finally heading to his ship to depart. After a brief embrace from Geeba, UU set out on his continuing efforts to ensure his gang could live free lives outside of Quadrant 4.

Chapter Seven

Being a native Heislerian carried with it an air of importance. Whether legitimate or not, many—and all Heislerians—viewed the populace as a princely lot, heirs to all things aristocratic. Heislerians viewed, for example, the Zhiloan museum at Eese as a cheap attempt to unseat the vaunted Heislerian position in the known universe.

Heislerians adored expensive wines, cherished fine arts of all types, and coveted their philosophical discourses at public halls around the planet. No other citizens of the quadrants spent as much time as the Heislerians cooing over all things luxurious. The word "lavish" was not in their native language's lexicon—such a word would have been redundant.

And then there was Rick. His mother claimed he was influenced by the "vulgar" Rojanis and the "hooligan" Andalians. Young Rytkjmk was discovered, on many occasions, to have hidden under his mattress magazines with tales of appalling Andalian atrocities committed with ruinous Rojani weapons of war. His father, who rarely stepped in during Rytkjmk's maturation process, finally reached his limit of patience and expelled the youngster from his home.

Sent off to Sanlandan with an aunt and uncle who relocated for a job, young Rytkjmk promptly left behind familial ties and joined the military, lying about his age for the sake of entry.

He did not like to kill, but he loved to fight—and he hated the arts. He was a proud Heislerian without all the trappings.

On Earth, Rick worked by day to improve his leg's strength and stability, and by night he shared evenings with Julie, learning about her and the ways of earthlings. He found television not only an enjoyable diversion, but an educational forum. One point of interest included the Egyptian pyramids—a sure sign of visitors from the planet Shershin.

Perched on the couch, wearing clothing recently purchased by Julie—she did not dare take him in public wearing his native clothing—Rick sat, adorned in a blue Kansas City Royals t-shirt and a pair of Wrangler jeans. Julie had stressed to him the importance of covering his large feet, so tennis shoes or work boots—it took her three trips to get the correct sizes—and socks were a must when he stepped outside.

"I'm surprised the Nonoans didn't invent this on their planet," Rick opined, out of the blue. Seated on the couch with legs in front of him, resting on another cushion, Rick projected comfort. His wrapped leg may have signaled otherwise, but Rick felt nothing but enjoyment at the moment.

"What?" Julie asked, knowing nothing of Rick's subject or the Nonoans.

"Television. We have what you call the 'internet,' but we don't have this." Rick paused as the off-screen narrator described Stonehenge. "I guess we don't need it; we have ways to filter what we want to see to big screens throughout public places and in our homes, but it's mostly news—not education or entertainment."

"Don't you have time for entertainment on Heisler?"

"Sure, but our entertainment is discussing the latest, or sometimes the oldest, philosophies on crop production or theories about liberty or tyranny."

"Ah." Julie enjoyed learning about these other, mysterious worlds Rick described. In a few brief weeks, she knew she had learned a lot, yet so much lay untouched.

After nearly a minute of silence between the two, and the advancements of theories on the TV about the "how" and "why" of the construction of Stonehenge, Julie stood and announced, "I have to finish the laundry."

Rick barely noticed. Fixated on every word and image on the television, he continued his habit of banter with the program's narrator and on-screen guests. "Ha ha! That's a great theory, but the Shersheen put it there! It's not just a giant calendar!" He laughed. "It's a portal, earthlings! A portal for the Shersheen! They did that on Heisler and Eemlurie! The calendar helps them when they arrive!"

As the program progressed, Rick's focus sank deeper into the show. He did not hear the brief commotion on the front porch steps.

Before Rick realized a problem existed, three men wearing ski masks burst through the front doorway and into the living room.

Annoyed at the interruption, Rick rotated his head to analyze the invaders as he swung his feet to the floor.

The three men spread out in the living room, apparently ready to steal after subduing who they assumed to be an average-sized human.

Once Rick grabbed his crutches and pulled himself to his feet, the possibility of "subduing" ended.

The man with the concealed face closest to Rick aimed a .40 caliber pistol at him. "Get back on the couch or I'll kill you! Do it! Now!" The command was clear and the voice serious.

"I'll do no such thing!"

Before the three could react, the pale-skinned native of Heisler let out a roar which resembled a mountain lion's, but in a lower pitch. Spikes shot out by three inches from his neck, forearms, and sides, pressing against, then tearing the loose Royals t-shirt which covered his torso. Jeans seams burst. In an instant, Rick's body mass increased by forty percent. His skull grew, his neck thickened, and his arms, chest, and legs followed suit. Even his socks ripped. The red headband which circled the top of his head expanded and then fell to the floor, still in one piece.

The leader of the group watched in horror at the monstrous display while his compatriots succumbed to mild shock; they did not move. The leader of the thugs gulped, lowered his gun hand to his side, then breathed in a blast of courage and re-aimed his semi-automatic pistol.

Rick's enormous appearance served as distraction; his bulky frame intimidating to anyone who saw him. The spikes alone would have frightened any earthling.

With one move, the pistol was snatched from the hands of the would-be killer and crushed, becoming twisted metal. The monstrous Rick backhanded the leader, which sent him flying through a picture-glass window near the front door. In another blink of an eye, Rick grabbed the second attacker and used one arm to throw him across the room, into a wall. The force of the man's head striking the wall brought an immediate end to his life.

The third man used the diversion created by his flying friend to reach for the door. In one long stride, Rick caught the man by the back of the neck, pushed the screen door open, and threw the man into the darkness. Enough illumination from a nearby streetlight, which was perched on a pole in Julie's yard, allowed Rick to observe the masked man as he struck a tree thirty feet away.

In horror at the disturbance, Julie raced into the room to gain an understanding of what had unfolded. As Rick reentered the house, she saw his appearance. She froze. She did not know whether she should fear or congratulate him. As Rick stopped in the doorway, looking like a monster from another planet, Julie covered her mouth with her hand. "Rick?"

Rick nodded.

She could see her new friend was indeed the monster, but she lacked confidence he was truly the same Rick. As she slowed her breathing, she watched as he shrunk back into the recognizable alien he had been the entire time she had known him.

Rick looked at her, then turned his attention to the messy scene. He walked to the other side of the room, past the television, and put his hand on the dead man, who moments before seemed bent on eradicating Rick. "He is no longer alive," Rick announced with a matter-of-fact tone.

As Julie watched in silent horror, Rick walked out the front door and onto the porch. She did not move.

"This earthling is no longer alive, as well," he shouted to be heard.

Out of sight from Julie, Rick turned and gazed into the darkened yard. "The third earthling is gone."

He reentered the house. "What do I do now? Do you want me to burn their carcasses?"

"No!" After a pause, Julie fought off a laugh, amused by the inquiry. "No. I will call authorities. But before they get here, I have some things to explain to you." She looked him over. "And you need to change clothes—and that headband." She looked at the headband on the floor. "Just lose the headband."

•　　•　　•

"Miss Pitts, is there anything else you saw?" The Sheriff's deputy knew of Julie and her large family enterprise, but he had never met her.

"Look," Julie pulled the officer to the side and glanced at the man's badge. "Officer Brunk."

"Deputy Brunk," he corrected in a polite tone.

"Deputy, Rick is a friend of mine, but he doesn't have I.D. He just acted in self-defense, so can you guys not worry too much about him? Please?"

"I understand," Brunk nodded. "We get a lot of farm help around here. When you've got good help, you don't want to lose them when they didn't do anything wrong."

"That's right," Julie nodded. Her implication led to the desired inference. The deputy had made the correct assumption and Julie knew she could not have stated it better on such a delicate subject. "So just list him as 'Rick Martinez' and we'll be good."

Brunk shook his head. "I'll list him as 'Rick Carbo,'" he announced. When Julie gave him a funny look, he explained. "If there's a 'Rick Martinez' in the system with a record, that could come back to bite you. But I'm from Boston originally, and my dad was a big fan of Bernie Carbo."

Again Julie flashed a confused expression.

"A baseball player. Don't worry about it, Ms. Pitts. I've got you covered."

Julie smiled and thanked him with a nod and pat on his shoulder.

The ploy worked. Officially, Rick had struck one assailant with his crutch, causing the intruder to find himself knocked into the wall, where he met a terrible end because of the fluky way he hit his head at a wall stud. The second intruder had leaped out of the window in fear, bleeding to death from a cut sustained from broken glass. The third man had fled into the night, never to be seen again. The story was believable enough the police did not question it.

The final matter of Rick's identity was cleared up by her implication that he was illegally in the country, which, in a way, he was.

Problem solved—other than replacement of the broken front window and repair to the wall next to the television.

"There is one thing I don't understand," Deputy Brunk said as he looked at Rick, who again found comfort on the couch. Deputy Brunk's partner paused his observations and stood next to Brunk.

Julie's heart seemed to stop. Rick had given his rehearsed statement and Julie attempted to answer random questions directed at her extraterrestrial visitor.

"Rick." The deputy's facial expression reflected a matter which escaped him. "We found the gun belonging to the guy on the front porch, but where is this guy's gun?" He pointed at the body of the invader, now covered by a sheet, who died next to the television.

Rick, now attired in another pair of jeans and a red Kansas City Chiefs t-shirt, sighed and flashed a quizzical look. "You know, I don't know what happened to it. Maybe in all the confusion the creature who ran off grabbed it."

Brunk thought for a moment then nodded, which was followed by a laugh. "Creature. That's funny." He laughed again, amused at the use of the term. His partner chuckled, then returned to reviewing his handwritten notes.

For the next hour, Sheriff's deputies surveyed the scene and waited for the coroner to arrive. Rick, under the guise of needing to recover from all the excitement, returned to his perch on the couch and watched a television show about Nikolai Tesla. Julie breathed easier knowing the gun Rick crushed had been explained away. Now on a shelf in the lower basement, Rick had promised to take it back to his side of the galaxy the next time he went through the portal.

Neither she nor Rick would have been able to explain how he possessed the strength to crush a steel handgun.

Deputy Brunk turned to Julie. "You know, you two really shouldn't be in here. You and your friend here don't seem fazed that there's a dead body in here."

Julie frowned. "Believe me, officer. I'm very upset about it." She turned a glance toward Rick before her eyes again met the Sheriff deputy's eyes. "He's just addicted to TV."

Rick's focus remained on the television.

"I'll let you finish your job," Julie said to the deputy as she left the room to check on her laundry. Before she could leave, Rick's voice stopped her in her tracks.

"Oh, come on! It's obvious!" Rick let out, unaware of his voice's volume.

She put a hand on his shoulder.

Feet on the couch, the comfortable alien looked up at Julie.

"It's obvious what happened," Rick explained, even though Julie remained unclear of the subject. "Either directly or indirectly, Tesla was influenced by the Shersheen. Either they left before teaching him what he needed to know, or he was incapable of learning the lesson."

The deputy glanced up at Rick. His partner seemed bewildered.

In a moment of awkward silence, the four adults in the room attempted to not look at each other. Still standing above Rick, Julie stared at the television, though she did not listen.

"We'll be right back," the deputy announced as the two officers headed to and then off the porch, apparently headed to their vehicles.

"Rick!" Julie began to admonish her alien friend as she felt comfortable the police were out of earshot. "I told you, honey. No one is going to understand when you say the Share-sing helped out Tesla and other people on this planet. And quit saying 'planet'!"

"Shersheen," Rick corrected. "Sorry."

Chapter Eight

Two dozen law enforcement officers, armed with standard police Drebehran laser rifles, raced into the deserted building situated on the outskirts of what was left of the Gigorline city of Umbr. For reasons unknown to UU, citizens of Umbr had chosen to remain at a higher rate than any other city in the quadrant. Whether they chose to disbelieve the predictions of scientists or did not care whether they died, UU did not know. He did know, from a kilometer away, the police were in the middle of tracking down a false lead.

UU's presence on Gigorl was the result of his desire to test Anthun's loyalty. Doubts about the Andalian's intentions were growing and spreading through several members of his band. The colonel was here to plant a "trip camera," as they called their motion-activated biometric sensors, in the gang's former hideout to see who would pay a visit to the facility over the coming months. Yane's equipment had been removed when UU decided to forego the location as a sanctuary, so UU had decided to plant a hidden device.

Through his auto-zoom binoculars, he could see the entire situation unfold. Unless another group had taken over the building, they would undoubtedly go home empty-handed. As UU sat on the hillside, peering over the small ridge and watching law enforcement move in, he pondered the purpose of their raid. Was he not now on the good side of the law? Why would they raid his former hideout?

UU's propitious timing gave him chills. Had he arrived five minutes earlier, he would have been inside the building when law enforcement arrived. His turn toward the good side of the law was too tenuous to believe he would have been quickly released.

He contemplated the false information he had planted with Anthun. That it would result in a police raid had never crossed UU's mind. He had anticipated thugs moving in, hoping to surprise and kill the gang, but not law enforcement.

Before he could allow his thoughts to follow their logical paths, he found himself ducking when a powerful wave raced toward him. The ear-splitting blast startled UU. The concussion leveled a building a block away and launched debris in all directions. The power of the explosion amazed UU as well as nearby residents who lived Spartan lives in their apocalyptic world.

The blast roared for kilometers until the sound and energy dissipated. A small sense of sadness crossed his mind, but for only a brief second, as he considered the loss of two dozen law enforcement officers; but, one thought—one overbearing, pressing notion—settled in his brain: the UU Gang would take the blame for this. The building had been a key hideout until just one Heislerian month prior.

The next problem he faced was his mere presence. When questioned, locals would remember seeing the colonel around the time of the blast—someone would recognize him. His brief jaunt into town to scavenge for food likely would haunt him.

The apparent—obvious—betrayal by Anthun left UU with a chilling sense of urgency. As the gentle Gigorl breeze tickled his face and the star called Mize warmed the air, the frenetic sounds of debris crashing to the ground served as a stark contrast to the environment. Despite the distractions, a thought dug deeper and deeper into UU's soul: his lie to Anthun—that they would return to this hideout—was to test the Andalian's loyalty. This was a simple test, and Anthun had failed, spectacularly so; in fact, the test started a chain of events which led through the death of two dozen officers and could bring about the end of the UU Gang.

He considered whether this could be a coincidence—an act or betrayal by someone else. *It's possible, but not likely.*

As UU's brain raced, encountering thought after thought and conspiracy theory after conspiracy theory, the realization of the explosion's impact pressed on his chest and shoulders. He failed to consider the dead officers, blown into oblivion in a split second, or their families. Such thoughts had fled the quadrant with the Great Exodus. No one showed much concern for the value of life; those days were gone.

In all of the confusion inside UU's mind, he returned to one concept—one fact—over and over: UU had told Anthun the gang would again use this hideout, and within a day, legal authorities raided the hideout.

The hideout itself had been an odd choice for bandits. At the edge of a mildly populated area, the gang had blended in with the other Remainers, but it still felt too public, too exposed.

And why the trap? Why send these law officers to their deaths? His mind settled on what seemed the most likely explanation. Either the perpetrator of the trap planted the explosives to prevent the UU Gang from going straight, which would point to Anthun, or to ensure the gang would be arrested and likely executed.

He did not trust Anthun even though he trusted the Andalian's prowess as a warrior. Almost too willing to fight, a reckless spirit resting in the souls of almost every native of their planet, Anthun seemed, at least in UU's mind, to be willing to act in the best interest of sustaining a fierce battle rather than that of the group.

Still, "traitor" did not seem to be a word which could be associated with the large beast.

UU put the pieces together: Anthun took the bait of the "next hideout" information, rigged—or more likely, hired someone to rig—the location with explosives, then informed law enforcement. UU's hunch had to be correct: he could not think of a better theory. Anthun had to know the UU Gang would receive the blame—a galling move on the Andalian's part.

Was Anthun's motive to kill law enforcement officers or to frame the entire gang of a crime which carried consequences they would not be able to escape? *He was opposed to us turning our backs on banditry.* That made sense. *If we're blamed for killing law enforcement, we'll never be able to turn to the good. We'll never live free again.*

Little time had passed since Anthun had received the news; yet, not only did the police launch a raid, but now two dozen officers were dead. Proving they were not involved—except Anthun—was going to prove challenging. The colonel needed more evidence against his fellow warrior, but UU's conclusion felt solid.

The colonel sat up on the hillside and further contemplated what this attack on law enforcement meant. On the horizon, he could see the green ocean on which the port city of Umbr rested. A mixture of pale green and the green-gray of an olive, the water supported life, despite possessing a chemical composition unique to the known universe. Out of sight to UU, Remainers and creatures of all types enjoyed the odd-colored water, unaware of the import of the explosion they heard and felt.

The scenic planet could not snatch dark thoughts from UU. One word rested in his mind and would not go away: betrayal. UU would wait until the right time—when he had additional evidence. His thoughts all gathered into one unified goal: *I will kill him.*

•　　•　　•

The first, most notable reason Geeba became a target of the filthy, malodorous group of Sanlandan males was because she was female. That was enough of a reason for the males to tease and surround her as the leader of their five-member group uttered vile, sexually suggestive comments to her. The vile fiends were not shy about giving explicit details of what was in store for the Corsan female.

Remainers had grown accustomed to the foul odors of decay and rot bestowed by the last gasps of life all around them. They were comfortable with body odor, bad breath, and other unpleasant byproducts of their meager lives, even though cleanliness once had been an important facet of all their cultures except the Andalians. These Sanlandan males, however, produced a new level of sickening stench.

The second reason she became a target was her beauty. The Sanlandan males proved incapable of conquering their urges.

The final reason was obvious: Geeba was alone and thus appeared vulnerable.

Her mistake was to not follow Alana into the latter's former home. Unbeknownst to the abhorrent brutes, Alana watched through a window, waiting only to choose the proper moment to help even the odds.

"You're making a mistake," Geeba warned, although her soft, feminine tone and voice did not help matters.

"Ha! A mistake!" the leader roared. "We're making a mistake, my friends!" They laughed together, raising their adrenaline levels further.

A change began to overtake the Corsan. Tall for a female of her species—taller than many males, in fact—her frail frame did not pose a deterrent to the excited vermin who examined her. Geeba's soft voice hardened a few degrees. "Do you wish to be crippled, or should I release you from your grimy existence and kill you?"

More laughter.

"Look at you!" the leader snarled. His long, black, mangy hair lay matted on top of his head. None of the creatures had bathed in many months; Geeba could not ignore their dreadful scent. His orange and white skin appeared light brown due to the dirt which coated his entire body. "You're tough! You're going to put up a fight and we like that!"

"You couldn't take on one of us, let alone five!" another grungy miscreant called out with a mocking tone.

Geeba relaxed her body, stood up straight, and folded her arms. "Then I have an idea." She spun in a slow circle to face each one. "Four of you back away and whoever is the bravest can attack me first."

From inside her now-dilapidated house, Alana smiled. Both Alana and Geeba knew she could not take on all five—both together could not take on all of them—so Geeba had a plan to thin the crowd.

"I'll go first," the leader snarled. He reached for his laser, causing Geeba to put a hand on her own. The Sanlandan then threw the weapon behind him, where it hit the ground more than ten meters away. "Now do the same, female."

"I will not." Geeba's resolve could not be missed.

The leader of the small gang growled and pondered the situation before taking three bold steps toward his intended victim. Geeba stepped to the side, out of his way, as she also took two steps backward. Geeba's move to cede ground caused the Sanlandan to move faster toward her, which fit the female Corsan's plans. Before the gang leader could adjust his attack, Geeba threw up her left arm to push her pursuer's right arm, then chopped his throat with her open right hand.

The Sanlandan gasped as he collapsed, fighting to breathe. He reached for a knife but the twin enemies of pain and lack of air prohibited his body from responding.

A small sound behind her caused Geeba to spin, just in time to avoid an onrushing attacker. Before he understood what happened, Geeba unsheathed her Corsan knife, which mimicked the Andalian Battle Knife, though a smaller version, and she sliced through the creature's shirt, laying open part of his right side. He screamed in pain as he spun to face her.

One of the other hoodlums saw the moment as the perfect time to shoot Geeba, but the moment he drew his laser, a blast emanated from Alana's doorway. The beast died within a half-second of the laser's strike.

"No one else will unholster their weapons!" Alana snarled. "I hope I am understood."

The two uninjured Sanlandan's stood in brief shock, eyes bulged, at the appearance of another female. They both backed away in fear.

Geeba took advantage of the diversion to leap toward the sliced attacker and deliver a flying kick to his side, amplifying the pain. The move only served to enrage the wounded combatant. He drew a blade, attempted to gain solid footing, and moved toward her. With a head feint to her left, she leaped to her right. The male reacted to the head feint and moved forward. Pain slowed his reactions and he could not stop the blade of Geeba's knife from slicing open his left side.

The screams from the wounded attacker easily drowned out the gurgling made by the leader, whose breathing had diminished over the brief lapse of time. The leader looked at his two unharmed friends and held out a hand. His attempts to plead for help would not have been audible even if the other attacker had not screamed without cessation.

Geeba turned to Alana. "Thanks for the help. Perhaps we should get off this planet while we still can."

Alana nodded. "That's a solid plan." She smiled as they jogged away from the dead and the dying and the one who wished he could die. As they departed the scene, they kept up consistent glances toward the unharmed Sanlandans, who within seconds disappeared around a corner and out of sight, abandoning the others.

"I'm sure this was a nice planet before the Great Exodus," Geeba offered as they quickened their steps.

"It was. It really was." Given the status of the entirety of Quadrant 4, no further explanation was needed.

Chapter Nine

The biggest open secret in Quadrant 4 was the fate of the Premier. While each planet had a premier as the top leader, only Aelo Seveen, the Premier of Asimon, remained. The others displayed wisdom and fled the doomed quadrant. The megalomaniacal Asimoni concocted other, greater plans. His plans fit in with his personality: a narcissist of the highest order, he could present a loud, forceful front while working with surreptitious machinations and unwavering dedication behind the scenes. He could appear honest and forthright while altering meanings of words in the Shersheen language to misdirect observers or delegitimize critics. Aelo Seveen, simply known as "the Premier," lived as a legend to some and demigod to others.

Law enforcement heard the rumors of the Premier as warlord—the godfather of quadrant crime—but no planetary official dared believe it. To the rational mind, the Premier had too much to lose and low odds of gaining anything. To law enforcement, the charge represented a foolish conspiracy theory. To the Premier, the failure to understand the obvious was a product of inferior minds: he had the known universe to gain.

Officially throughout the known universe, the Premier sat in a dungeon on Asimon, a prisoner and hostage of desperate, conniving outlaws bent on reaping riches in exchange for their celebrated captive. Through misfortune or the good fortune of the criminals or both, on three separate occasions, riches were transferred but the famed hostage was not.

After the third failed purchase of the Premier's freedom, some in law enforcement began to give credence to the rumors. Either the criminals never planned to return the Premier or the leader himself directed his minions—either way the result repeated itself.

Asimonis, while heralded for their intellect and cunning—they made great negotiators, politicians, financiers, and detectives—like the Heislerians, they were not known to undervalue their self-worth.

And the Premier never under-valued his own abilities.

Whether victim or perpetrator, others knew the outlaws surrounding the Premier were rich, intelligent, and doomed like everyone else. What escaped most observers, steering them toward the belief of the leader's innocence, was the lack of an end game. How could he pull off such an audacious ruse and get away with it? Just as with the UU Gang, without turning to embrace the law, those who fled Quadrant 4 and returned to civil society would be captured and tried for their crimes.

But the Premier, brilliant Asimoni that he was, had a plan.

In one of the few places in the quadrant with functioning energy supplies, the Premier stood behind a microphone which rested on a podium. In the dead language of Asimoni, the planetary seal read, "Honor, Integrity, Service,

Compassion"—utter irony for the occasion. The leader who claimed the lofty ideals as his own stood before his consortium of criminals in a large hall which previously hosted massive political rallies and conventions.

The tall, well-dressed Asimoni had always encountered female admirers and sycophantic groupies wherever he went—even on a planet he fully controlled he lacked the power to quell their desires to bestow praise—and more—on him. Pre-astronomical panic, Premier Aelo Seveen held the title of a mere democratically elected leader. His quiet aspirations seemed destined to be unrealized. He flirted and cavorted with beautiful females and spent much of his free time in the throes of the best, most expensive alcoholic beverages. The males hated him—unless they were part of his inner circle and grabbed hold of the unfortunate females or the liquor he cast aside.

Scandals brewed in the days before the chaos hit; no one marked the news of the impending supernova the way the Premier did. Before the Great Exodus began, he hosted a party to celebrate the event for which others had coined a name: "Nova Quadrant." In the midst of a crisis, Aelo Seveen hosted a delightful drunken gala, relieved he could bury the indignities of his debaucheries forever on the simple premise of "no evidence, no sin." Within weeks of the announcement, gone were the charges of corruption and illegitimate offspring.

If anyone in the quadrants was built for controlling the populace, it was the Premier. He adored the trappings of office and engaged in them as often as possible. He needed praise. Mere acclaim was not enough: he needed adoration, adulation. He wanted to be a god, and only mortality stopped him from reaching that goal. He considered himself a living legend, an untouchable force the public needed, required.

"We are succeeding, my dear friends," the Premier cooed into the microphone, his smile growing by the second. "But there are those who oppose us." The smile skidded to a halt, then retreated. He did not raise his voice as he hissed the pronouncement; instead, he eyed the crowd of 200 with a slow, deliberate sweep of his head, as though he could make eye contact with each member in attendance. The slender Asimoni, with pale white skin and light-brown stripes covering most of his body, commanded the room.

"Before this cosmic opportunity arose," he said, referring to what others termed an existential crisis, "I learned of my Shersheen heritage. Asimoni blood came much later in my family history," he lied. The Premier knew the falsity of the statement; at least half his audience knew it was a lie; yet, they all nodded with reverence and approval. "And I want to stay true to that heritage." No scientist could even prove the existence of Shersheen DNA.

The Premier's cadence and timing demonstrated his oratorical brilliance. His voice remained low, causing his audience to lean forward—mentally if not physically. Shouts would come later.

"It is my duty—my calling—to take our cause to all beings." He again hesitated, allowing his subordinates to inquire—inside their own minds and without consideration of any truth except that which the Premier placed in their gray matter—what that "cause" could be. "And what is that cause, you ask yourself? It is better life through reliance on superior minds."

The equation did not include the concepts of liberty, principles, populism, or even desires. The equation evoked nothing similar to self-reliance or independence. The equation could only contain input supported by the mathematician—and that mathematician, of course, was behind the microphone.

"Perhaps you have heard the shield around our entire planet has been completed." What began as a question ended as a statement. "Law enforcement supports us; they understand our mission," he lied again. "We can bring about the improvement of countless billions upon billions of lives." His pace quickened. "This is not about power. No! This is about making poverty, crime, hunger, and war obsolete. This is about a healthy, happy, and heroic future. This is our time!" He stressed "our" so his audience felt part of the despotic diatribe. "This is not just about us! This is about a secure future! Free from the starving masses! Free from senseless murders and wretched thieves!" His voice increased by another 40 decibels. "This is about making sure our civilization survives!"

He had said nothing in all those words, yet the crowd roared its approval all the same. Each member of the audience either controlled planets or regions of planets, or they served the Premier in some capacity at his lavish mansion, which until recently had garnered support through taxation.

The Premier's overriding theme—that all would benefit from his rule simply because the Premier would be the ruler—

remained consistent in these brief speeches to his underlings before the group settled down to the business of managing the criminal activity throughout the quadrant.

Before he could continue with his despotic discourse, an aide limped toward their leader. The limp resulted from a battle with another gang in the days immediately after the onset of the crisis. Transferred to the palace, the gangster found a safer, more pleasant life. He whispered in the Premier's ear before turning to limp away.

"I have great news!" The Premier bellowed with a resounding growl as he regurgitated the final word. He then pounded his fist for effect. "We have found the hideout of that despicable colonel, Untas Ursulanus!" He paused for the crowd to cheer, which it did as expected.

"If UU does not wish to join us, he will die! We have found him and he will not escape our grasp!" Premier Aelo Seveen lacked the knowledge to confirm the veracity of his words, but he knew those words needed to be uttered. "He has been making money and gaining wealth that belongs to us!" Thunderous applause from the 200 rang out at a louder volume than would have been expected by so few. "He will be ours! Or he will die!"

The Premier failed to learn that his minions made a habit of only giving good news and the UU Gang had already escaped the grasp of the would-be tyrant and vacated the hideout; but, such facts did not matter to the bellicose crime boss. Whether ultimate victory was at hand or not, most subordinates did not know what the ultimate plan would mean for them. They never asked such questions.

Chapter Ten

Laser fire of all colors volleyed back and forth, signifying the various weapons of assorted manufacturers on many planets throughout the quadrants. Pinned down behind a burned out Rojani Cargo Craft, Chabdab and Kimberlina—both Rojanis—fought with fearless fervor as they attempted to protect the gang's right flank.

The intel showed a weak spot which UU said they could overcome; at this point, UU's prediction proved unfounded. For his part, the frontal assault he led with Geeba, Bill, and Mookie faced much heavier fire than predicted.

"Where did all these creatures come from?!" UU shouted in the direction of his cohorts. Though it seemed like an odd time to shout a rhetorical question, such was the colonel's frustration level. "We were promised a weak defense!"

Indeed, law enforcement made such a guarantee. The message from Abuss Onuss indicated a Trerzon Gang hideout—a bombed out compound, really—ripe for conquering. Authorities knew the Trerzon Gang well, supposedly because their criminal reign over Ceratofs had exhausted what few resources survived the Great Exodus.

The city of Trerzon, the third-largest on Ceratofs, lay devoid of life and resource, thanks to the eponymous gang. Fearing they would migrate to another planet like a swarm of insects bringing famine, apprehending the gang seemed like an easy way for the UU Gang to earn their reputation as "reformed." Instead, explosions from grenades told a different story.

"Kimbyk!" Geeba shouted, using her friend's given first name. "Kimberlina" sounded like a much more affectionate name than Kimbyk Parlina.

"We're trapped!" Kimberlina shouted back. The separation of 35 meters proved more of a problem than had been foreseen. When they initially hid behind the cargo craft, it was fully intact. Now, to call it a shell of a vehicle would be an overstatement.

An explosion near Chabdab sent a small piece of metal into the Rojani's head, knocking him unconscious. The explosion knocked Kimberlina backward, exposing her entire body to enemy fire. The enemy did not miss.

Kimberlina's screams unnerved the group. Already down to 11 due to Rick's absence, they stood on the precipice of losing two more friends—and facing even worse odds of survival, let alone success.

Certatofs all, the Trerzon gang members swooped in on the UU Gang's right flank as Chabdab and Kimberlina faltered. A sudden and heavy volley aimed at UU's position left the team struggling to find adequate cover. The left flank, held by Kreeg, Yane, Blik, Anthun, and Alana, lay too far away for assistance.

"Damn!" UU shouted. Surveillance had shown two could cover the right flank; yet, in retrospect, six might not have been able to hold it. He glanced at Mookie. "What are you shooting at?!"

In the heat of the battle and chaos, Mookie declined to answer. Three successive stray shots had not accomplished anything, but he did not wish to make such an admission at the moment.

"Chabdab!" With desperation in her voice and weakened movements, Kimberlina grabbed her comrade by his shirt with both hands, under his chin, as he fought to regain consciousness.

An explosion from a Ceratofs Rocket Grenade sent more shrapnel into both combatants. Kimberlina cried out again as hot steel blasted into her right leg and hip. Chabdab again struggled with consciousness, but his bleeding head brought far more concern to Kimberlina.

"If I don't get some help we're both going to die!" Resignation peppered her words. Her fate seemed sealed.

The twilight attack had turned to nighttime during the battle. Despite search lights and the light from fires and explosions, Anthun shocked the entire band—especially UU. Without warning to his mates on the left flank, he leaped to his feet, away from the compound wall which served as cover, and ran to the forward position. The wall, which jutted out from the main wall of the structure, apparently served at one time as a fourth wall for a separate structure. Now it served as their left flank. Anthun abandoned safety for his critically injured friends.

"Anthun, what are you doing?" their concerned leader asked from behind one of the two overturned cargo trucks.

"They're going to die if we don't do something!"

"Congratulations, Anthun," Mookie could not hide his disdain. "You're pinned down with us."

"I'll use my personal shields," Anthun insisted.

"I'm glad you have shields left," Mookie moaned. "We're out of shields here." Only later would they realize recharging batteries or replacing personal shield kits were impossible tasks. Demand outstripped supply more every day.

Before Anthun could respond with words, he let his actions do the talking. Three steps into his charge to the right flank, a laser overwhelmed his personal shield and struck him in the leg before shrapnel from another rocket grenade felled him, leaving him out in the open. Mookie and Bill stood up together, opening cover fire.

"Crawl!" Geeba shouted.

"I'm going!" Mookie yelled at UU and Bill. "Keep firing!"

Mookie reached Anthun without sustaining return fire. He grabbed his fellow Andalian by the arm and half-dragged him toward the frontal position's cover. Just as they reached the relative safety of a cargo truck, a hellacious attack drowned out sound and darkness. Explosions from lasers and grenades rocked the UU Gang's positions. When it stopped 10 seconds later, Chabdab and Kimberlina were nowhere to be found.

"You are lucky!" Bill shouted at Mookie.

On a whim, Kreeg and Yane rushed forward from the left flank. With a boost from Yane, Kreeg peered over the main wall of the compound to get an idea of the enemy's location. A yellow laser round blasted by his right ear, causing him to leap backward, off Yane's shoulders. He crashed to the ground, unhurt.

The two raced to the cover of a large cargo ship. The left flank's cover proved safe, but too far to assist trapped comrades on the right or in the front.

"What did you see?" Blik asked.

"Oh, we're gonna have some fun!" Kreeg laughed. "You ready for this?" As the others looked at him in anticipation, he opened up a box he had carried with him to the battle. He pulled out a grenade for the Rojani Hyper Grenade launcher. "It seems like a long time ago we were in the diamond mine on Zhilo."

"It was last week," Blik chuckled.

"Oh so long ago." Kreeg turned his attention back to Yane. "I only got to fire off one that day. Do you have the tube?"

Yane handed him the launcher, which was less than a meter long.

"Everybody grab two. We're going to blow these things up as fast as we can." Again Kreeg laughed. Destruction excited him, but especially when that destruction came in the form of explosives.

In rapid succession, Kreeg launched Yane's two grenades, then changed his stance with only a twist of his shoulders to select new targets a few degrees from the original victims. Two quick launches of Alana's grenades were met by another pause as he stopped to listen to the explosive roars. Realizing the lack of return fire, he looked at Yane and nodded. Two more grenades launched, followed by two more from Alana.

Within a few more seconds, all twelve grenades had been launched—two hitting approximately the same area before moving on to another area of the compound where he would land two more. The ferocity of the fire fight lessened with only a few, sparse laser shots illuminating the night.

Kreeg would have loved for his grenade attack to have been the opening salvo of the battle, but the fighting had been too intense to scout the targets.

"Hand grenades ready!" Kreeg shouted to the frontal position. "The UU Gang!" he announced in a thunderous voice, which had become his typical battle cry.

In near unison, nine grenades flooded the compound grounds. Dirt, building materials, and body parts filled the air, then settled back down to the ground. After ten long seconds of silence, they knew the matter had become a cleanup operation.

"Wait a minute!" From his forward position, an epiphany struck UU. He looked at the right flank, then shouted "Follow me!" as he ran toward the spot where Chabdab and Kimberlina had endured punishing bombardments. He looked toward the left flank and yelled. "Kreeg! Yane! Wait!"

Behind the extended wall, Kreeg looked at Yane. "Apparently, he thinks we've left our cover."

"It sounds to me like I'm staying right here," Yane replied.

"Hopefully, he's trying to find something else we can blow up," Kreeg said with a tinge of glee.

"There will be more, you crazy Eemlurian. There will be more, just maybe not today." Yane laughed as he admonished his friend.

Return fire ceased. Voices carried as they began to understand the battlefield better.

At the left flank position, Mookie arrived out of breath. He had followed UU, but only to Kimberlina's last known position, then made his way to give the word to Yane. "UU doesn't want to storm in just yet." He paused to catch his breath. "They got Chabdab and Kimberlina—they're gone, and we're sure they didn't surrender."

"Any idea where they are?" Alana asked.

"UU, Geeba, and Bill are trying to find them."

"Okay," Yane took command for the moment. "Let's go hold the frontal position in case there's anyone left in there to rush out and attack us." He looked at Blik. "You stay behind."

Leaving Blik behind, the others reclaimed the middle.

After several minutes, Geeba approached the frontal position. Walking with a slow, deliberate stride, she joined the others. She eyed Mookie, Alana, Kreeg, Yane, and the injured Anthun. "It's not a good time to speak to UU." She paused, her emotions fighting to get the best of her. "We caught up to a Ceratofs. He said they took Chabdab and Kimberlina away."

"To where?!" Alana asked, her emotions beginning to rise.

Geeba shook her head. As an afterthought, she answered the question. "We don't know. The creature wouldn't tell us, so UU snapped his neck."

"Sounds like UU," Kreeg reasoned.

"The creature said they were going to keep them alive to get information."

"Then UU should have kept the Ceratofs alive for information," Yane countered.

"That's what Bill said." Geeba hesitated again. "But there's more." Her halted speech continued. "Bill recognized him as law enforcement—or at least someone who has worked with them."

Before anyone could respond, UU and Bill approached them from the darkened right flank, the faded embers of the land craft behind which Chabdab and Kimberlina had hidden no longer supplied much light.

"It's probably too late to find anymore Ceratofs alive," UU said, reasoning the Trerzon Gang had all been killed or fled. "Kill anyone you find."

Surprised, the others looked at each other.

"What about our contract to bring them in alive?" Yane asked, unable to hide his incredulity.

UU shook his head, as if to say, "That's not going to happen."

"But UU," Yane pleaded. "I'm angry, too; but, law enforcement is looking at this as part of the test. They want us to bring back prisoners."

UU fixed his angry gaze on Yane. "Tell me I care about a test. Kill them all!"

No one in the group spoke up. They were used to the volatility of their leader. This was UU. This was his attitude when angered. Even so, most members of the group had a history of being enthused when orders were "Kill them all."

Chapter Eleven

When UU walked into the conference room, law enforcement boss Abuss Onuss and fellow Board of Ten members Bingus Jam and Pracen fought off nerves. All three struggled to conceal the trembling sensation they felt in their hands, stomachs, and hearts. In their own minds, separately they knew they did not want to show fear, but they also knew they were destined to fail in the attempt. Their expressions looked more like that of youngsters caught committing petty theft. Untas Ursulanus had grown into The Legend of UU, and they feared both creature and legend.

UU sported an angry face—a look of a warrior on the verge of rage. His uncharacteristic expression added immediate tension to the room, as though he carried a ticking time bomb strapped to his chest. He brought a reputation of being intense, stubborn, and fiery, yet the fieriness seemed reserved for the battlefield—never the board room.

Yane accompanied his friend and colleague. He knew how to guide a conversation as well as keep UU calm—two talents about to become necessary ingredients in the concoction of conversation about to be stirred.

The surviving friends had only found two members of the Trerzon Gang still alive. Both badly wounded, UU relented from his prior order and permitted his team to transport them back to law enforcement on one condition: no medical treatment was to be provided during the trip back.

Yane felt better because of law enforcement's concerns, and UU felt better because he showed no mercy to those who abducted his friends.

Unable to find Trerzon gangsters to kill, UU's rage had not abated. They remained concerned about Bill's recognition of one of the gang members. In these unprecedented times, they had witnessed many ruffians switching sides from law enforcement to outlaw and back again. Still, the ramifications concerned them. Many observers failed to realize the changes *from* law enforcement were never by actual members of law enforcement. Police and other officials did not stay to become rich, rather out of humanitarian reasons. Law enforcement was paid too well and provided with too hefty of pension plans to risk switching sides; but, to the observer, without knowing the individuals, they were unaware many criminals and opportunists posed as law enforcement.

Common courtesies and niceties were dispensed with as UU and Yane reached the large boardroom table. The one Drebehran and two Zhiloan legal officials did not greet the retired colonel. As he took the final steps and reached his chair, UU reached into his pocket and tossed onto the table a piece of plastic. The item slid to a stop in front of the flinching Abuss Onuss.

Abuss Onuss picked up the item and recognized it as an identity card. In silence, he looked up at UU.

"Run it. I want to know who he is and what his connection is to law enforcement," UU demanded, his voice and tone lacking any indication of a request. He sat directly in front of the head of law enforcement while Yane deposited himself in front of Pracen.

Abuss Onuss slid back in his chair and touched a spot on the table. A keyboard in the Shersheen language lit up a small square on top of the table—a dim light represented a computer which allowed the user to access any data needed. He hit a few buttons, then ran the card over the lit area with a quick swiping motion.

The portion of the table in between UU and Abuss Onuss displayed a depiction of the dead Ceratofs. Abuss Onuss looked on in horror—everyone in the room realized he recognized the dead fighter. Abuss Onuss lifted his head up and looked UU in the eye.

"Colonel," the nervous law enforcement boss said, attempting to hide a quivering voice. "It's been a long time."

"Who is he?!" UU's quiet voice could not hide his harsh tone.

"His name is Tookas."

Yane laughed. "Tookas? His mother must've hated him." Yane's attempt at levity failed.

"Who is he?!" UU repeated, his tone no different than seconds prior.

"I'm afraid you're not going to like my answer, Colonel."

"Who is he?!"

"He's secret police." Abuss Onuss stopped, as though considering his words with careful attention."

"Don't make me ask again."

"Now, UU!" Bingus Jam interrupted the exchange between the two. "If you're here to threaten, that can be remedied."

UU rotated his head to flash a menacing stare at the creature he considered to be a bloviating waste of Zhiloan blood. Without delay, UU returned his gaze to Abuss Onuss. After several seconds, the Drebehran knew he had to provide an answer.

"Tookas the Ceratofs, as he is referred to while off planet, was an agent for the Ceratofs secret police—the Zanzi—when the Great Exodus began." The legal leader paused in order to keep himself calm. "There were rumors he began playing both sides." He looked from side to side. "Apparently, that is true, judging by your tone and demeanor."

"He *was* playing both sides," Yane interjected as he stressed the updated tense of Tookas' existence. "But keep going."

"Law enforcement doesn't play both sides!" UU snarled. "There was more to this vile creature."

"At first," Abuss Onuss followed Yane's orders and continued. "He told our offices he was going undercover. We found that odd given the entire Ceratofs societal structure had fled. They moved out everyone, regardless of their age, wealth—or lack thereof—or standing. They made everyone go, yet some stayed somehow, including him.”

UU’s tone did not relax. “Was he working for you or any other organization before last night?”

“Maybe you can tell us what this is all about, Colonel,” Bingus Jam interjected for the second time. “You come in here real—“

“Was he working for you or any other organization before last night?” UU repeated his question.

“No.” Abuss Onuss’ head shake illustrated resolve. “No, he was not.” After a pause to gain more courage, he asked, “May we know what upset you?”

“Tookas is dead because he kidnapped two of my comrades.” UU’s cadence reflected a precision in word choice and clarity of meaning.

“We’ve been informed you only brought back two prisoners.”

“There wasn’t a whole lot of surrendering happening.”

“Oh. I see.” Abuss Onuss struggled with meaningful conversation.

“They were ready for us,” Yane added. “They had enough of a force to wipe us out; we just barely made it out.”

“We did not set you up, Colonel,” Abuss Onuss proclaimed with a burst of energy. “I want you to succeed! We get dozens of requests a day to escort Returners back to their home worlds so they can get more of their possessions—which they don't realize have been looted already." The apparent non sequitur made perfect sense to the law enforcement leader.

"There is very little wealth left in the quadrant," Bingus Jam added.

"How is that a convincing argument?" UU inquired. He failed to understand Abuss Onuss' supposed logic, and he continued to ignore Bingus Jam.

"The sooner law enforcement succeeds, the sooner we can all get out of here," Bingus Jam said. "If you can help us, I can put away my distaste for you."

"I'm impressed but not moved." UU mocked his fellow Zhiloan with a dismissive tone. He turned his attention back to Abuss Onuss. "Do you know how often we encounter creatures trying to play both sides of the law?"

"I know there are criminals who switch sides, back and forth, helping law enforcement. I don't know of any officers of the law who switch back and forth," the head of the Board of Ten responded. "That generally doesn't happen. They have too much to lose and not enough to gain."

For the first time, Pracen spoke up. "How did Tookas die?"

"Quickly," was all UU would volunteer.

"Colonel," Abuss Onuss changed the subject. "You have our support. We want you to succeed."

UU stood, using his bulky frame to play a role in his message. "Then you'd better eliminate leaks. Those Trerzons knew we were coming."

Yane read UU's cue and stood, then followed his boss out the door as the meeting came to an abrupt end.

When the door closed, Abuss Onuss turned to his colleagues. "It would be beneficial if he succeeds."

"It would be beneficial if he dies," Bingus Jam riposted.

Pracen looked into the empty space of the conference room as he spoke. "He's like the Motrinx Fever. You can't kill him. You just hope he goes away."

Chapter Twelve

The brilliance of the light caused all vision to fade to white. He could see nothing—not that he could see anything before the light appeared. Thoughts swirled around a nebulous idea: *This should hurt. I should be in pain.* Yet pain never followed the light. The light and subsequent lack of reaction displayed a disconnect between what he observed and felt.

Muffled sounds carried the cadence of voices; notes of a song, lingering in the air. He felt as though he were under the murky waves of the TyBar Sea on his home planet of Rojan, struggling to come up to break the surface; yet he could breathe.

Somewhere in the distance, a dull roar smothered all sounds which attempted to enter his ear drums. On occasion, he felt the warm breath of someone who tested him for reactions, yet the disconnect prohibited him from responding.

He possessed knowledge that something—perhaps a medical laser—pierced his skull and probed his brain. *I can't feel it.* Turbulence rocked his thoughts, leaving unfinished notions to disintegrate; brainwaves breaking on the rocky mental coastline, falling apart. He waited for the next set of waves to roll in only to dissipate into a pool of useless neurons, never to become complete thoughts.

What is happening? He struggled with an occasional burst of emotion; yet, like his attempts at thought, they, too, dissolved into nothingness.

Chabdab felt himself melt away from consciousness and into a dream world. The probing into his brain seemed to leave him no choice; decisions were being made for his brain—not by him.

"Chabdab! Over here!" The masculine voice conveyed not a request but a command.

"Yes sir!"

"Lieutenant Chabdab, your soldiers are disobeying my orders!"

The lieutenant recognized the face, yet the voice seemed off; different. It was Colonel Ursulanus.

"Yes, sir! They are disobeying your orders, sir! Because they are obeying mine." To the colonel's surprise, Chabdab uttered his retort with the utmost confidence.

"What?!" Colonel Ursulanus asked in obvious shock. "You countermanded my order, Lieutenant?!"

"What happened to your voice, sir?" Chabdab asked, though the whiff of confused innocence went ignored.

"What?!"

"Your voice, sir. You sound." Chabdab fought to find the correct description. "Different."

"Lieutenant! I ordered you and your soldiers to board that craft and take them to our hideout! Do it now!"

"No, sir. I will not."

The large, blue-skinned colonel grabbed Chabdab by the throat. The smaller creature struggled to breathe until he began to thrash. After several seconds of struggling, he struck the colonel in the throat, causing the latter to release his deadly hold. As he let go, Colonel Ursulanus pushed Chabdab backward, causing the lieutenant to fall on his back on the rocky soil.

When he sat up, his grandmother rushed to his side. "Oh Chabdab! Are you all right?!" Her long, partially webbed fingers caressed his face. She rubbed the back of her hands across his forehead as her scale-like pinkish skin soothed the young soldier's pain. Her tall, cylindrical ears, so adored in their culture, gave her the appearance of a Rojani female model, despite her age.

"Tell them what they want to know," a stern male voice scolded. Twice as large as the female, Chabdab's grandfather sounded just as he did in the younger's memories.

"Father capitulated," Chabdab responded, the disapproval in his voice evident.

"But you're not capitulating," his grandmother answered, as though she expected the refrain. "You're not giving up secrets to the enemy—you're helping Rojanis everywhere."

"How?"

With a display of impatience, the grandfather attempted to steer the conversation back on track. "We love you, Chabdab, but you've got to help us. You've got to help all Rojanis. Just tell them what they need so they can save our planet from destruction."

"Tell them where the hideout is, honey."

"I don't know," Chabdab answered.

"Sure you do," she admonished. "You know but you're being childish by not telling us." She turned her hand over and began to use her sharp, thick nails on his cheeks and forehead, scraping away his scaly skin.

"But I don't," he insisted. "I don't know."

"We have complete faith in you, Chabdab." The grandmother dug deeper with her nails. "We know Colonel Ursulanus would trust you with the information."

"Grandmother! You're hurting me!"

"These officials need to know," she prodded further. "You have to tell them. You could help all Rojanis."

Chabdab faded away, watching his grandparents slowly disappear below him as he rose upward, into the sky, as a chill overtook his body.

The painless white light returned along with the muffled sounds which seemed to be voices. The light seemed to shake, but Chabdab lacked the ability to determine whether the movement was his own body or the light itself. Then, after only seconds of awareness, he found himself on the side of a pockmarked hill devoid of vegetation.

"Private Chabdab!" a voice penetrated the sounds of explosions and laser fire. "Continue your mission! Get up the hill!"

He looked upward in time to see a comrade step on a landmine. The subsequent explosion rained dirt, blood, and body parts down onto him.

"Move, Private!" The officer ordered from ten meters away.

"This is not my mission!" Chabdab answered. "I don't know where the objective is!" He shouted every word in order for his commanding officer to hear him.

"If you don't get up that hill, we're all going to die!" The officer's voice contained a mix of command and pained request. "Come on, Chabdab! We need you!"

This isn't my war. I've never been here. Chabdab surveyed his surroundings. *I've never seen this place.*

"Now, Chabdab! Let's go! We've got a mission to fulfill!"

"It's not my mission!"

"I need you to lead us! Get on your feet! We're going to die unless we get to the hideout!"

An explosion obliterated the commanding officer. Another storm of dirt, blood, and body parts rained down on Private Chabdab. When the gruesome mix of "rain" ceased,

Chabdab leaped to his feet and ran down the hill. As he neared the bottom, intense pain shot through his chest and radiated through his torso. He dropped to the ground. He could feel life slipping away. Breathing became a struggle. Pain more intense than he had ever felt plagued him. Thoughts faded. Consciousness faded.

•　　•　　•

Quiet alarms sounded at the nurse's station down the hall, unheard by the perpetrators. A nurse entered the hospital room. "What are you doing?!" The female, from the planet Mang, made an instinctive dash toward the patient. The two males, both from Asimon, barged past her and through the doorway.

A small, hand-held medical laser remained next to Chabdab's head, injecting a potentially lethal dose of small laser blasts into the patient's body. The nurse grabbed the instrument and turned it off.

Caregivers with differing skills rushed in to provide assistance. "Where's the doctor?!" one of them shouted. "I don't think he's going to make it!"

Chapter Thirteen

"Give me an update."

"Our sources tell us law enforcement has adopted a strategy of ignoring us to clean up other hot spots."

"That's not good," the Premier responded, annoyance cutting into his words. "We want them focused on us."

"Sir, I understand that." The Premier's chief aide, Rocash, sounded as though he were paddling upstream before he even climbed into the boat. "I understand we want the focus on 'rescuing' you, but I think we're strong enough to make a move soon."

"You do?" A smile crossed the Asimoni's face. As of late, the gentlemanly premier of the planet had ceased viewing the traditional atmosphere of the palace as acceptable and evolved into someone who preferred a stuffy regality. He now preferred "Premier" over "Premier Seveen;" a business suit had been replaced by a purple robe; his head was frequently adorned with a tall, thin hat ordinarily reserved for Asimoni clergy.

"Yes, sir. I do."

"You think we can just dance right out of the quadrant, set up shop in another quadrant, and begin taking over the galaxy."

"We have the riches," Rocash implored. The young apprentice appeared even younger than he was, and the Premier enjoyed the verbal pokes of reminding him of this fact, which led the aide to employ a defensive demeanor whenever around his boss. "We can buy the best contacts, the best 'garshanes,' the best — "

"The best garshanes?" The Premier referred to the colloquial term for mercenaries. "I don't want garshanes, Rocash. I want the best armies."

"Yes sir. That will take time."

"We don't have—" The Premier interrupted himself. "You know, I appreciate that you're thinking, Rocash. But don't. Don't do that. It's my job to think."

"Sir? I know what you pay me for, but some of those around you are more interested in glory."

"I'm interested in glory!" The Premier thumped his chest with his fist as he stressed the importance of accolades and recognition for himself. "I want to rule the galaxy—not 'us.' Not you. Not my minions—but me. Me! Do you understand?!" The Premier stepped forward and looked down at his small-statured lackey.

"Yes sir." Rocash turned his head away in obvious disgust. His frown would not allow him to mask his feelings.

"Are we clear, Rocash?"

"I just don't have the same faith in the bravery of the outlaws as you do."

The Premier lifted a hand and, with the back of his fingers, turned Rocash's face until their eyes met. "Are we clear?"

"Yes, Premier. We are."

•   •   •

"Has anyone heard from Chabdab or Kimberlina?"

"No." UU's somber response answered Geeba's question on multiple levels.

"I'm not going to lie," Blik added. Known for his blunt manner of speaking and wild ideas for inflicting pain and revenge, Geeba cringed at what might follow. Instead, she relaxed as he responded with a pained yet sane reply. "I cannot foresee a scenario in which they were allowed to survive. I'm sorry to say it."

The eyes of Blik and UU met. The latter understood the former meant well. "I'm hoping they were just captured for information," UU said, his dark brown eyes sad.

UU wandered away from the group, basking in the cool breeze which pushed away the warm rays of the midday sun. The yellow star Lucan turned the atmosphere a deep blue—a perfect afternoon. Fields of dead crops, unattended since the announcement of the impending supernova, gave the impression harvest had occurred only a few Heislerian weeks ago.

Geeba saw a chance to soothe UU's concerns, but she chose to stay away. Because she remained so close to him, she realized others had talked about their relationship behind her back, filling in the blanks with their own lack of knowledge. Imaginations had kicked in about the depths of their feelings for each other and what the coziness actually meant. UU and Geeba understood that relationship, but others simply leaned on conjecture and rumor as a substitute for facts. She chose to allow the misgivings of others to shape her actions at this moment.

Little conversation ensued. The bandits kept to themselves, slumber setting in on a few of the gang when the roar of an engine scuttled thoughts, imaginations, and sleep. It was Yane's craft, bringing a report from their meetings with law enforcement.

.   .   .

"What kind of fools do they think we are?!" Anthun roared.

A half dozen voices erupted at once. Geeba and Kreeg expressed their level of concern; Anthun expressed his predictable anger; Blik and Bill engaged in a brief side conversation, their amazement expressed with a healthy coating of gall. The splintered moment would end soon, so UU stood motionless, a wry smile adorned his rough face.

As was their unplanned tradition, the group sat on the ground as UU paced. He allowed the conversations to drown each other out until, after a half minute, he lost his patience. "All right!" His voice boomed across the deserted farmland. Within two seconds the group sat in silence.

"Yane, are they that foolish to believe the Premier is a captive?" UU did not attempt to hide his disdain.

"Alana and I tried to explain it to them," Yane said as he nodded.

"Yane was forceful about it," Alana added.

"And yet, here we are," UU shook his head.

"Here we are," Yane said in a failed attempt to suppress a smile.

"What's so funny?" UU did not sound angry, but he could not conceal his obvious confusion.

"They are sold on the Premier being legitimately in peril," Yane answered.

"They spoke of his predicament in somber terms," Alana concluded. "It was rather pathetic."

"Why does everyone in the quadrant understand what he's doing except law enforcement?" Blik asked in a baffled tone.

"I'll tell you why," Yane answered. "They have so few actual law enforcement officials acting as law enforcement they don't know who to believe." Yane looked around at the group as he climbed to his feet. "There are a lot of creatures throughout the quadrant who've never been with the police in their lives, but now they're deciding who to arrest and working on complex strategies."

"It's a series of fiefdoms, Colonel," Alana explained. "They're riddled with spies and they don't even know it."

"So how can we trust them?" Mookie asked. "How can we operate if we may be betrayed at any moment?"

UU's head motions mirrored that of someone who had just escaped from the Zhilo Institute for the Mentally Decrepit. His neck twitched, dragging his head with it, and he alternated between head nods and shakes.

Geeba recognized UU was about to explode in anger. "Maybe we shouldn't take this at face value," she interjected as she tried to calm UU. "Maybe if we remember we're only dealing with certain creatures, which will limit leaks. Yane, do you think we can trust our contacts?"

"Limit leaks?" Anthun could not contain himself. "You saw what happened on Ceratofs! You were there!" Anthun looked around at the group members. "We can't trust any of them."

Before the conversation could collapse into a cacophony of complaints, UU repeated Geeba's question. "Yane, do you think we can trust our contacts?"

"I would like to be able to say we can trust them," Yane said, a certain lack of enthusiasm for his message dominating his tone. "Abuss Onus is a politician more than law enforcement. Bingus Jam and Pracen both hate you." He looked at UU with a chagrined smile. "While they want what's best for the quadrant, I don't trust any of them. The old structure is gone—they fled in the Great Exodus, so I don't know any of them. But I still think we can trust the Board of Ten. They were in place before the madness."

"I completely agree," Alana injected her opinion. "They may hate you, and by extension us, but they've already seen our value. Pracen was amazed we were able to dismantle a large portion of the Trerzon Gang."

"They did tell us they were working to get rid of some of the squids," Yane added, using a slang word for criminals who infiltrate a legitimate organization.

Kreeg seized on a pause in the conversation. "Colonel, is this plan of yours working?"

"Every chance I get, I try to communicate with military friends in the other quadrants," UU answered in his own roundabout way. "Media in the other quadrants are focused on sob stories of those who lost everything or the Premier or the science behind the nova." He paused as he considered his words. "Because I'm not on their minds, it will make it easier for all of us to restore our names. The plan is working. That's what makes this next step so important."

"So, you want to go through with this?" Bill asked.

UU and Geeba exchanged a glance, both allowing their eyes to express shock. Bill rarely spoke up, especially when the conversation turned contentious.

"Yes, Bill. I do." UU again slowed his speech to choose his words with care. "The odds may be against us gaining anything out of it, but normal lives will be impossible if we don't try to change our reputations, so this is the next step."

"We're going to be incredibly outnumbered," Bill added. "More than usual."

"It's a reconnaissance mission, Bill."

"Okay." Bill did not add an explanation to his acceptance.

•　　•　　•

Recovering from his recent assault, Chabdab remained in a coma. The nurse, a short, brown Corsan, listened with solemn intensity to the Zhiloan doctor. Her thick, matted hair was less a product of her species and more due to the long hours of the job and her failure to find time to wash it.

"Okay, nurse. Now don't move the clamp."

She gripped the steel holders, which were attached to the clamp, with steady pressure as the doctor held onto Chabdab's wrist. The small medical gun found its mark atop the steel plate and he pulled the trigger with a slow, easy motion. The *pop* of metal striking metal caused the nurse's head to flinch but her hands remained steady.

"Okay." The doctor took a deep breath as he stood back in apparent admiration of his work. "Nothing imperative hit, so it's a good, clean attachment."

The nurse looked down at the patient as she shook her head. "I don't know what they want with you, mister, but I sure hope they don't cut off your arm if they want to abduct you."

Her chagrined statement caught the doctor off guard. "Yes. That would be terrible!" His pronouncement seemed punctuated by the shock of the thought.

"That's what I would do, doctor," she explained, unable to hide her incredulity at his naiveté. "If I kidnapped someone with a Universal Tracking Device on his arm, I'd just cut off his arm."

The blue-skinned doctor lifted his eyebrows. "I hadn't thought of that." With that, he left the room, leaving the nurse alone with Chabdab.

"They almost killed you," she said with empathy in her voice. "Something tells me if they come back again, it won't go well." She stared at his round face as she added. "Whoever you are."

She shook her head as she walked out of the patient's room.

Chapter Fourteen

Yane piloted his Drebehran Armed Shuttle, a craft his friends found to be an odd choice for someone who should attempt to appear inconspicuous while traveling. The Mangan did not care whether his choice of ships led to derision—he had survived many scrapes while in the craft.

Kreeg, in the co-pilot's chair, kept track of instrument readings for Yane. Blik sat behind the cockpit, alone in a row of seats, with a sullen expression plastered on his face. He made his third and final attempt to convince Yane of his intentions.

"Yane, if I don't monitor the communications as we drop out of light," he said, referring to light speed. "Then it could be too late by the time we figure out whether we've been spotted."

Aggravated by Blik's persistence, Yane rotated his chair to look at his friend. "Blik, I told you. We'll be fine. It's not like it's pre-exodus."

Blik took a long, deep breath but kept his opinions to himself.

In the back of the craft, UU and Geeba engaged in a quiet conversation which was not meant for the ears of the others. They stood facing each other, within reach of one another.

"Untas, you know I trust you." She put a hand on his chest, below his shoulder. "I'm not afraid of dying, I just want to have a life after all this insanity."

"I'll get you out alive. I promise."

"I'm not convinced we will." Her sigh lifted up her torso for a couple of seconds before culminating in a slow release of air and a low groan. She took her hand off the colonel and let it fall to her side.

"I know you trust me, and I know we've had some close calls." UU seemed to stop mid-thought. He stared into Geeba's bright blue eyes.

She took advantage of his truncated statement. "Don't you want to start all over? Spend your life with someone?"

"I haven't, no. Not since Karesh died."

She looked into his eyes as though she could heal his emotional wounds.

"I know it's been three Heislerian years." He hesitated again.

"You can torture yourself for only so long."

He smiled. "I am pretty good at it." He dropped his head.

"You're lonely, whether or not you'll admit it to yourself."

"Well." He lifted a hand to her neck and brushed his thumb across the bottom of her jaw, feeling her soft face. "You know how I feel about you."

"No. I don't," Geeba responded. "I really don't."

"Colonel!" It was Yane. "We're about to drop out of light speed."

"Coming." UU winked at Geeba before leading the way to the large but already-crowded cockpit.

The shuttle dropped out of light speed and approached the planet of Asimon, watching as the brown, blue, and green planet grew larger in front of them.

UU and Geeba took seats to Blik's right and looked on as Kreeg, still in the co-pilot's chair, checked readouts to ensure potential threats did not close in on their position.

"How is the digital view?" Yane asked, referring to Kreeg's diligent study of all objects which could turn out to be other ships.

"All's quiet so far."

Yane spun around in his seat to address his seated passengers. "Enter at the south pole, get as close to Roandan as reasonable, and then put Blik to work with his gadgets to measure their activities."

All eyes turned to Blik. With his specialty of communications, surveillance and decoding, responsibilities fell to him. He enjoyed every opportunity to display his expertise. His customary laugh launched right on schedule when the subject of his electronic wizardry came to the fore. The loud, penetrating chortle signaled his happiness, and the team had grown to appreciate the annoying, comical wheeze of a cackle. "If all goes well," he explained the reason for his latest laughing outburst. "Next time we're here, I'll get to play with my toys and kill some bad beasts!" He laughed again, this time with a deeper, louder laugh which signaled his satisfaction.

"Uh. Uh! Uh, we have a problem!" Unsure how to react, Kreeg managed to blurt out his words after a brief struggle.

"This is why I needed to monitor communications as we left light speed!" There was no time to argue, but Blik felt the need.

Having spun in his chair again at Kreeg's weak announcement, Yane entered instructions to the ship via its computer and pressed a button. Before the over-sized laser cannon round could reach the shuttle, the ship launched itself away at a 90-degree angle. With only one second to spare, the large red laser beam sliced through space to the starboard side of the craft.

"Was that a planet-based laser?!" Yane shouted as he continued to manipulate the shuttle. "Blik, you were right and I was wrong. Monitor their communications, please!" His eyes remained fixed on the planet. After a moment, he returned his gaze to the control panel to punch in more commands to the computer as he exclaimed, "Who has a planet-based laser cannon?!"

Leaning over Kreeg's shoulder, Blik made quick work of his task. With a dover in his ear, Blik announced his discovery. "It's not planet based. There's a battle cruiser orbiting Asimon. I think Kreeg missed it because it's so close to the outer atmosphere."

"Sorry."

"Don't worry about it, Kreeg," Blik said with an unemotional tone. "We'd have to have military equipment to destroy that thing."

"What do we do now?" Kreeg asked.

"We go find a beach somewhere and enjoy some sunshine." With that, Yane punched in a series of commands on the computer and the craft leaped forward. After only a few seconds, the blur of Asimon now far behind them, the shuttle slowed out of light speed again.

"Where are we?" UU asked.

"About a million kilometers from that cannon's reach," Yane answered in a deadpan tone.

"We'll never get in there," Geeba spoke up. "Unless we take care of that battle cruiser."

"Abuss Onuss seemed to think they had gotten their hands on one—but just one, he says. A very old one." Yane moved his head back and forth, then up and down, conveying his skepticism with a combination of simultaneous nods and shakes. He turned to face Geeba as he added, "Just one. They didn't know whether it was air-worthy."

Blik clapped once, startling his friends. "I believe you're correct: the Asimonis only possess one such craft," he declared. "The ship communicated with a command center on the ground, and no other ships were contacted."

UU narrowed his dark brown eyes. "We have a new layer to the plan."

"Destroy that ship?" Geeba asked, knowing how the friend she admired viewed life.

"Destroy that ship." He paused, still in thought. "And, it could provide a perfect diversion."

For once, Blik did not laugh; he frowned. "I like killing creatures face-to-face. I don't like this spacecraft stuff."

"If you want to kill face-to-face, we're going to have to take out that battle cruiser," Yane said.

"Fine." Blik nodded. "But can we board the ship?"

Yane shook his head and closed his eyes.

Chapter Fifteen

Rick exited the farmhouse out the back door and headed toward Julie's office—a metal shed perched on a concrete foundation. The building, 30 feet long and 20 feet wide, housed records—the important ones were stored in the house—and featured a desk for Julie and a wheeled office chair she adored. Rick had found amusement in her attachment to the chair and wondered aloud about the strange behaviors of earthlings.

As Rick left the house, a young man walked out of Julie's office. He turned and walked away from Rick, leaving the Heislerian to only see the back of the man's head.

Something seemed familiar.

Before he could continue with his thoughts, Julie opened the door to her office. His eyes wondered back to the man, but the latter rounded a corner of a large wooden barn which housed many of their tools and equipment.

"Rick! I'm happy you're awake." She ran up to him and hugged him.

"That's the last time I will allow you to give me a shot of medicine."

Embarrassed, she put her head down. As they stood on the gravel driveway in relative solitude, she felt the need for a mea culpa. "I thought I calculated the weight of a cow versus the weight of a—you. Your weight."

"I'm still rather groggy."

"I'm sorry, Rick!" The Kansas breeze lifted her hair upward from behind, partially obscuring her face.

"I'm not in pain anymore, so I guess it worked." He reached to his head and adjusted his red headband.

Her genuine smile radiated as brightly as the Sun which hit her face. "Come on. I'll drive you into town and I'll buy you a burger. I know you like them." Julie had learned that, as long as she kept the Heislerian well-covered, with only his face and hands exposed, Rick could pass for an earthling, albeit it a rough-looking earthling.

"I like burgers. I wish we had them where I come from." The wave of satisfaction which overtook the alien told Julie that his 12 hours of sleep was worth it.

•   •   •

"Are you sure about this?"

"Yes, I'm sure. I heard her say they're going to get a burger." Ricardo—or 'Ricky,' as he was known in the area—had only worked for the Pitts family for eight months.

"So, they'll be gone for a while then, huh?" His co-worker and friend Allen was not the smartest guy. He had worked for the Pitts family for three years. Julie frequently chastised the pale skinned, lanky young man for allowing himself to sunburn so often while working with the machinery.

The two hurried through the house. As they headed down the steps to reach the first basement, Allen's doubts rose again. "What's a portal?"

"I don't know, but I heard him say something about it one day."

"What's it do?"

"I don't know."

"What's it look like?"

Ricky stopped on the stairway and tried to look into Allen's eyes through the darkness. "We'll know it when we see it, I'm sure. Stop asking your dumb questions!"

When they reached the bottom of the concrete stairs, a naked bulb, already illuminated and hanging from the ceiling, provided a faint amount of light. Items for storage populated shelves—over a dozen shelves and tables littered the large, stone "second" basement. A lone flashlight rested on a nearby table; Ricky grabbed it, tested it, then after a quick scan of the room proceeded to walk to the next set of stairs.

"I ain't going down there. It's dark!"

"Yes, Allen. It's dark. That's why I grabbed a flashlight."

Without a response, Allen continued to play the role he carried out so well: follower.

"Rick scares me."

"Yes! He scares me, too." Ricky failed to hide his fear. "I saw what he did to Julio and Jonathan!"

"But how can he be a monster?"

"I don't know. I just know I saw him get real huge before he threw me out into the yard."

The brief silence provided Allen time to think of his next question. "If Rick killed Julio and Jonathan, why didn't they arrest him?"

"Who's gonna believe an illegal Guatemalan that a monster killed them when he just looks like an ugly person?"

Allen did not have a retort, so he continued following Ricky and the flashlight.

After a full minute of silent searching, Ricky spoke first. "There is nothing down here. Nothing!"

"Just darkness and walls." Allen could not see Ricky shake his head in derision.

They entered a small room—the "lower" basement. Ceiling, floor, and walls all made of stone, they felt as though they had entered a dungeon—minus the torture devices.

"I can't believe it!" In frustration, Ricky slapped the rear wall of the room. Before Allen could respond, a brilliant flash of white light momentarily blinded the pair. With arms over their faces, they stepped back in unison.

When the light dissipated, they found themselves in the labyrinth of dark rooms and hallways which served the Eese Planetary Museum. The two young men lacked the understanding they had just traversed the galaxy within seconds.

•   •   •

After half an hour, the two humans—now aliens themselves—emerged from the bowels of the museum and sucked in their first breaths of the Zhiloan night air.

"Hey!" Allen looked around as he quizzed his friend. "Where the hell are we?"

"Well, I know where we're not."

"How did it get night?"

"I don't know."

"It's dark."

"Yes, I know."

The natives of Kansas and Guatemala walked down the moonlit city street. The eerie scene was deepened by a glass building which reflected moonbeams at odd angles, lighting up the street as though artificially powered. A streak of light highlighted Ricky's chest when he stopped to look behind them.

Looking upward, Allen pointed. "Look at the Moon. It's gigantic!" The gray disc appeared to be four times larger than the moon they had left. The glass building broke the light into individual beams, which gave the appearance of a thousand spotlights illuminating their path.

"We don't need this," Ricky announced as he clicked the button on the side of the flashlight.

"You just didn't like me seeing you shake," Allen mocked.

"I'm not shaking!" With that he strode with an air of confidence into the bright section of the city.

Allen followed, but they had only marched a few more seconds before they saw what lay ahead. "Ricky!" was all Allen could manage.

"I see them." Ricky's voice trembled. He looked around—for what, he did not know.

"Maybe we should go the other way."

Ricky did not see the need. "What for? They ain't gonna do nothing to us."

"How can you be sure?"

"Just watch, man. Just watch."

As they neared the two creatures walking toward them, the size of the individuals became apparent. Ricky muttered under his breath, "They're huge." But he kept walking. The large, gray individuals both stood over six-feet-nine in American terms. Both sported large muscles, a thick frame, dark eyes, and vicious expressions.

One spoke to the other in Zhiloan, which seemed to be gibberish to the earthlings. When the second creature chuckled, cold sweat lit the earthlings' necks and arms.

"Who are you scrawny creatures?" The first Zhiloan asked in Shersheen. He did not have the light blue skin of royal heritage as Colonel UU did. These Zhiloans were dirty, layers of grime adding on by the Heislerian week as time separated these Remainers from the day the Great Exodus began.

Before either man could respond, four additional Zhiloans rounded a corner on the other side of the brightly lit building. With hundreds of moonbeams glancing off the glass and highlighting the men's anxiety, the natives never felt threatened.

"We're earthlings. Who are you?" Allen continued his penchant for asking questions.

"What's an earthling?" the second Zhiloan retorted.

"That means we come from Earth." Allen puffed out his skinny chest as though he felt a surge of superiority—he understood what an "earthling" was and they did not.

The first Zhiloan summed up the situation as their friends neared. "If they don't work hard, maybe they'll taste good."

"Boiled?" the second Zhiloan asked with a laugh.

"Probably. As scrawny as they are, I hope they know how to be good slaves."

Chapter Sixteen

The sleek, silver ship slowed below light speed, transitioning from a flash of light into a recognizable Rojani fighter craft. Krokreeg Grust never felt comfortable in an unarmed vehicle, and he long ago decided that, if he wanted to travel safely, he needed to always be armed, regardless of the setting. While he feared an armed ship would draw undue attention, he considered being unprepared to defend himself was foolishness of the highest order. In this post-exodus existence, survival loomed over every decision.

On Rojan's second moon, a secret colony of a Rojan religious order lay hidden in a desert, deep in a canyon. Having completed their mission to rescue art and artifacts, they then focused their energies on efforts to extricate the irreplaceable religious valuables to the "safe" quadrants. Had an observer taken time to notice, that observer would have witnessed ship after ship come and go as those involved in their mission of saving what remained of Quadrant 4 culture continued to off-load from the moon what the religious order had removed from various planets. Now a Heislerian year removed from the Great Exodus, little remained to salvage; the religious order focused on rescuing the innocent and getting themselves out.

Though not part of the religious order, a female Eemlurian and her young child resided among the fervent followers, tucked safely away in one of a canyon's many caves.

Lacking the amenities of her home planet and comfort of her former life on Rojan, Rokila Grust could only pray life would soon change.

Rokila recognized the roar of the engine; the single-engine fighter craft produced a sound like no other. From within the cave, she emerged, daughter's hand in hers, to greet her husband. The religious order had rubbed off on her, and when her prayers were answered, she felt closer still to her protectors.

A short, slender Eemlurian with typical pale-red skin tone and deep facial features, Rokila raced toward her husband—though not too quickly lest her young daughter Rekil should fall to the ground. She slowed as she neared the ship, catching her breath in the process. As Kreeg climbed down the short ladder into view, her heart seemed to skip a beat.

"Daddy!" Rekil squealed, too young to feel tired from the brief dash from the cave. "Daddy!" she shouted again. The young girl escaped her mother's grasp and rushed ahead.

Kreeg dropped to a knee and absorbed the crash from the little girl's body. Without delay, he began kissing his daughter on her pink cheeks. After a big, loving squeeze, he stood to greet his wife of fifteen Heislerian years. "Oh, love!"

Rokila could not speak and did not try. In silence, her tears dripped onto her husband's shoulder while others streamed down her light-red cheeks made redder by the moment. She pulled away to ask the question he knew she would ask. "When?"

He shook his head as a frown enveloped his face. "I don't know, love. UU has a plan, though."

Without a word, her forehead drifted into his chest as though pushed from behind by an unseen hand.

"I will get you out of here, I promise," Kreeg consoled as he ran his fingers through the hair on the back of her head. "I promise."

She pulled her head back and gazed into his green eyes which matched her own. "Rekil and I can't stand this much longer." Her tone reflected neither anger nor demand, rather a level of sadness which eschewed description. "I don't know how much longer I can live like this."

"I already have a plan to get you out." He paused as he became lost in her eyes. He looked away to regain his focus. "It won't be long. It won't be long."

"How long are you here this time?"

"Not as long as last time," Kreeg responded with a chuckle. "I was late, and I don't want to do anything that will bring attention to your existence. We must keep you hidden."

As little Rekil continued to hug her father's thigh, Kreeg and Rokila embraced and kissed away their sorrow and pain.

•　　•　　•

In the bowels of the massive Asimoni capitol building, allegedly safe from bombs of war, the Premier met with his inner circle as well as leaders of various gangs and syndicates. He held no concerns about bombs or war—he knew that he was safe; no one could get to him with their planetary shield and the powerful battleship which patrolled the planet.

The Premier's penchant for wearing purple robes abated somewhat as the "days of action," as he dubbed the execution of his upcoming plans, approached. Nevertheless, his attire seemed to always include the color purple. In this instance, his purple buttoned-down dress shirt brought to mind a king garbed in casual apparel. The seated leader, dressed in black pants and matching shoes, his white skin with brown stripes visible on his neck and part of his face, exuded the confidence fit for an absolute ruler.

"Everyone understands this conversation is privileged, correct?" The Premier moved his head with a slow, deliberate pace, eyes glaring at each associate seated at the long, rectangular table. After receiving the requisite nods, he continued. "When we leave, you will have chosen your most loyal staff to accompany you. Only the most loyal and the toughest fighters will make the journey."

Before he could explain his words, a Gigorl boss allowed his eyebrows to shoot upward in surprise. "Sir?"

The mere implication of disagreement brought a small sample of the Premier's wrath. "Would you like to finish my presentation, Wocumb?" The sneering question cut into the crime leader's ego.

His meek voice and demeanor cleared up the matter as he posited a weak response. "I am only trying to understand your wishes, sir."

"Then perhaps you should allow me to finish giving you my wishes." Despite the smile, the Premier's acidic snarl delivered the caustic message. After a brief pause designed to continue the discomfort for the subordinate, their leader continued. "My entire staff of palace personnel will make the journey, as will our best fighters here." He looked around the room at each face as he continued. "I want each field leader to choose his best creatures. The rest have to be left behind. To exit too large of a group would provoke suspicion throughout the quadrants."

Not accustomed to cowering, the criminal known as Wocumb again spoke up, his resolved hardened. "Premier, you are asking me to betray my gang. Why would I betray anyone? My entire organization is exceptional, from top to bottom!" The strong-willed Gigorline punctuated his last sentence with a strong voice—stronger with every word.

"Are you questioning me?!" the Premier demanded with a shout.

"Yes." Wocumb's confidence soared with the one-word response.

The Premier seemed to relax. His body language exhibited a calm demeanor. His shoulders dropped and the intensity in his eyes diminished. "I understand. You feel loyal to your subordinates."

"And not a blind loyalty; an *earned* loyalty." Wocumb's confidence blossomed into cockiness. "There is no better gang in the quadrants. My team can pick any lock, destroy any building, hunt down any beast, and persuade a city to turn on its own leadership. We are the best, and I need them all."

The Premier nodded as his face communicated warmth and reflection. "All is well then. We will discuss this further, in private."

An aura of triumph overcame the Gigorline. His species, like the Heislerians and Zhiloans, failed to see themselves inferior to anyone. "Thank you, Premier," was all he added.

"Our operation has become too large to include everyone in the days of action," the Premier continued. "Besides, a nice diversion will aid us as we relocate. When we arrive in Quadrant 3—Xaveis is my choice—we already have enough military force to follow through with my plans for an immediate coup." He paused to allow his plan to be processed by his minions. They all knew the planet Xaveis was a good choice for their next step in dominating the quadrants. "My friends in the Xaveisir military have assured me now is the time to overthrow their premier."

"Xaveis will be a base of operations, then?" a Ceratofs leader asked.

"Yes. From there we will conquer Quadrant Three. This fits in perfectly with my original plans," the Premier answered, his smile deepening. "I will have prepared a message for those left behind," he explained. "I will make sure they understand they will perish with honor. They have served us well. If they escape the nova, they will be arrested wherever they turn up. If they stay, they will die glorious and honorable deaths."

The Premier provided a prolonged description of his plans. Despite Wocumb's expressed concerns, no one else felt emboldened to disagree with any aspect of the details.

•　　•　　•

A creature in a bright gold uniform exited the small transport craft. The flying machine had been built to move military or police troops into locations for quick strikes or to impose strength through numbers. In this case, only three officers emerged.

Air cycles, utilized by individual police officers, littered the urban area, parked in front of a large warehouse which had been used by a bread factory before the Great Exodus.

The ranking officer on the scene walked away from the police transport. His face shield remained in place until the ranking officer already present reached him. The gold shield, which matched his uniform, reflected the rays from the nearby star, Mize. The Fankan afternoon sky was known to be brighter than what most foreigners, and some Fankans, could handle. The ranking officer at the scene, a Lieutenant Ashken, was reminded of the blinding star as he caught his own reflection in his Police Chief's visor. The reflection proved sharp enough to display Lt. Ashken's squinting, crumpled face.

"How bad is it?" Police Chief Rolan Crui asked as he raised his visor.

"Bad. Bloody." Ashken turned away from his boss and put his back to the source of the light. "This is one thing I won't miss when we finally get out of here," the officer added, referring to the star.

"Do we know who did this?"

"I think so. Follow me, please." Ashken motioned with a hand as they walked passed the crowd of officers and paramedics. "There's a lot of red, blue, and orange blood—the most I've seen in a while."

Once inside the warehouse, the Chief glanced with a casual attitude, unfazed by laser-scorched torsos and severed limbs; brief rivers of blood flowed from wounds not seared by laser blasts. "I hear there's over fifty dead females and children here," Crui said, although his tone led Ashken to infer confirmation was needed.

Ashken stopped and looked at the Chief. "Over one hundred. It's sick."

Crui shook his head as the pair resumed their brief walk.

"Over here." Ashken led Chief Crui to the far end of the facility, away from most of the carnage. They stopped over the body of a pink-skinned female. Lying on her back, her black hair lay to the sides of her head to reveal tall ears. One look at the webbing connecting the base of each finger on each hand left no doubt the carcass had hailed from Rojan.

"The cause of death is obvious," Lt. Ashken said as he motioned with his foot at the laser-burned lower torso.

"Is that who I think it is?" Chief Crui asked.

"That's right. We now know the identity of the gang who massacred these innocents. How they got them here and why they killed them is a mystery, but now we know." Ashken paused before adding. "We checked the small village where these victims were living. It's been picked clean of valuables. Weapons, currency, everything."

"Maybe they were going for no witnesses?" Chief Crui shrugged. With sadness overwhelming his facial expression, the police chief could only muster a thought about the logistics of the matter. "I'll spread the word when I get back to headquarters." The pair exchanged melancholy glances before walking away from the dead body of Kimbyk Parlina, known to the UU Gang as Kimberlina.

Chapter Seventeen

The large Rojani male had reached his limit of patience. As he watched the Mangan female nurse disappear around the corner, out of his hospital room, Chabdab reached under his sheet and pulled out a large knife he had pilfered when the nurse on a prior shift had turned her head. As he pondered what a native of the planet Mang would be doing in Quadrant 4, he drove the blade into his arm, careful to miss the main artery.

Red blood dripped, then poured into the pan beside him as the Rojani fought off a shout of pain. *Well, Yane is Mangan, too. He's in our quadrant.* The knife plunged deeper yet. His pained expression grew into a look of agony. For a moment, he feared he would faint from the intense throbbing sensation which made his stomach queasy. *But Yane's crazy. I wonder why the nurse is here.*

At last, cutting complete, Chabdab dropped the knife with a gentle action designed to avoid splashing his blood into the plastic pan. He then extended three fingers and the thumb of his right hand into his forearm. Once comfortable he had a solid grip, he pulled out the small, rectangular electronic device designed to track his every move. He felt pleased that he kept the scream of pain low in decibels. As he paused to recover from the pain, he realized that he did not hear rushing nurses or doctors, so his exclamations were not loud enough to derail his plan.

He pulled the electronic "identifier" close to his face to study it, allowing an inadvertent drop of blood to fall on his hospital gown, just below his neck. He discovered what appeared to be a weak point, then grasped the device with both hands. He snapped one end of the identifier, rendering it useless. The audible groan which escaped his throat as he broke the electronic gadget was louder than he expected.

Confident it was now useless, Chabdab threw the identifier into a nearby trash can. Still on his back, he knew a doctor should sew his arm to close the wound. *How should I do this?* Before another thought could enter his head, he let out a scream which may have awakened the latest arrivals to the basement morgue.

The scream itself wore him out as blood continued to flow into the pan. The Mangan nurse rushed into the room, perhaps fearful another mysterious attacker had paid a visit to her patient. When she saw the blood and the innocent expression on Chabdab's face, she faltered for a moment, thrusting one hand out to brace herself against the wall. Before he could speak, she rushed out the door to hail a doctor.

•   •   •

The angry look on the Corsan doctor's face caused Chabdab to remain silent. Usually a calm, even-tempered race, the Corsan made clear his anger and disdain for Chabdab and his actions.

"If I had more time I'd wait for another identifier!" the doctor snarled, his large head remained motionless as he continued sewing on his patient. With gritted teeth, he continued his mumbles and grumbles. "It was the government who put this in you, you foolish reprobate!" He jerked the stitching tight. "I'm not allowed to let anyone go without one!" He snickered before continuing. "You are going to be in so much trouble without an identifier." He looked into Chabdab's eyes for a brief second before continuing his work—and grumbling. "Everyone in the known universe has an identifier in his arm. You'll never get far!" He laughed under his breath. "You'll never get out of the hospital. I'll have to cut you open to put another one in!"

While it was true everyone in the quadrants had an identifier inserted into their arms when they turned ten Heislerian years old, only the newer devices could transmit data. This meant individuals over the age of fifteen Heislerian years could not be tracked. The five-year-old advancement in instant tracking could not be inserted into current adults in the quadrants without incurring an enormous, prohibitive expense. The device did, however, make escape from quadrants or through checkpoints, including inter-quadrant transport stations, impossible.

With a deep breath, the Corsan doctor glared at Chabdab. His chocolate-brown skin, common among Corsans, seemed to almost obscure his beady eyes. He pulled his body back from his patient and exhaled with a loud and angry blow.

"Why didn't you give me a pain killer?" Chabdab inquired.

The doctor sneered. "You didn't need a pain killer when you cut yourself open; you don't need it when I stitch you back together." He let out a small growl. He leaned in again to finish the job. "I don't have time to be stitching back fools when I have patients on the edge of death everywhere!"

Although in pain, Chabdab's feeling of triumph conquered the needle work in progress.

"Almost done," the doctor mumbled. "I hope this hurt."

Chabdab nodded. "You delivered on your promise, doctor. It felt like I was stung by a Drebehran wasp."

"Good!"

•　　•　　•

Julie Pitts found herself in a quandary—every day. She wanted Rick to accompany her everywhere she went, but the thought of Rick in public made her skin crawl. She wanted to leave him home every day, but the thought of what could happen with him alone in her house frightened her. She feared letting him out of her sight.

As she drove her Ford down her driveway, on the way to park in the separate structure garage, she noticed multiple males—certainly not human—on her front porch. With anticipation building in her stomach, she carried two bags of groceries and entered her house through the side door, near the kitchen.

She could wait no longer. She had to know. She set the two bags onto the kitchen countertop and hustled to the front porch. As she walked through the front doorway, she felt relief flood her. In rocking chairs on the large porch sat Rick and UU along with three aliens she did not recognize.

When the door opened, the sound of the creaking produced by the storm door caused the five aliens to look in her direction. She froze—not from fear, anger, or trepidation, but due to a sense of relief she did not bother to ponder. With Rick and his friends, she felt a sense of security; she was simply relieved problems were not about to confront her.

"We like these rocking chairs," Yane called out.

Rick stood, causing his wooden rocking chair to move in his absence. "Julie!" Rick strode across the wooden porch, which extended halfway across the breadth of the house, and grabbed her by the arm. "Blik, Kreeg, Yane," he began. "This is our portal host."

Blik laughed. "I did not know portals had hosts."

The others chuckled as Rick pulled Julie closer to them.

Rick pointed to his friends. "This is Blik, Kreeg, and Yane."

For their parts, each nodded his head and stood as introductions were made. Rick put his hand on Julie's shoulder. "This is Julie. The earthling."

A bit uncomfortable due to the presence of more aliens, Julie let out a small chuckle as she said, "That's me. An earthling. I have been all my life." Her eyes bulged as she considered the sizes of the aliens. She had never been around a human who stood over seven-feet tall, and now she stood next to five aliens who were close to or over such a rare height.

"You can change species on Earth?" Yane asked, surprise in his voice.

The aliens settled back into their rocking chairs.

"Uh, no." Julie's discomfort continued. "I was joking." She shifted her feet as her awkwardness rose.

"Earthlings do that a lot," Rick said without humor in his voice. "They place value on laughter."

Odd expressions greeted Rick's observation.

"We laugh," Yane said.

"Yeah, at Blik and Kreeg," UU added.

"But they do a lot," Rick countered. "A lot."

"Blik, Kreeg, Yane, welcome to Earth," Julie's comfort level improved as she spoke.

"We'd like to tour the planet, but UU says we can't," Kreeg said with mild disappointment in his voice.

In his own attempt to make conversation, Blik spoke up. "UU tells us this planet could easily be taken over."

"Uh, yeah. Okay." Julie flashed a horrified look at the colonel.

"I just mean if it were in our universe—part of the galaxy," UU stuttered as he tried to make the statement sound less menacing.

"Don't worry, Julie." Blik tried to supply reassurance. "If we were going to take over, I would have already killed the entire population in this area."

"Oh. Okay." Julie attempted to sound reassured. "Well, that's nice you're not going to."

Kreeg smiled. "We're good creatures now."

"Ooooookay." Julie nodded.

"We only kill bad creatures now." Kreeg continued the reassurances.

Rick laughed. "It's okay, Julie. They don't understand Earth yet—or earthlings." He turned to his comrades. "They're not as violent as we are. They fight a war every few years and they end it. Then they fight another one and end it. They don't fight all the time as we do."

"Really?!" Julie's surprise could not be concealed. "We think we go to war too often!" The surprise in her voice coated her words like chocolate on candy.

"You do?" Rick mirrored her disbelief.

"Earthlings think we fight too much," Julie answered.

"Not like we do," Rick answered. "We just fight in space most of the time so we don't destroy our cultures."

"Well, I guess if you don't tear anything up..." Julie's sarcasm sailed over the heads of her guests.

"Exactly," Rick responded in earnest. "We don't want to destroy our Heislerian society."

"Listen to the ugly Heislerian," Blik mocked. "We don't want to destroy the wonderful Heislerian supremacy."

"Exactly," Rick said again. "We have to protect it."

Blik shook his head, then turned to Yane. "Remind me to go pay the great planet of Heisler another visit before we leave."

Rick looked at Blik with disgust until the large Andalian laughed, causing Rick to smile.

"See," Yane said with a triumphant tone. "We laugh."

·   ·   ·

The setting Kansas Sun provided one last opportunity for the aliens to view Julie's planet. Maple, hackberry, and elm trees swayed in the breeze in the front yard as birds scurried to a nearby feeder for the final time. A red-winged blackbird chirped with a sharp warning to the visitors that they should not approach his feeder.

Julie emerged from the house carrying a tray of sandwiches, causing the few remaining birds to escape the perceived danger. As she allowed her guests to take from the tray, she explained the contents of turkey, cheese, lettuce, tomato, mayonnaise, and bread.

"What have I missed?" Julie asked, wide-eyed and hopeful they would tell her.

"We're planning our next moves," UU answered with an intentional vagueness.

"And we're thinking about making this our hideout," Rick added.

"But we'll have to set up a command center in your basement," UU added as he prepared to take his first bite of Earth food.

Julie watched with a detached smile. Any earthling would have recognized her timid approach to her guests. Her feelings of excitement for having actual aliens at her house were balanced with the thought of more coming and staying longer.

With a light gulp, Blik spoke first. "These were good." He looked at his friends. "We'll have to kill our own turkeys when we come back."

"We can't interact with the locals," UU admonished his communications expert.

"You ate that in one bite!" Julie exclaimed.

"I was hungry," Blik explained.

She looked at the others; their sandwiches had all disappeared. Her gaze turned to Rick. "You don't eat like that."

"I'm Heislerian," Rick deadpanned.

"Oh, not again!" Kreeg pushed Rick away with both hands, causing the latter to rock faster in his chair.

Yane smiled as he looked at Julie. "See, we laugh a lot."

"At Rick," Kreeg shot back.

"And if they don't laugh, we kill them," Blik added as he glared at Julie.

UU closed his eyes and shook his head.

"He's kidding," Yane interjected.

With that, a broad smile crossed Blik's rough, hairy Andalian face.

"You scared me for a minute," Julie laughed as she tried to make light of her racing heart.

"That's his job," UU said with a straight face. "Well, part of it."

Blik tugged on the bottom of his t-shirt so she could read it.

"Bliktos Kilz," Julie read the writing. "Yes I do." Her quizzical expression betrayed her thoughts. "I don't understand the rest."

"The rest is in several languages: Andalian, Heislerian, Zhiloan, Drebehran, and Corsan."

After a squint and a frown, Rick understood his Earth friend enough to interject. "It essentially says, "Yes, I kill creatures, but it's his name."

"Okay," Julie nodded. "I get it. But I didn't know you wore t-shirts in your world."

Again Rick came to the rescue. "Very few creatures in our world wear articles of clothing with wording."

"Just 'kilz' on your own planet and we'll get along fine," Julie ordered with a smile.

Blik turned to Rick. "Are all earthling females this fearful of blood?"

"I only know one earthling female." Rick's response ended the conversation.

A brief few seconds of silence was interrupted with a mild shout from Kreeg. He slapped himself on the forearm as he pushed backward in his rocking chair with a hard lurch. "That little demon attacked me," he said with an indignant tone as he wiped the remains from his arm.

"Don't you have creatures on your planets that suck the blood of other creatures?" Julie asked.

"Yes, and they suck you dry and you die!" Kreeg intoned with a concerned look at his arm, his blood pressure obviously high.

"These bugs only take a little blood," Julie snickered.

"Where we're from, everything that bites you can kill you," Yane explained.

"We call them 'clean-up crews' where we're from," Rick said. "They clean up the weak among us."

"Oh, gee. I can't wait to go to your world." Again Julie's sarcasm was missed by the group.

"Let's get back to business," UU ordered. Julie caught a glance from the colonel, swept her eyes across the other guests, then turned to leave the group, who had now entered their sixth hour of strategizing.

•   •   •

What each planet dubbed "law enforcement" was but a shadow of those same forces before the Great Exodus began. While a large percentage of law enforcement officers fled the quadrant, just as almost every other sentient being had done, enough stayed behind to keep a small degree of order. Even on the other side of the Milky Way galaxy, Nature abhorred a vacuum, thus the decimated forces found themselves infiltrated by thugs, scoundrels, and other ne'er-do-wells who pounced on an opportunity to profit from mayhem. Some members of law enforcement saw the futility in the situation and became part of the second wave of those who escaped the impending doom, while others attempted to underscore the "servant" implied in "civil servant" until as close to the end as possible.

Of the Corsan assault team members lined up, armed to the greatest degree conceivable and about to burst into

Chabdab's room, none had been involved in serving the public when impending doom had been announced. These infiltrators worked not for the public, but for a gang whose leader reported to an aide who reported to the Premier. On the planet Corsar, the Rule of Law had been murdered within a Heislerian month of the supernova announcement.

All dressed in blue uniforms—to mimic local police—and covered by black tactical gear, on the leader's command, they burst into the hospital room, weapons at the ready, only to discover the unconscious body of the one tasked with keeping Chabdab in sight.

When attempts to revive the living but motionless comrade failed, the leader understood Chabdab could have escaped hours prior. Like the hot Corsan wind known to blow down frail structures and scatter unsecured items, Chabdab had snuck away—or had been carried away—without a trace.

The leader of the Corsan gang had to report unhappy news to his superior. The announcement would doom he and his gang's opportunity to find safe haven from the soon-to-be exploding star. The Premier did not appreciate disappointment.

Chapter Eighteen

"I need off this planet and out of this quadrant!" Despite his feeble voice, the ferocity of the statement resonated with the recipient. "If you can put in another identifier, with a new identity, I'll be grateful." Chabdab's tone communicated command, yet his demeanor was that of a beggar.

"Leave it to you to ask at just the right time." Jomono Ah looked like the quintessential Corsan. His smooth brown skin served as contrast to his friend's pale, scaly appearance made worse by the lack of a recent bath. Despite the look of an office worker who had avoided strenuous work throughout life, the aging Corsan had endured hardship and setbacks his entire existence. It was during one of those hardships—he was caught in the middle of a battle while trying to escape the Quadrant 3 planet Aabaa during a business visit—he met the soldier who saved his life. In the opening moments of the war, Chabdab spotted the literally misguided civilian, rushed into the open, and hurried him to safety.

Chabdab found a chair in the small apartment, which lacked electricity and running water. "The right time; how so?"

"I'm leaving behind my tools of the trade," Jomono said, referring to his recent business of selling on the black market. From weapons to toilet paper, Jomono had a way of getting his hands on whatever was needed—and selling it for a significant profit.

"Everything?"

"Everything. How would it look if I tried to cross into Quadrant 3 with a bunch of untraceable identifiers on me? And everyday items are not a rarity in the rest of the known universe."

"Makes sense." Chabdab shifted in the uncomfortable wooden chair; his arm, chest, and shoulders producing severe pain. "Got any painkillers?"

"Of course I do!" the host laughed. "Of course. What I don't have I can get my hands on anytime."

"When do you leave?"

"Tomorrow."

"I'd like to come with you."

"In a couple of hours, after I finish making my preparations," Jomono said with glee dripping off every word. "I will insert a new identifier and we will be on our way to civilization!"

"Yeah. Great." Chabdab tried to be excited about the great news, but the combination of pain and fatigue tamped down the desired exuberance.

"Listen, my friend." Jomono's energy rose further. "Once I was almost killed because of faulty directions. I will now repay the hero who saved my life with perfect directions in a flawless plan to get us both out of here."

"That's great." Chabdab paused to take a breath, his words flowed from his mouth as though full of ice cubes. "Why didn't you get out sooner?"

"Oh, that's a story! A long, drawn-out story. I shall tell you the story while I insert an identifier. The story will keep you distracted."

"But you do have painkillers, don't you?"

Jomono flashed a look of insult. "Me? Not have painkillers? I have everything, my friend! Everything!"

"Well, let's gas me up now," Chabdab said without humor, using the colloquial expression of the known universe. "The more you gas me the better."

The Corsan smiled. "I will gas you. Rest assured."

Chabdab slid down in his chair, hopeful drugs would soon flood his body.

•　　•　　•

"I don't see what anyone sees in Zhilo." Chief Crui seemed to forget about the ferocity of the Fankan sun. "This is hot."

A Zhiloan who acted as a guide for the small group of law enforcement officers turned and glared at the foreign police chief. Once a farmer but now a survivor, the Zhiloan survived on leading Returners back to what was left of their properties. Of the Returners, authorities estimated more than 50% never made it out again. Life in the Nova Quadrant had become a dangerous place beyond the imaginations of most creatures.

This time, Zhiloan law enforcement hired the farmer-turned-guide. Too few Zhiloan officers remained, and the loss of bodies resulted in the loss of knowledge, as well.

"I've been to Fank. I know how hot it gets." The Zhiloan officer was one of the few residents of the planet who had been part of law enforcement before the chaos.

"Yeah, you're right," Chief Crui allowed. "I guess I'm not used to this humid, wet heat."

"There!" the guide interrupted. After a ten-minute walk made necessary by an extreme amount of debris in the plain leading up to the hideout, the guide pointed to a small, low-signature building at the base of the mountain ahead.

"I don't understand," Crui said. He could not hide his baffled reaction. "If this is it, then why did we walk so far?"

The guide looked at the police chief with disgust. "It's called a 'hideout' for a reason. I didn't know where it was."

"I see." Crui shook his head.

"From above, there must be a tech shield." The former Zhiloan police officer referred to the Zhiloan name for an electronic shield which allowed the occupants and materials of anyone in the area to blend in with the topography when viewed from the air.

Chief Crui paused to rest, then turned to the six officers who lagged behind him. "You know the drill. Cameras. microphones. Motion detectors. If you hide it well, they'll never find it."

Quiet responses of "yes sir" and "got it" quickly melted in the heat from Ma'eek, the star which gave life to the planet.

"You have enough provision to stay here for a week. Replacements will let you know when you can leave." The chief eyed his officers with careful study. Not everyone exceled at following orders these days.

•   •   •

"We go now," UU announced as he entered the basement.

Julie rose from her chair and turned away from her artwork. "When will I see you again?" Her comfort level with her guests had risen over the course of the visit.

"I would tell you if I knew," UU smiled as he answered. "We still don't know how to judge the time differences—how long we're here." He stopped, as though in thought. "We could be getting back the same moment we left."

"No," Kreeg corrected his boss as he reached the bottom stair of the first basement. "You would have been caught the first time you returned if that were true."

Blik, Yane, and finally Rick descended the stairway. All looked at her artwork before Blik offered an observation. "As much as I don't care about art, I wish our kind still had time for such luxuries."

"Never again in Quadrant Four," Kreeg nodded his agreement.

"Never again," Rick concurred.

"Okay, you Ruun worm," UU mocked his weapons expert. "What happens if the nova explodes while we're here? What happens if we go through the portal?"

"I don't know," Kreeg answered, raising his thick eyebrows as he pondered the question. "Either the portal will disappear because the other side is gone—so no portal if there's not two ends—or we get trapped in the portal and can't get out."

"Or!" Yane interjected. "We get in the portal and then return to this place."

"Earth," Rick added.

"Earth," Yane nodded as he recalled the planet's name.

"And by the way," Kreeg added as an afterthought. "I am not a Ruun worm. If you're going to insult me, at least call me something from my home planet."

They all laughed at Kreeg's display of faux offense.

Now weary of the postulations, UU reminded the group of the plan just put in place. "It's time. I don't know when that is when we get home, but we go now." He stopped himself after a single step and turned back to Rick. "As soon as you are healthy enough, wait for us at the Eemlurian base until we return."

"It will be done," Rick responded to the order.

The four made eye contact with Rick and then proceeded down the stairs to the second basement.

"You need to hurry up and get well," Julie implored her extraterrestrial friend. After observing Rick's quizzical expression, she continued. "I've had two employees quit with no notice and I'll be hiring some new help. Get well so you can have a job."

Rick walked with an exaggerated limp toward the stairs leading up to the main floor of the house. "Sorry!" He fought off a smile.

"Funny!" Julie laughed.

•   •   •

Despite increased security, alerted by the local dominant gang that a Rojani terrorist was on the loose and likely to flee the planet, Chabdab and Jomono boarded the "interstellar transport," as the services between quadrants were known, without incident. Once aboard, Chabdab's demeanor improved. He had listened to too many of his friend's stories, missing the point of Jomono's attempts to calm him.

The jumbo spaceliners, which served as comfortable transportation, could easily host 5,000 passengers, including sleeping cabins. Despite the vast size of the quadrants—or, "the known universe," as most citizens referred to the collective quadrants—most life could be found within relatively small areas in each quadrant. Only a few planets, such as Feinzuk in Quadrant 1, inhabited a section of a quadrant so remote, most residents in that quadrant had never visited the place, and many in other quadrants did not know its location.

Despite the 600-light-year-length of the known universe, most of the planets in the quadrants could be reached within two months, particularly if faster, more expensive interstellar transports were used. Travel within each quadrant was the most common form of long-distance travel; most rarely ventured outside their own regions.

Travel beyond the approximated quadrant boundaries never reached far simply because no inhabited stars within reasonable range existed and no one knew of life outside of the known universe. The edge of the Milky Way galaxy arm they inhabited presented dark, starless night skies for three of the six Quadrant 4 boundaries and two boundaries each for the other quadrants. Exploration beyond Quadrant 1 had been limited to uninhabited probes, which reported back mostly planet-less stars and dangerous nebulae, quasars, and a presumed black hole.

Cost dictated speed, and vice versa, with the fastest ships charging the most money. The standard interstellar transport on which Chabdab and his newfound guardian found themselves would reach their destination, the planet Pnkaj, within three Heislerian weeks.

"So far, so good," Chabdab muttered just loud enough for Jomono to hear. Seats taken, heads down, the duo appeared to be two more weary travelers during these chaotic days.

"Good fortune follows you again, Cha — " He caught himself before speaking the Rojani's name. The possible catastrophe caused him to lower his voice further, until Chabdab had to strain to hear his friend. "I came upon identifiers not properly wiped by a hospital," Jomono said, referring to the hospitals' duty to delete certain electronic data the average citizen could not replace. "Even if they dug it out of your arm they'd have no way of knowing it was illegal."

Before Chabdab could respond, one of the gang members who had stormed the hospital room stopped at the sight of a Rojani. "Identification, please," the faux police officer growled.

Chabdab reached into a coat pocket and pulled out his new ID, which he had roughed up the prior evening to take away the fresh look of the card.

The surly beast snatched the identification card from Chabdab. After eyeing the plastic, the gang member made another demand. "Let me scan your identifier." He then reached out with a palm-sized electronic device and scanned the identifier, which was completely buried by Rojani flesh. The thug looked at the readout and called out the name. "Ocollomomololo Luriji," the creature said, struggling with every syllable. He looked back to Chabdab. "What kind of name is that?!"

"Ocollomomonollo Lrji. Please pronounce my family name correctly." Chabdab's faux anger jolted the armed thug. "This is a family name that has been around for Rojani centuries and I would appreciate if you pronounce it correctly and respectfully!"

The rough-looking Corsan, with pock marks in his face and a permanently-swollen jaw, glared at Chabdab. He thrust the ID card out for the owner to retrieve and walked away without another word to exit the craft. The creature never noticed the slight, nearly invisible scar around the identifier, on Chabdab's forearm. Besides running hustles throughout Quadrant 4, Jomono had also learned to use the medical equipment which cleaned up scars.

"Well, Ocollomomonollo," Jomono teased. "Let's go start our lives over."

Within minutes, the interstellar transport lifted off, ensuring Chabdab and his friend would not be obliterated by the explosion of the impending supernova.

Chapter Nineteen

"Premier." The long-haired male, a white Asimoni with brown stripes across his body, though only his neck and face were visible at the moment, approached the Premier with reverence. "We have found a family in one of the farming sectors of the planet."

"And?" The Premier found little room for patience when conversing with those he found beneath his social status, which happened to be everyone currently on the planet. In case his lowly aide forgot his own station in life, he could not forget Premier Seveen's standing—the purple robe left no doubt.

"Well, they said they wish to meet with you."

"Why?"

"They are having second thoughts about being Remainers."

Premier Seveen hesitated before delivering a response. First a frown, then a grimace preceded a slow smile. "It took them long enough. A little slow of mind, wouldn't you say?" He paused before adding, "I will see them."

The Asimoni aide made a hasty retreat and left the room only to return seconds later with a middle-aged Asimoni couple. He with brown skin and white stripes and she the opposite, the couple strode into the Premier's chamber with looks of awe covering their faces. Their awe grew into prideful satisfaction as Premier Seveen greeted the couple with kind hands to their shoulders before inviting them to sit in large, comfortable chairs which looked crafted for royalty.

As the Premier took his seat, he engaged the couple. "What brings you here?"

"Well," the husband squirmed in his seat as he glanced at his wife. "We chose to be Remainers when the news first hit, figuring it could be many years before the nova exploded."

"And now you've changed your mind, I take it?" The Premier's tone dripped with kindness and even understanding. His voice seemed to be a sugary salve for their frightened existence.

"Yes, yes we have." The husband's response sounded as much resignation as hope. "We have made a grave mistake. I have heard the star could go nova within the next Heislerian year."

"Yes," the Premier intoned with a gentle quality flowing from his eyes and lips. "And you would like to escape now?"

"Yes, we would."

"Where are your children?"

"They're on the farm, working," the husband responded. "Our eldest child is of a responsible age. He watches them in our absence."

"How many children do you have?"

"Six total—four males and two females." The husband again glanced at his wife as a flash from his eyes seemed to communicate his uncertainty about the prospects for the conversation.

"Listen." The Premier leaned forward in his chair as he exuded compassion. "Let's get you and your family off the planet, out of the quadrant. What do you think?"

"Oh, thank you!" As gratitude gasped from the male's mouth, the female leaped from her chair with outstretched arms. She could not speak; she squeezed Seveen as he stood to absorb the grateful embrace.

The Premier motioned for the male to stand. "You are quite welcome. You made a miscalculation, but at least you have time to correct it. Am I to assume you cannot afford to make the journey with your own funds?"

The Asimoni wife spoke for the first time. With tears streaming down her cheeks and appreciation flowing from her eyes, she nodded as part of her answer to the one who provided them redemption. "You are correct. We could only afford to get four of us out, and that was not an acceptable option for us."

"But governments provided for free escape," the Premier responded, clearly baffled.

"Oh, she means when opportunists offered to send us out." An embarrassed husband glanced at his wife. "This was long after our initial." His voice trailed off for a moment. "Miscalculation was made."

The Premier presented a look of understanding as he nodded. "I see." He began a slow but methodical walk toward the chamber door. "Let's have you go home, gather possessions, and you can make it off the planet tomorrow morning."

The couple exchanged an excited hug.

"The journey will take some time. We have a cargo craft leaving tomorrow morning, and it will take you several stops and ships to get you out." The Premier flashed a reassuring smile. "But we'll have you on an interstellar transport within days."

"Thank you! Thank you so much!" The husband's energy grew by the second.

"Yes, thank you! You are more than kind!" The wife echoed her husband's sentiments before adding. "You are truly a great leader!"

The female again hugged the Premier and the male exchanged caring pats on the shoulders with their political leader.

The Premier motioned toward the door. "Go and my aides will give you details of the arrangements."

As they opened the door, the couple was greeted by the aide who made the conversation possible.

"Please see this family gets off the planet tomorrow morning," the Premier ordered.

The aide nodded and led the couple away.

Before the door could close, Rocash and another aide entered the chambers.

"Close the door," Premier Seveen ordered.

The three sat as the two minions sat in the same chairs most recently occupied by the farmers.

"I assume you have the status report I requested."

"We do," Rocash said. "The last we informed you, there were five significant gangs working against our interest."

"And now?" The Premier did not like guessing games.

"And now there are three."

"Unacceptable." The Premier's judgment came with a flat, even tone. "And UU's gang?"

"One of the three." Rocash frowned, knowing how the news would be received.

The Premier squinted, as though narrowing his eyes would help him think. "I will dispatch Wocumb and his gang today to search Zhilo. UU must be there! I will tell him to search for three Heislerian weeks. If not on Zhilo, then his gang can search every other planet in the quadrants!"

"Won't he miss the day of action?" Rocash asked, surprised at the proposed command.

"You are correct. What a shame," the Premier said without emotion. "There is a price to pay for questioning me in front of others."

"One way or another, we will destroy the UU Gang," the aide assured his boss. He looked at Rocash for reassurance.

Rocash nodded in agreement with the aide but the Premier had yet to expend his unhappiness.

"I hope you understand — " The Premier caught himself before unleashing only mild anger. Perhaps the kindness he had shown the farmers soothed his temper. "We will squeeze out all the raw materials, all the wealth, and all the assets physically possible to transport from this quadrant, and we will do so for as long as possible, up until the last possible moment. But time is running out." He hesitated for effect. "I have over one-hundred-and-fifty transports—jumbo transports—at the ready. We are sending out transports full of riches every day. Every asset and every material UU and his gang gets their hands on is less wealth for the rest of us." He hesitated again, but this time to control the boiling rage which threatened to erupt like a rumbling volcano. "Do you understand?"

In unison, Rocash and the aide responded with "We do," and in unison the pair rose to their feet. Without another word, the pair hurried out of the chamber.

"I no longer want him alive!" the Premier shouted after them. "I believe I have previously made that clear."

Later that evening, rewards for killing the UU Gang and the two other bands of outlaws increased ten-fold. The word spread throughout the quadrant; bandits and the Premier's enforcers alike took notice of the rewards. The acquisition of riches was why they had stayed in the quadrant for as long as they had, and they could not allow others to take part of their spoils.

•　　•　　•

When he stepped through the portal, UU realized that, with one exception, he had only been on post-Great-Exodus Zhilo at night. He had not taken the time to visit his home planet for any reason other than banditry. As each creature re-entered the home world, he reached into a pocket and pulled out a small yet powerful flashlight. Kreeg followed his boss through the portal, followed by Blik and Yane.

The foursome wound their way through the museum's maze of hallways before finally emerging in the large exhibit hall. Light from the planet's moon provided illumination for maneuvering.

"How far was it to our craft?" Blik half-closed his eyes while trying to recall the layout of the city.

"On the roof of that building over there," UU motioned with no specificity. "Let's just hope the tarps didn't blow off the ship."

As the group stepped outside, UU stopped after four steps. "Listen!" he hissed.

"What is it?" Kreeg whispered.

"Something's not right," UU whispered. The seriousness of the moment could not be missed by his comrades. "Something is here. Watching us." He clicked his flashlight off, so the others followed suit.

Yane shook his head. "UU and his eight senses."

"Eight?" Blik's shock turned to amazement.

"It's a joke, Blik!" Yane yelled in a whisper. "But he does feel when he's being watched."

UU pointed to the building two away from their current location and across the street. "It's the same building where we left our ship. He's been waiting for us, I'm sure."

"I don't see anything." Blik looked at his friends.

"Over here," UU ordered.

The four scurried around a corner.

"Here's the plan." UU could only see Kreeg's eyes but knew the others were attempting to look at him. "Blik, you stay here. Walk around. Talk to yourself. Be noticed."

"Will do."

A thought struck UU. "Does anyone have personal shields left?"

"No," Kreeg answered.

"Same," Yane confirmed. "I think the whole team is out. We're naked. No energy sources, no power packs."

"I ran out at Ceratofs," Yane added.

"Kreeg, you and Yane find a place near here where you can keep an eye on Blik." UU hesitated, as though he heard a noise. "I will go around and then go into the building and see if I can find whoever is waiting for us." He turned to slip deeper into the darkness.

"Wait!" Kreeg called out, just above a whisper.

"What?" UU stopped and turned as he asked his question.

"What if there are several creatures hiding out?"

"Then I'll have to kill several creatures," UU retorted. With that, the fierce Zhiloan turned and disappeared into the night.

"Now what?" Kreeg seemed unsure of his instructions.

"You heard him," Yane offered. "Let's let Blik be the bait and we'll capture the predator."

"What is someone going to do?" Blik asked with incredulity. "Run up and try to carry me off? He could shoot me from up there!" He motioned toward the building UU had pointed out.

"Turn your flashlight on and march," Kreeg told his friend. "Talk loud. Be like a crazed Andalian. That's easy for you to do. Just be yourself."

"I'm the calmest Andalian you'll ever meet!" Blik shot back.

"But you're still crazy." With a slap on Yane's shoulder, Kreeg communicated his desire to have his comrade follow him. "And besides, you're not calmer than Mookie."

Within a few steps, the pair faded from sight. Blik turned on his flashlight and began pacing on the flat section of concrete at the top of the stairs to the great museum.

•　　•　　•

Kreeg and Yane made their way down the darkened Zhiloan street as though walking through a field of broken glass while barefooted. They carefully dodged debris they could barely see and made as little noise as possible. Even though it was just one block removed from the street in front of the museum, the street lacked the glass buildings designed to reflect moonlight. Tall, dark buildings limited light from the moon.

"This would be a perfect location for drones or machines," Kreeg spoke first.

"Drones are possible," Yane answered.

"Not really," Kreeg responded. "Very few gangs or organizations possess the technology, let alone the energy to operate them."

"True," Yane said.

"Once the energy sources depleted, the drone is useless."

"True," Yane repeated. "Too bad they didn't invent solid fuel for the drones."

"Yeah, so a drone could swoop down and kill us now," Kreeg scoffed at his friend. "Besides, they're illegal."

"Like we're not?!" Yane chuckled.

They referred to the quadrants-wide treaty which banned artificial intelligence and drones for everything except some military use. The first cautionary tale came from the Shersheen who, according to legend and historians, had made great strides in artificial intelligence technology before abandoning it. They then included in their messages reticence about reliance on artificial intelligence as they spread their knowledge throughout the galaxy.

Before the quadrants had established formal treaties, several planets used artificial intelligence in wide-ranging capacities. While confident machines could not conquer them—after all, the machines were extensions of sentient intelligence but incapable of reasoning—they did learn that, if they could communicate with a device, then someone else could hack into their communication network and communicate with it. If the owner could not communicate with the artificial intelligence, it could become dangerous.

Artificial intelligence followed commands written in binary programming; it could not evaluate moral situations— it simply acted based on computer programs. Fear of giving artificial intelligence the ability to kill and having that ability hijacked by fiendish forces led to banning machines from engaging in some military and all civilian roles.

"Did you hear that?" Yane asked, concern in his voice evident.

"Yes! It must be UU!"

Kreeg and Yane clicked on their flashlights and sprinted toward the sound of laser fire, all the while dodging debris strewn in the streets from wrecked, burned, and looted vehicles of all types. Kreeg's red Eemlurian skin glowed in the light cast from Yane's flashlight, the latter only steps behind the former. Orders to stay with Blik were long forgotten.

"Kreeg! Wait."

Both stopped running.

"We have to turn off our flashlights."

"It'll take us longer to get there, to watch where we're walking."

Now side-by-side, they tried to navigate the street without the aid of light.

"This might not work," Yane advised. "I may be wrong."

"Get behind me!"

Yane followed the order. Kreeg and his bright green eyes allowed for better night vision. His eyes glowed from the faintest of light, and they retained enough of a reflective quality to allow his vision to pierce through darkness to a reasonable degree, thus allowing the pair to pass through the littered streets.

More laser shots announced the resumption of a battle. Whether UU was involved would take time to ascertain.

•　　•　　•

Blik tired of pacing after only minutes. He had become unnerved at the thought of focusing his attention on the streets and surrounding buildings, but not considering anyone could assault him from the museum itself. Once he stopped being the bait, he felt better, then he stepped behind a nearby pillar. The tall, concrete column rose to meet the front façade which attached to the museum's roof.

Unwittingly, by disappearing from sight, Blik lured an adversary from the shadows. As the Andalian alternated between attempting to stay hidden and attempting to see his opponent, he noticed a peculiar sight: the silhouette of a creature using its flashlight as a signaling device. Blik did not understand the meaning of the flashing patterns, but it soon became apparent the signal was one of recognition.

To his left, the signaling from the figure in the street continued. To his right, he saw a small squadron of perhaps a dozen creatures approaching from the opposite direction. Blik gave a brief thought to disappearing down the same alley in which UU, Kreeg, and Yane had departed. Instead, he retreated into the building, briefly exposing his whereabouts to the original lookout who, at the sight of Blik, resumed sending signals to the approaching outlaws.

As Blik raced through the doorway, six gangsters spotted him as they reached the bottom of the stairs.

Chapter Twenty

In the darkened building, UU crept forward. His target stood only meters away.

The creature from the Quadrant 1 planet Ruu leaned out of the opening which had once held a glass window in place. Wearing a night vision monocle, the combatant's thoughts appeared to be focused only on the museum. On the street seven stories below, another Ruun flashed lights to communicate Blik's whereabouts.

UU shook his head in disgust at himself. His own night vision monocle sat undisturbed in the "duty kit" in his craft. He had not bothered to take it with him during his trip to Earth, through the portal, so he now faced an adversary in the dark, at an extreme disadvantage should the Ruun decide to turn and scan the room. The realization sunk in he should have sent Kreeg, with his natural night vision abilities, to take out this sniper.

The Zhiloan moon's light accorded UU the ability to watch the Ruun as he turned and set his Drebehran laser rifle on the floor, then rotated his body to stretch his tired muscles.

UU sensed the moment had arrived. Delay could mean discovery. With three quick strides, the large Zhiloan reached his opponent, jumped into the air, and kicked the sniper with both feet. UU landed with a thud, his back striking the floor with great force. His instincts caused him to leap to his feet, ready to fight, but the room was empty. Out of curiosity, he stuck his head out the opening to peer down to the street. His action was greeted by a blinding white laser blast which shot past his head and into the room he occupied, striking the ceiling and causing debris to fall with a crash.

Unable to confirm what he knew had happened, UU's wish to see the splattered Ruun sniper's body abated as self-preservation took over. *Of course the Ruun is dead. That's how the other beast knew to fire at me immediately.* He briefly considered another attempt to view the street, this time to return fire at the enemy below, but thought better of it.

UU stepped away from the window opening and began to plot his escape. He reached down and picked up the sniper's rifle before heading toward the doorway. Before he could exit the room, the area lit up with a flood of brilliant white light. Explosions rocked the side of the building and the energy knocked UU off his feet, through the doorway. The cacophony of laser fire proved louder than what the colonel's ears could tolerate, but he chose to flee over worrying about discomfort from the stentorian laser impacts behind him.

•   •   •

"That's gotta be UU!"

"Probably right. Let's cut through this building." Kreeg turned into what used to be a hotel and completed a cautious run through the blackened lobby.

Ten steps in, Yane called out, concern dripping from every word. "I can't see. I'm losing you."

"Stay with me!" Kreeg ordered. "I can't see much, either."

"Did you hear that?" Yane sounded bewildered.

Kreeg stopped running, wanting to hear whatever noise Yane had heard. Yane crashed into his friend and fell backward, onto the floor.

"Hear what?" Kreeg asked in a whisper.

"Hear you?!" Yane shot back. "You told me to stick with you, but you can't see, either!"

"You stopped me for that?!"

"No! I didn't stop you! I was just amazed at what you said. I'm blindly following a blind brute."

"I can't help it. To see in the dark there must be at least a little light. Now stick with me. Come on!" Kreeg's last sentence reached Yane's ears from a greater distance.

"Wait!" Yane began his pursuit into blackness.

The pair reached the other side of the large hotel lobby in time to see three warriors on the street standing together while one shouted and pointed.

"You take cover across the street," the gangster commanded the third fighter. "You! Come with me and we'll find this intruder and neutralize him." He looked back to the first comrade he addressed. "The odds are he'll try to go out a different way, so we'll try to drive him toward you."

Across the street, in the darkness, Kreeg patted Yane on the shoulder and extended his Drebehran laser pistol. Yane aimed his Zhiloan laser in response. The two opened fire with blasts of white and green exploding into the night. Both gang members fired four rounds each, then stopped as three bodies hit the street.

"I told you to follow me," Kreeg teased with a mocking, almost childish tone.

"Yeah, yeah, yeah. Follow you into a fire fight. I like it." Yane laughed before his attention was averted down the street, to his right. "Look!"

"Four more!" Kreeg muted his shout the best he could under the exciting circumstances. "They're bound to have night vision, so be careful."

"We have to get them now while they're close together."

"From this distance?" Kreeg was concerned about firing pistols at moving targets one hundred meters away—in the dark.

"What are our alternatives?"

"No alternatives. We fight." The resignation in Kreeg's voice made the moment almost comedic to Yane. Kreeg then dropped to a knee and peered around the corner. Yane peered around the same corner, his head a meter above the crouching Eemlurian's head.

With the whisper of "Now!" from Yane, the pair launched salvos which struck and wounded two of the adversaries. The third raced for a nearby obstruction created by a monument—or what remained of the looted symbol—on the curb, on the same side of the street which Kreeg and Yane inhabited. Attention focused on the running hoodlum as both UU Gang members aimed at the running warrior. Attention refocused when a laser blast from a wounded combatant obliterated a piece of the building above Yane's head, sending concrete debris crashing to the ground and onto both of them.

"Oh!" Kreeg shouted in pain.

"That hurt!" Yane responded as they leaped backward, searching for safety from the crash of debris.

Before either could continue the battle, an explosion of white laser fire ripped through the air directly across from them. It was UU.

"Haa!" UU shouted. "Got him!" He then leaped back into a doorway for cover.

"Well, our insane leader is still alive," Yane deadpanned. Without delay, he raced into the street, toward the threesome they eliminated first—or thought they had eliminated. One had lived to fire another shot before UU snuffed out his existence.

After a moment of surprise, Kreeg's training guided his brain and he opened fire down the street, providing cover for Yane's sudden urge to run to the dead bodies.

UU followed suit, opening cover fire, though he, too, remained perplexed at Yane's maneuver.

Repeated blasts from UU's newly-acquired rifle and Kreeg's pistol filled the air as Yane yanked night vision monocles off the fallen enemies. Yane jerked his head downward, a double-take at his sudden realization. Despite the tumultuous fire fight, Yane yelled at UU. "They're 'Civics!' They're the Premier's minions!"

UU ceased firing. "What?" His tone signaled not a lack of hearing but a lack of belief. "I killed what looked to me was a Ruun."

Yane ripped at one dead fighter's sleeve, tearing a patch away from the cloth.

•　　•　　•

Blik dived away from a laser blast and rolled out of sight, away from his pursuer and behind a pillar. When he turned to look back, he saw nothing but blackness. Horror overtook him as the realization sunk in: as he scurried to safety he lost his night vision monocle. Without a search with a flashlight, he had no way of knowing its location.

He could only sit, catch his breath, and wait.

•　　•　　•

UU, Kreeg, and Yane committed each step forward with great care, careful to not bring attention to their position along the sidewalk. In low voices, they tried to make sense of the situation.

"You sure he was a Civic?" UU asked Yane. The latter stepped into an entryway of a shop, an inset into the building's opening. He turned on a flashlight and held out his hand so UU could see the insignia he had ripped from the shirt of the deceased fighter.

UU nodded.

Kreeg stepped into the entryway. "What are Civics doing here? Why aren't they on Asimon?"

"I think it confirms the rumors," UU answered.

"But you said you killed a Ruun," Kreeg struggled to understand why a native of the Quadrant 1 planet would be working as a member of Asimon's civilian military force.

"I agree." Yane nodded out of habit, even though only Kreeg and his innate night vision could see him. "It confirms the rumors, and one of the dead gangsters was definitely a Ruun."

"So that means what?" Kreeg asked.

"They're here for a reason," UU said. "I don't think they want to mop up every planet for sheer power. They want the riches. They're doing exactly what every gang is doing."

"But the museums and rich houses have all been plundered," Kreeg pointed out. "What's left?"

"Natural resources," Yane said with firmness in his voice. "Just like we were in the diamond mine. What else could it be? You haul out a lot of natural resources—as much as you can before leaving—and the Premier is going to be wealthy. Wealthier. It's why he's still here."

"Makes sense." Kreeg's voice faded away, enveloped by his thoughts.

"That would explain why they keep trying to kill us," UU chimed in.

"To what end?" Kreeg emerged from his brief mental journey. "He was already wealthy."

"Power. What else is there for a beast like him?" Yane's rhetorical question carried enough validity their minds seemed to simultaneously close the subject as they turned back toward the sidewalk.

"We have to find Blik," UU said in a hushed voice. "I left him on his own thinking we were battling two soldiers."

"He's probably killing riffraff with his bare hands by now," Yane chuckled.

•　　　•　　　•

Crouched behind the remnants of a large stone tablet, engulfed by the darkness, Blik waited for the sound to draw nearer. Exposing his head too soon would surely prove fatal.

The footsteps approached, a slow cadence of taps faded and increased as the pursuer stopped and started. Despite the use of a night vision monocle, the would-be killer moved with a nervous, uneven stride.

"Caggis!" A voice shattered the silence. Down the hall and around the corner from Blik's position, he wondered how his pursuer would react. "Caggis! Over here!" The urgency in the gangster's voice caused Caggis, unknowingly within two meters of Blik, to turn and retreat.

The distraction proved enough for Blik. He rose, spotted the flashlight which flickered in Caggis' hand, and launched two rounds. The first struck the retreating gang member's arm, sending him spinning and stumbling. The light from the first pale green laser blast proved to be a visual aid for Blik's subsequent shot, which struck his opponent's upper torso and ended his life.

The consequences for successful shooting became immediately evident. Blik dived to the floor and crawled toward his fallen opponent as two warriors rounded a corner across the debris-littered display room. Works of art not deemed important had been smashed long ago, when the Great Exodus was only partially underway. Now, they served as alarms as Blik bumped into broken statues and crawled over crumpled metallic artwork.

Blik needed to get to his opponent's weapon and monocle.

The sound of a small piece of bust in the image of a long-dead citizen of ancient Zhilo provided the alert the attackers sought. The two opened up their guns with a frenzied fire, obliterating everything in sight. Blik covered his head and lay motionless, enduring the murderous rain of lasers and debris. When the shooting stopped, the attackers listened with an intent focus, determined to find their prey.

Blik did not move. Any motion would create noise now that debris covered every square centimeter of the display gallery's floor he inhabited. Certain death closed in as the pursuers took small, slow, almost dainty steps toward Blik's location.

The two Civics spread out, limiting the danger of both being struck by Blik's anticipated laser fire. After separating by more than ten meters, the attacker to Blik's left made an arm motion, giving the signal to open fire while the other waited for Blik to expose himself.

Unsure of Blik's location, the first blast ricocheted off a piece of steel artwork which now could only be identified as a lump of metal. The sudden blast alarmed Blik and caused an involuntary startled movement which caught his attacker's eye. The opponent on Blik's left fired a shot which narrowly missed his torso.

Trapped and running out of time, Blik made the decision to die fighting. He lifted up enough to shoot at the position of the last laser blast's source. Just as he squeezed the trigger, he heard a shout from behind. The Civic in Blik's general aim ducked for cover as the room behind the action lit the night. The opponent to Blik's right dropped.

"Blik!" It was Kreeg.

Confident he had been rescued from certain death, Blik opened fire toward the approximate position of the bandit on his left. When the creature moved to respond, a white blast from Blik obliterated the shooter.

"I believe that's it," Blik yelled.

"Got it. We'll keep checking," Kreeg said with assurance.

Blik trudged through the debris and bent down when he reached a dead body. He pulled the night vision monocle from the gangster's head. "Got a new monocle!" Blik shouted with a laugh, as though the tense situation moments ago had already escaped his memory. He turned on the flashlight to determine the identity of his adversary. "Hey! Look at this, guys!" He stood up to be better heard. "This guy's a Civic. I haven't seen this emblem in a while."

"Yeah," UU shouted. "We found another one, too.

"Hey," Blik came to life. "Civics always have great rifles!" He grabbed the Drebehran laser rifle lying near the lifeless body—this particular model contained better sights and a low-resistance trigger compared to commercial models. Turning back toward the general direction of his friends, he continued. "What is an Asimoni civil soldier doing on Zhilo?"

"Trying to kill us," came UU's laconic response.

"Well, I should be dead right now, so thanks." No one had time to respond to Blik's gratitude. The room brightened with a tremendous roar from lasers as two enemy combatants opened fire. A shout of alarm from Yane's direction pierced the air. UU and Kreeg scrambled for cover as Blik dropped to hide behind the dead body at his feet.

Spread throughout the gallery, the UU Gang members stayed on defense until Civic shooting stopped. Without delay, Blik blasted a shot aided by his new-found monocle and Kreeg did the same from across the room. After a long five seconds, the firing waned. The attackers lay dead. The battle, at long last, ended.

"Everyone survive?" It was UU. Given the savagery of the attack, he feared the worst.

"Good here," Kreeg yelled.

"Same. Good," Yane responded, though with little enthusiasm.

"If we don't kill everyone, we're going to deal with this every time we go near that portal." Blik, always one to want to kill "everyone," made a point they all accepted: keeping the location of the portal hidden carried great importance.

After a brief reminiscence of the fire fight, the surviving four comrades agreed they could not wait to leave UU's native planet. Despite their desire, they could not leave.

Chapter Twenty-One

The long, slow-rolling hills of west-central Kansas farmland extended in every direction until the wheat fields, cattle farms, and hog farms seemed to meet the sky. The unsavory smell of cattle farming had been present Julie's entire life, so she never noticed; besides, it was better than the stench of hog farming, she always reasoned. Her companion and new friend had no similar experiences from which to draw.

Twenty miles from her house, Julie walked with Rick on an infrequently traveled dirt road used primarily by combines headed to the nearby wheat field and semis loaded with cattle, exiting the neighboring farm which they owned, headed in the direction of Interstate 70.

He had grown accustomed to earthling clothes and enjoyed wearing jeans; but, for whatever reason, Julie could not convince him to get rid of the ever-present red headband. The only time he failed to wear it was when Julie threw it into the washing machine.

The brilliant cobalt sky was still months from being shrouded in smoke when farmers burned their fields. Instead, only wispy white clouds created by jet airliner contrails erased portions of the blue. Accustomed to skies of varying colors on various planets, the alien paid little heed to the landscape or sky; Julie felt enthralled by it.

"I never get tired of the beauty of the countryside."

"Is this beautiful to you?"

"Yes!" Julie seemed to take a little offense at the question, but Rick failed to notice. "It's not the ocean or the mountains, but it's still beautiful! And you can see the horizon."

The alien shrugged. "Makes sense. But the scenery here does not contain many colors. You should see Heisler!"

"Your home planet, right?"

"Yes. Heisler is recognized as the most beautiful planet *and* having the most intelligent inhabitants."

Julie looked at him with a skeptical glance, unsure whether the Heislerian's chest expanded in reality or just in her imagination.

"It's true. The planet is gorgeous."

Julie stopped and faced her friend. "Rick, do you like it here?"

Rick stopped to face her and took a deep breath. "I have to go back, Julie. It's where I belong."

She fought back a tear as she struggled for words. "I know. I just—I just. I—I'm enjoying you being here."

His face tightened. "I have to go back. I can't think about it any other way. I'm a soldier and must think like a soldier." Rick looked around before facing Julie again. "To do so would be to inhibit my judgment."

"Cloud." Julie smiled. "On Earth we say, it would 'cloud' my judgment.'"

"You do understand we say many of the same things, including some expressions."

Julie nodded. "Yes, it's amazing."

"It's just proof the Shersheen were here, although I haven't figured out how recent that was." The thought changed Rick's expression to one of puzzlement.

She reached out and put a hand on his shoulder. She tried to remind herself that he was not who he seemed to be at this moment. At this very moment, Rick was a bulky human with differences not readily perceptible to the human eye. At any given moment—at least, any angry moment—he could become a being which grew by 40% of his current size. No matter what she thought—felt—she had to remind herself that he was not human.

"I gotta remember." Julie shook her head.

"What?"

"That you—that you." She verbally caught herself. "You don't belong here."

"That's right."

She frowned. A light breeze lifted her brown hair away from her shoulders as it bounced behind her head.

"My limping is a lot better and I can walk for several minutes at a time without hurting," he announced with pride in his voice. "It won't be long."

“Maybe I can come with you.”

“I’d have to ask UU, but do you believe you’re strong enough to live our kind of life?”

Julie pondered the thought for a moment before turning to head back toward her pickup truck. “Maybe.”

“Who would run your farms?”

A sense of defeat pervaded her body. “I don’t know.”

“You have to know.” Rick paused for effect. “You can’t get there and find out, when we’re in a heated battle and you have a job to do, that you can’t handle it. Someone could be killed because of it. It might be you or someone in our gang.”

“You say ‘gang’ a lot.” Julie crinkled her nose. “That has a little different connotation on Earth.”

“For us, it’s just a group of like-minded creatures.”

Julie dropped her head, her mind on what hurt her heart. “Let’s get you off your feet.”

Rick nodded.

The pair walked back to her truck, side-by-side and together in spirit, though not in word. Neither spoke again until after they climbed into her pickup truck.

•   •   •

Kreeg, Yane, and Blik felt lost, but their boss continued with confidence toward a small mountain, outside the city of Eese. The once-spectacular city was surrounded by a barren brown desert, teeming with small animals suited for arid emptiness, yet those same small animals were difficult to find when hiding from the blazing star Ma'eek, which had risen within the prior hour.

UU recognized the small mountain and led his cohorts to the nondescript block building which blended in with its surroundings. The Zhiloan native did not get lost when anywhere near his favorite city.

Their lightly armed shuttle craft's best weapon was its agility. UU had piloted it with adroit zigs and zags throughout the city to throw off any ground-based pursuers, then took a circuitous route on the outskirts of town to allow for greater opportunities to pick up scans from craft in the atmosphere or above. Confident of an undetected journey, he piloted the ship directly to the remote building which served as the gang's original, and now occasional, refuge from the evil which sought to find and destroy them.

Only meters from the building, UU planted the shuttle onto the barren soil. The four exited the craft and waited as Yane prepared to exhibit one of his skills.

"Hey, UU," Yane called out as he approached the building. "Do you think I need to check for booby traps first, or does anyone come near here?"

"You need to check for everything, especially booby traps." UU's flat tone gave no comfort to the concern Yane felt when he heard them.

"Then I will," Yane replied with an unhappy disposition. He continued to walk, then replied when he knew he could not be heard. "No sense in getting blown up today when I can die in a blaze of lasers and bombs."

"You don't think anyone's been here, do you?" Kreeg asked.

"Killers like to kill, Kreeg." Blik's answer was just as much mockery as information. "I know."

"Yes, I know you like to kill, Blik," Kreeg said as he shook his head.

"That's why my last name is Kilz." As he always did, Blik laughed heartily at the thought of the aptness of his name—of which he reminded everyone often.

"That's why you're such a useful team member, Blik," UU said with a laugh. "I need all kinds of skills, including killing."

"You got the right warrior then," Kreeg answered with a straight face as he shook his head.

"Yes, he does!" Blik roared, his voice deepening with each word. The belly laugh which followed added an aura of the enjoyment Blik gained from the conversation.

All three checked their surroundings every few seconds as they spoke. No one wanted to find themselves arrested, let alone at Death's door in a fire fight.

Kreeg eyed Blik before asking a question. "Why do you like killing so much?"

A smile crawled across Blik's large Andalian face before he responded. "Just so you know, I don't kill innocent creatures. But I enjoy it because it's a challenge, and I know I'm making the universe better. Andalians are like the parasitic heroes of the universe." He paused and doubled the size of his grin at the thought. "We get rid of the evil-doers and vicious murderers. We make life better. We clean places up."

"Oh." Kreeg looked at UU before continuing. "Is that how you see yourselves? I see."

"Don't look at me," UU begged in a mocking tone. "I couldn't convince him otherwise if all the liquor in Gigorl was at stake."

"I think you Andalians are — "

As he began his sentence, Kreeg found himself interrupted by the mad Mangan running from the headquarters. "We've got to leave! Now! We've got to leave!"

Kreeg and Blik stared at Yane, whose arms were flapping while he leaped into the air as he sprinted. UU stared away from the building, in the direction of Eese.

"We've got to leave!" Yane approached with all the speed his legs could muster.

"It's too late," UU said with a flat tone.

As Yane came to a halt in front of his three friends, he peered in the same direction as they did. The two dozen or so columns of dust rising up in the distance approached at an alarming speed. They could not react in time to board their vessel and fly away, so they simply stared at the fast-approaching land-based craft which kicked up the columns of dust.

Chapter Twenty-Two

Over five minutes elapsed before every member of the law enforcement team exited every craft which had screamed up to the scene.

While looking around, hands up in the air, UU surveyed the situation. "They would've blown us out of the sky had we fled."

The others frowned to display their agreement with their leader, but no one looked at the other. Instead, they all stared ahead, at the impressive display of force.

As they left their craft, some law enforcement officers dropped to a knee and aimed their weapons. Four strategically-placed officers set up long guns on tripods, ready to disintegrate the bandits if they chose to take flight. Police Chief Rolan Crui and Lieutenant Ashken took the lead, flanked by two Quadrant Police members, although UU and company did not know whether they were members of law enforcement before the known universe entered its apocalyptic chaos.

The group of four officers approached UU without a word; they did not slow their pace until within a few meters of their subjects, then they came to a stop a mere two meters from UU.

"Untas Ursulanus! You and your team must drop your weapons immediately!"

"It's Colonel Untas Ursulanus." UU stressed the title. "And we will comply."

UU led by example, loosening his combat belt, allowing his sidearm and holster to fall to the Zhiloan desert ground. The others followed his lead. Within seconds, additional weapons plopped to the brown soil, bounced, then settled into the dirt.

"You are under arrest for the massacre of one hundred and twenty-one souls: females and children, young and old."

UU's eyes bulged. He expected a lot of different accusations, but not this. "What? Massacre?! Females and children? What is this insanity?!"

Crui laughed. "Such a ploy is not going to work, UU. We have proof."

A look of anger flashed across UU's face. He felt his blood pressure and urge to retaliate rise. "We have committed no such crime! You cannot possibly have proof of our involvement in something we did not perpetrate!"

Chief Crui turned to his lieutenant. "Go ahead."

"Wait! This is not right!" Kreeg shouted.

"Gag them if you must," Chief Crui added, disdain dripping with every word.

•　　•　　•

The Fankan prison had a distinct odor thanks to the pungent smell which emanated from a nearby silver mine. The planet Fank was rich in high quality silver and had been a source of wealth for millennia. Unfortunately for prisoners in the massive complex, the Fankans employed a unique chemical in the mining process designed to keep cutting tools cool and render the surrounding rock weak. Weaker rocks brought faster, easier cutting, which led to reaching the silver sooner.

UU and company did not know much about Fankan silver, other than mining it was lucrative over time; thieves and gangs did not bother with attempting to collect silver when other riches could be gathered quickly.

The day-long journey from Zhilo to Fank had proven uneventful, with each of the four captives held in solitary confinement in tight, uncomfortable, upright boxes which passed as holding cells. Communication with each other had been impossible, and each had no way of knowing whether the others had been released, killed, or were being held in the same manner. The Fankans were largely an unremarkable species without unique talents or features, and they lacked notoriety for anything other than the silver mines.

As UU's thoughts stewed and raged, he felt grateful that, in his prison cell on Fank, he had the ability to pace.

The cell itself was encompassed by thick concrete. Windowless, the room was lit by a light fixture built into the ceiling. The three-meter-high walls allowed access to the light by an enterprising criminal bent on escape, but every wannabe fugitive made the same discovery: the concrete ceiling sported a hole to allow the light fixture to fit in, with only small holes drilled to allow for the fixture to receive electricity. There was not even enough electrical cord for a suicide attempt, let alone to use as a weapon on an unsuspecting guard.

The fourth wall included a door made from steel bars, but an extra, exterior door sealed the occupant from the outside world. The small window in the exterior door allowed for authorities to peer inside, but it's composition and distance from the barred door made meaningful viewing out of the cell impossible. Prisoners on Fankan were held in solitude as much as possible with little contact with fellow inmates.

Two Fankan guards interrupted UU's thoughts of anger and revenge. UU made an immediate observation that he could easily disable both guards and flee his cell, but he knew such actions would not only be interpreted as signs of guilt, but his lack of knowledge of the prison's layout would doom him.

"Turn around," the skinnier of the two guards ordered, his meek voice made him sound as though he had just entered puberty.

UU complied with the instructions and provided no resistance as the frail guard locked the steel electronic handcuffs together, leaving UU to stand with his hands secured behind his back.

A third guard entered, carrying two metal chairs. In a wordless flurry of brief activity, the guard set the chairs on the cell floor, facing each other, then exited.

"Sit there." The frail guard pointed at the nearest chair, then moved the other chair to almost two meters away.

UU glared at the second guard, an equally frail looking young Fankan who allowed fear to show in his eyes when the beefy colonel's expression changed to a snarling, simmering face of anger. UU sat in the prescribed chair.

The guards left without delay and did not close either door behind them.

UU felt a twinge of surprise when the official who entered his cell was not Police Chief Rolan Crui, but a short, well-dressed skinny Fankan who arrived empty-handed.

"Hello, Mister Ursulanus." Wearing a thin jumpsuit which looked like a modern military uniform throughout the quadrants, but adorned with an animal hide jacket and matching belt, the Fankan looked like he was fit to enter a courtroom.

UU rose from his chair in a deliberate, slow manner. "Colonel Ursulanus," he growled as he stressed his former military rank. As he reached his feet and stood at full height, he leaned forward, as if to look down on his apparent adversary. "Address me properly." His final thought flowed from his mouth as smoothly as a cat going over a waterfall. His voice cracked and deepened as it approached a roar. "I will not allow my team and myself to be prosecuted for crimes we did not commit."

The visitor's voice deepened, but it still sounded shrill and fragile when compared to the colonel's. "Sit down, Mister—Colonel Ursulanus."

UU squinted, glared for another couple of seconds, then eased into the small chair. The short Fankan followed suit.

"Colonel, I am Dextair, federal prosecutor, and the only creature who stands between you and a death sentence."

UU's expression failed to change. He gave the look of an unimpressed warrior.

"There is some damning evidence against you and I would like to discuss it." Dextair smiled as though he held every card, which he did. "Your friends have been giving us valuable information, and I suggest you do the same."

If the statement had been made so UU's reaction could be analyzed, the mission failed. UU's burst of laughter reached a decibel level which caused the prosecutor to flinch, surprised and in mild pain by the aural assault.

After the laughter died down, UU gave a more intelligible response to the obvious lie. "Kreeg would rather blow you into a thousand pieces than cooperate with you." UU paused for effect. "Yane has probably already bartered for a more comfortable bed and a tub of Xorbonis candy so he can laugh at the show you entertainers put on." UU laughed at the mental image conjured by his statement. "And Blik. Blik!" UU laughed again. "Blik would rather kill you with his own hands, boil you, and eat you for a meal."

The little prosecutor gulped, then mustered up the courage to respond. "Colonel, you're going to be executed for these crimes."

"You say you're a federal prosecutor?"

"Yes."

"Have you considered presenting evidence and allowing us to do so?" UU's tone changed from threatening to flat. "Even on your backward planet, the rule of law is valued."

"If the evidence were not so damning," Dextair paused, as though arguing with his thoughts. "But between the terrorist you left behind and the types of weapons used, there is no doubt."

"Wait!" Concern dominated UU's face, suddenly plastered onto his skull from ear to ear. "What do you mean, left behind? Who?"

"Colonel!" Dextair's soft voice dripped of faux offense. "You play me for a fool. As though you don't know your own gang members."

Thoughts of Chabdab and Kimberlina flooded UU's thoughts. His countenance dropped and toughness faded.

"That's better," Dextair mocked the caged criminal. "You know who."

"Fankan, so help me if you don't tell me who you found!" UU truncated his own words but could not cut off the thoughts.

Sensing an opportunity to display dominance over the much larger creature, Dextair poured on more of his acidic mockery. "Or you'll what? The guards outside would vaporize you before you could—"

"Are my teammates alive?! Tell me!" UU roared like the caged animal he was.

"Teammates?" Confusion grasped Dextair by the shoulders. "Surely you realize you only left one female behind."

"Kimberlina?! Is she alive?"

"Yes, it was Kimbyk Parlina." Dextair paused. "No, she is not alive."

UU's head dropped. His shoulder's slumped. Energy drained out of his body. For the first time, UU displayed a desire to cooperate, although his reasons had nothing to do with dead females and children. He lifted his head and allowed his eyes to meet the prosecutor's haughty stare.

"She was kidnapped on a law enforcement mission to Ceratofs to capture the Trerzon Gang." UU paused in an attempt to conquer his rebellious emotions. "I lost Kimberlina and Chabdab. Kidnapped."

"So, you're telling me they joined another gang, and that gang perpetrated this heinous crime." The prosecutor's words composed neither a question nor a satisfactory statement, at least in his mind. Tone skeptical, words biting, Dextair did not take UU's words as a legitimate attempt at truth.

UU glared through the pain and into Dextair's eyes. "I'm telling you they were badly hurt and kidnapped. One of the Trerzon gang members told me."

"And where is this Trerzon criminal now?"

"Eaten by the Xin buzzards, for all I know," UU referenced the large bird that preyed on Ceratof carcasses. "I snapped his neck after he told me."

"Killing comes easily for you."

The pain in UU's eyes faded and anger found new strength. "Yes, it does."

"How did Kimbyk come to die on Fank?"

UU recognized the hope in the prosecutor's voice, as though the latter could draw a damning admission from the gang leader.

"I have no idea." UU looked around the room as he paused, still fighting emotions over thoughts of Kimberlina and Chabdab. "Someone in law enforcement set us up and we were close to being wiped out." His eyes settled on Dextair again. "We haven't seen Kimberlina or Chabdab since then."

For the first time, the prosecutor seemed content to listen.

"We've been working with law enforcement throughout the quadrant. Abuss Onuss has been coordinating our work." UU paused in thought before continuing. "But they have a leak. Probably many. In fact, on Ceratofs, we encountered a law enforcement agent working with them—I don't remember what police force Bill knew him from."

"Bill. Is that Blbbb—I see why you call him Bill." Along with most creatures, the prosecutor proved incapable of pronouncing "Blbbbimukx" or remembering Bill's tutoring on the matter.

"Yes. That's him."

For the first time since the disjointed interview began, Dextair climbed out of his chair and paced the room in a slow, deliberate manner. UU's squinting told Dextair the colonel was trying to ascertain the prosecutor's thoughts.

"Colonel," the prosecutor began, a hint of befuddlement in his voice. "Colonel, we have several of your team in custody."

UU's expression did not change until the meaning of Dextair's statement hit him.

"Yes, more than just the four of you."

A slow nod from UU informed the prosecutor that he understood Dextair's meaning.

"I don't know if we have the whole gang or not, but you will tell us that later. Right now, I'm struck by something." Dextair ceased his pacing long enough to decide how to word his next sentence, then continued his zigzag pattern around the small cell. "You all have the same story about Kimbyk and Chabdab."

"You don't have Chabdab?" UU interrupted.

Dextair stopped pacing again to answer. "No." UU's frown caught Dextair's eye. He then turned away and resumed pacing. "I realize many of you are ex-military and you're well-trained, so I recognize this could all be a charade; but, the evidence is overwhelming."

"What evidence?"

The prosecutor shook his head with vigorous jerks. "No. No." He laughed. "Not a chance, colonel. Not a chance."

"You said I may be executed yet I cannot be told of the evidence against me?"

"In due time. Probably at sentencing."

"I've heard the quadrant described as 'lawless,' but you're certainly underscoring that fact."

In anger, Dextair marched up to UU with swift strides. His voice rose in volume with every word. "Those of us who have remained in order to protect the innocent are protecting them from the likes of you and your gang!" His last few words had reached a shout.

"You're not very scary, mister," UU said in a flat voice. "I am telling you the truth. Kimberlina and Chabdab were kidnapped and we haven't seen them since."

Dextair yanked his body with a jolt away from his prisoner.

"If you at least let me know when," UU counseled. "I can tell you where we were at the time of this massacre you described."

With his back to UU, Dextair was not listening, choosing instead to formulate his next line of attack. "Colonel, my next communication off planet will be to Abuss Onuss." With dramatic flair, as though he were baiting a criminal on the witness stand into an admission of guilt, the veteran prosecutor spun on a heel and faced his suspect. "And what is Abuss Onuss going to tell me? Is he going to back up your fantastical concoction? Is he, colonel? Or is he going to say exactly what I expect him to say: you are a killer, not working with authorities, and you were never commissioned to do anything on behalf of law enforcement? What is he going to say, Mister Ursulanus?!" He stressed the title to rub in his salty point.

"Contact him and find out."

"That's exactly what I'm going to do, Colonel." With that, Dextair marched in long, angry strides out of the cell and out of sight.

As UU sat deflated, mourning the death of Kimberlina and the loss of Chabdab, one of the guards closed both cell doors, sealing UU into his lonely world, left to think about his friends and ponder how they could escape their apparent fate. Only later would they remove his manacles.

Chapter Twenty-Three

When the cell door opened, UU would never have guessed who would follow the guards in. After the usual addition of chairs and handcuffing, Abuss Onuss entered the cell. To add to the surreal moment for UU, Abuss Onuss carried with him a concerned, caring expression — one UU assumed he would never see from the officer of the law.

The leader of the Board of Ten, his slightly oversized forehead and small frame providing a contradiction which UU found appropriate, strode to the errant colonel with surprising alarm.

"Have they abused you?"

"No." UU laughed. "I think they fear I will retaliate somehow, but I have been a model prisoner."

"Good for you." Abuss Onuss nodded, his bulbous head rocking to and fro. "I'm sure you have already deduced that Bingus Jam and Pracen are furious at me." A small, wry smile grew into a larger one as he considered his own words.

UU laughed. "I haven't had time to process the meaning of your presence, but I'm not surprised."

"It's been a challenge, but you should be grateful I have tracked your every move—well, most of your moves."

"So, you know we didn't commit that massacre." UU posed a statement rather than a question.

"First, it's not your way. Second, you were on Zhilo at the time."

"That I didn't know." UU stressed the first word, unaware of the timing of the crime.

"How could you not know where you were?"

"They haven't told me anything," UU answered. "Including when this happened."

"I had someone following you," Abuss Onuss explained. "He was supposed to place a tracking device on your craft but proved incapable."

"We didn't kill him, did we?"

Abuss Onuss closed his eyes for a long moment, then reopened them and shook his head. "No. Fortunately."

"We've been on Zhilo several times, so I still don't know when the massacre took place. The last time there we killed a number of creatures—Civics—and we almost didn't make it off planet."

"Civics?"

UU nodded.

"But — " Abuss Onuss interrupted his own thought. To follow the thought to its logical conclusion would be to accept the widespread belief the Premier was THE puppet master, not a hostage. "I don't understand."

"It's what we've been trying to tell you." UU stared into Abuss Onuss' eyes with an intense search for some sort of recognition from the career law enforcement officer.

"Why would Asimoni civilian military be on Zhilo?" The expression on Abuss Onuss' face told UU the law enforcement veteran did not wish to accept the obvious.

"Abuss Onuss," UU began, a slow, steady narrative developing in his own mind. "You know why Civics were there. The Premier controls them. Not terrorists. Not kidnappers. The Premier." He paused to allow his words to sink in. "Not out of misguided allegiance. But for the Premier."

The reaction was obvious to UU. Abuss Onuss experienced a rapid increase in blood pressure and mental discomfort. Words and belief were passing by each other—not connecting, but close enough in proximity to elicit confusion. The law enforcement leader struggled to accept the conclusion which hovered over him. "But," was all he could manage.

"But the rumors are true." UU did not continue his thought; he wanted Abuss Onuss to do so. He wanted—needed—the Board of Ten to understand and accept the truth. If UU could get the leader of the Board to accept the obvious, he knew the rest of the Board would, in time, separate from their persistent denials.

•   •   •

"I have not told UU yet."

"Why?"

"Because," Abuss Onuss explained. "If I tell him who murdered Kimbyk Parlina, he'll go into a rage and hunt the killers. I need him to stay focused."

"You forget, Mister Chairman," Dextair said with cold confidence. "UU and his murderous gang aren't going anywhere."

"I've explained it to you," Abuss Onuss replied in a firm tone. "They weren't there."

"Then that can come out in trial." Dextair's eyes narrowed. His confidence did not abate. He believed he possessed the dominant argument.

"How are you even having legitimate trials during these times?" Abuss Onuss asked, indignation growing.

"We are functioning," was all the prosecutor would offer.

"Do you plan on getting out of the quadrant before the nova explodes?"

Dextair felt his head make an involuntary jerk backward. He did not anticipate the question. "Well, yes. Of course."

"It's our job in law enforcement to ensure the wrong creatures don't make it back." The small-framed Drebehran glared at his fellow officer of the law. He fought to suppress his anger. "No matter his reputation, UU is brilliant. I need him."

"Do you plan on making the jump in time?" Dextair asked the question out of genuine curiosity.

"I do. And so does UU." Abuss Onuss paused. "And so does his gang. And they will."

•   •   •

"The Fankan Freedom Liberators?!" UU roared his reaction to Abuss Onuss. "I've never heard of that gang!" Out of his cell for the first time in a Heislerian month, UU felt at ease without his handcuffs until now. Now, he simply wanted to crush the throats of his newfound enemies.

UU, Abuss Onuss, and Dextair sat at a table large enough for thirty. The chairs varied in sizes to accommodate various humanoids who wished to conduct business with Fankan law enforcement. The walls, with drab gray paint and a lack of windows, held a smattering of paintings and photos from the planet's varied landscape.

"UU, I'm sorry." Abuss Onuss said with a genuine tone of sadness. "I wasn't going to tell you the true demise of your Kimberlina, but we agreed you deserve to know."

"We?" Dextair flashed anger from his eyes at Abuss Onuss. "I don't even want him released, let alone know they were citizens from my planet!"

"You were protecting your own kind and ready to allow me to die?!" UU struggled to hold back the building rage.

"But you know he's innocent. They are innocent." Abuss Onuss stressed "they" to remind the prosecutor of the illegitimate detainment of most of UU's gang.

"That should've been for a court to decide." The prosecutor glared at his guest. "I don't know they're innocent!" He stressed "know" as though he were trying to convince the two of his own legitimacy. "You are the one who claims the 'FFL' committed the act, not me!" Dextair turned his attention to UU, then back to Abuss Onuss.

Abuss Onuss ignored the statement. That line of argument no longer served a purpose; with the freeing of UU, the subject of standing trial became moot. "I have given to the prosecutor security camera footage. You should not view it, but I have."

UU's anger rose higher. "Why shouldn't I view it?"

"Because you do not need to see the badly injured Rojani meet her demise." Abuss Onuss had lost the battle of telling UU the truth about how Kimberlina died, but he had no intention of allowing him to see the graphic act. "She was killed on Ceratofs. They certainly transported her body to Fank to aid in framing you."

UU dropped his head for a moment. His eyes involuntarily closed. He took a deep breath before continuing. "I can accept that. Abuss Onuss, you have trusted me and I will return the favor." UU's noble recognition of Abuss Onuss' intentions was a common attribute throughout the quadrants. They believed such quid pro quo served a valued function in the progress of civility.

"Where's the rest of my gang?" UU had neither seen nor spoken to his compatriots since his incarceration.

"They will be here soon." Dextair's comment was shrouded in a deep layer of regret. Releasing UU and his gang was an act the prosecutor thought he would not have to commit.

"We are innocent, Dextair." UU slowed his speech with every word. "You know it."

The Fankan pursed his lips and avoided a verbal response, although his facial expression was worth a thousand-word speech.

•　　•　　•

"UU, you have to do this."

"No." UU shook his head with vigor.

Abuss Onuss looked the Zhiloan leader over, then turned his attention to his gang members. "Kreeg. Yane. I need your assistance."

The rest of the gang stayed away from the main conversation, several meters away, squinting in the fierce white light from the Fankan sun under the pale blue sky. They chatted among themselves as the animated conversation continued not far away, where arms flailed and fingers pointed as each one spoke. The shadow of the prison ended just meters from their current location; none realized the poetic significance of the fact.

Kreeg laughed as he spoke. "We are going to find Kimberlina's killers and destroy them." His voice became weak and melancholy as he thought about his missing friend. "We suspect they also killed Chabdab. We shall see."

Abuss Onuss again focused his attention on the team leader. "But UU, I need for you to understand," he pleaded. "I communicated with the Board, and they want you to stop the Civics."

"That is acceptable; we can do that, but it will be right after we avenge Kimberlina and Chabdab." The colonel pondered his own words. "We must make the guilty pay. Then we can live with ourselves, and only then can we worry about our own futures." UU never considered how badly outnumbered his group would be up against the Asimoni civilian military.

"All those years in the military but now you've lost your discipline." Abuss Onuss seemed to understand an attack on UU was an attack on them all, so he took a physical step back as he did the same with his verbal approach. "Let me put it another way." He paused. "Whether you are correct about the Premier or not, this will lead you closer to him."

Attention gained, UU's facial expression communicated a willingness to listen. Beads of sweat had formed on the top of his head and a drop streaked down his face near his left ear, such was the heat from Mize, the star which kept them uncomfortable.

Abuss Onuss continued his efforts. "Think about how you will look if you can rescue the Premier. And if he really is as evil as you say, you can capture him and bring him to justice."

UU snorted his disapproval of the thought of rescuing the mastermind behind much of the murder and opportunistic thievery in the quadrant.

"You will be a hero with law enforcement," the leader of the Board of Ten punctuated his belief as his arms gesticulated and his fingers poked the air.

"I see."

"But I need you to bring someone back alive," Abuss Onuss continued. "I need Weektu the Corsan captured." An afterthought caused him to repeat himself. "I need him alive."

"Why?"

"Because he seems to be the head gang leader of gang leaders," Abuss Onuss explained as he wiped sweat from his forehead with a large blue handkerchief. "You seem to be one of the few gangs not controlled by Weektu."

"I don't follow your reasoning," Yane interrupted. "We're not controlled by him. Does that not make it more difficult for us to find him?"

"He's taken refuge on Jermibu," Abuss Onuss answered. "We know where he is—at least what planet he's on. I'll check our intelligence again before you go."

"No." UU shook his head with vigor. "We're not interested in that until after we kill Kimberlina's killer."

Once again Abuss Onuss turned his attention to UU's friends for help. "Kreeg. Yane. I need your assistance."

Police Chief Rolan Crui spoke before Kreeg could start a sentence. Yane and Blik exchanged glances while UU and Abuss Onuss looked to the police chief. "The Fankan Freedom Liberators are not on Fank right now."

"Then where are they?" Abuss Onuss could not hide his incredulity.

"We did not follow them. We assume they'll never come back."

UU needed to be convinced. "Why wouldn't they come back? This is their home."

Abuss Onuss joined in with his own skepticism. "Why would they go anywhere else? Their contacts off-planet are limited."

Blik, the large Andalian with the hair-trigger mind, responded with cynicism wrapped by a growl. "This sounds like the words of someone who doesn't wish us to find what we're looking for." He paused before adding. "I would hope that's not the case, Chief."

"I will disregard the threat," Crui responded with venom on his tongue.

Abuss Onuss, ever the pliant one, took an approach which surprised the entire little group. "If they've gone off-planet, tell me why and where. I want to know."

"I told you, we did not follow them." Following the lead of the others, Crui's frustration level increased.

"You must have heard from someone, somewhere, where they might have gone," UU half-asked.

Crui surveyed the eyes of UU, then Abuss Onuss. After a hesitation, he looked at Kreeg and Yane but avoided eye contact with Blik. A deep breath preceded his answer. "Jermibu."

Chapter Twenty-Four

Desolation knew no better definition than the arid, bleak, dreadful vastness of the dead planet Jermibu and its nearby sister planet Jamabu. To visit one was to visit the other, so similar were the two ancient, useless planets good only for archaeologists. Even plunderers found the planet of little value, with few sites containing jewels or artifacts of any sort and little shelter except for the deep caves used by archaeologists during their stays. Uninhabited for more than two millennia, historians believed they knew everything which possibly could be discovered about the dwellers of the now-dead planets.

The former residents of the sister planets were one species: the Jubu. These intelligent, advanced, yet aloof creatures allowed their misanthropic species to be overtaken by a backward, warrior race which did not share the natives' love of science, the arts, and education. Instead, these galactic Visigoths eradicated a great civilization which spanned two planets. In time, and unrelated to the invasions on the surface, the planet's core died and it entered its death throes. Rains ceased; crops withered; soil eroded. Unaccustomed to the harsh climate, the conquerors retreated to their home world and developed into what were now known as Andalians.

The planets lacked the charm and attraction which could be found in deserts by those who appreciated such barren beauty. Besides ancient buildings which had decayed to little more than masonry clumps, the planets' top "resource"—if it could be labeled with such a vaunted title—was sodium borate, but the substance was too acidic to be used by industry, and thus mined, for any conceivable purpose.

An approaching ship would see a brown world with wisps of thin white clouds circling the emptiness. Eventually, even the scant cloud cover would disappear as the atmosphere continued its gradual decay. Scans from space could only detect the life forms present to research the forsaken planet. Neither creature nor plant indigenous to Jermibu or Jamabu still survived. Experiments to see whether plant life could be revived failed. No one dared attempt to reintroduce animal life of any type.

The few scientists who still desired to study the planets built little villages in the caves in order to have temporary homes when on their brief expeditions. The cavernous underground respites from the hot sun Rif provided enough comfort to dine and sleep when not on the surface digging through layered cities or photographing ruins which became a little less spectacular after each year of dry winds which devoured their once-lavish features.

To the inhabitants of Quadrant Four, the sister planets represented Hell.

Because everyone avoided the planets—they had no incentive to do otherwise—the two planets became perfect hideouts for criminals before the Great Exodus and plundering gangs seeking short-term sanctuary afterward. With two targets in their sights, the UU Gang relished their trip to the planet closer to the yellow star.

"You do realize, UU," Yane began. "There are well over one hundred potential sites for us to search."

UU shook his head. "Abuss Onuss showed me tracking data. If we're in the wrong place we'll figure it out." He paused to chuckle. "If we're in the wrong place, we'll probably see combat, anyway." He again paused, this time to think about his words before delivering them. "Abuss Onuss wants us to capture a thug for him first, then kill Kimberlina's killers. Either way, I have information for both, even if he intentionally reversed the intelligence."

Sitting in a bench seat, alone and in thought, Blik smiled. Killing Time approached. He looked up to see Anthun and nodded. Anthun returned the nod, both understanding the other's thoughts.

The entire gang was doing something it rarely did: traveling together in one craft. The entire surviving gang, sans Rick, was present: Alana, the Sanlandan who found herself back in her own star system, though her native planet looked nothing like the sisters Jermibu and Jamabu; Bill, the native of the Quadrant Two planet Ozkzokoj; Mookie, a warrior, yet the Andalian seemed a bit too meek, and certainly too small, to hail from such a militarized planet; Anthun, the stereotypical Andalian who would be just as likely to strangle his enemy for the sake of laughs as attempt to gain needed intelligence from the victim; Geeba, the sweet, squeaky-voiced weapons expert from Corsar who held a special place for UU in her heart; Blik, the Andalian communication expert who garnered respect rather than fear from UU, but sought the latter from others; Yane, one of few Mangans UU would go to battle with; Kreeg, the red-skinned, green-eyed conundrum of a beast; and UU, the trusted leader, fierce warrior, and calm tactician.

The gang of nine—ten, if one counted Rick convalescing on Earth—was a small yet effective gang. Now they were of one mind: avenge Kimberlina and find Chabdab—if he was still alive.

. . .

The Drebehran Armed Shuttle flew low to the ground. As requested by Kreeg and approved by UU, the former piloted the ship and entered the planet's atmosphere out of sight from potential guards who protected the still-unseen cave. Flying at 100 meters above the ground for over 200 kilometers, the team felt confident they had not been detected.

Less than two kilometers away from their target, they settled onto the hard sand of the hot planet. As they did, UU finished his briefing.

"Our top target is the alleged head of the Civics, the one they call 'Weektu the Corsan.'" A thought struck the Zhiloan. "Actually, any Civic is our target, but the main one is Weektu."

Yane raised his hand, as though in a classroom. He spoke after UU nodded at him. "Weektu is who Abuss Onuss wants us to capture. What about Kimberlina's killer?"

A small grin crawled across UU's face. "At first, I assumed her killer was unknown. But after observing Chief Crui, I believe they are the same."

Glances and brief exclamations were exchanged by his team.

"Rolan Crui did not want us to know where to find Kimberlina's killers because he knew we would figure out their secret."

Again surprise overtook the gang.

"The Fankans don't care what the Civics or the Fankan Freedom Liberators or anyone else does so long as they stay off their planet." UU winked before continuing. "They are trying to clean up their planet and identify all thugs before they finally evacuate. But they don't wish to be there too long, so instead of arresting thugs, they have chosen to drive them off the planet."

"It's quicker that way," Yane chimed in as he considered UU's most recent example of his heightened abilities of perception and wisdom. "You don't have to battle raiders if you can urge them somehow to leave."

"But how?" Bill asked.

"By paying them off with riches," UU stated what was obvious to the others. "Rather than fight them, pay them off. Nobody dies during a payoff."

"So how do you know Weektu killed Kimberlina—and maybe Chabdab?" Geeba understood the link between the Fankan Freedom Liberators and the Civics, but not to

Kimberlina's death. "We didn't see Civics the night she was taken. We only saw Ceratofs."

"True." UU agreed. "If I think about our encounter that night, it was dark. We couldn't see well. I suspect the Asimonis and Corsans stayed in the rear, allowing the Ceratofs to hold the front line—and die. We only killed Ceratofs."

A brief amount of chatter ended when UU began to speak again. "Even so, I would think the Civics would not want their Asimoni appearance to be seen."

Everyone in the group understood. The Asimoni Civics would not wish to be spotted on the planet Ceratofs due to their long-running rivalry, when such subjects as rivalries mattered, before the Great Exodus. It all made sense to the others.

•   •   •

Eight warriors advanced toward the cave they believed their target inhabited. UU spoke as they approached. The ninth, Kreeg, waited in the craft, ready for his signal to proceed.

UU's gang took up positions on either side of the cave's ten-meter-wide opening, above it, and a dozen meters in front of it. Positioned in four pairs, the team stood at the ready, hidden behind various boulders. UU gave the command into his wristband communicator and within a Heislerian minute their craft, piloted by Kreeg, climbed high into the sky, then descended. It approached the site just meters above the rocky ground, at a low speed.

On one side of the opening, Yane noticed a camera mounted on a thin pole, then motioned to Bill to get his attention. He noticed the camera seemed to be pointed in a non-helpful direction, away from the cave's mouth and upward at 20 degrees into the pale blue sky. He took note of the camera's worn condition and concluded the device did not work.

As planned, Civics emerged to investigate the roar of the approaching craft. Within seconds, the strategic superiority of the gang's positioning allowed them to remain hidden until a fifth Civic exited the cave.

Then the UU Gang opened fire. All five Civics fell to the ground, dead, before they knew who had eliminated them.

The gang ducked behind the rocks used for cover and waited for Civic reinforcements to arrive as Kreeg landed the shuttle on the planet. Three more Asimoni fighters emerged and, in a display of zeal which Abuss Onuss would have feared, UU and his team put an end to the additional enemies.

UU walked to the opening of the cave, looked at Blik, and called his name. The Andalian removed a two-meter-long backpack from his back, then pulled out a 90-centimeter-long tube and corresponding grenade. While UU watched the opening, Blik loaded the grenade into the tube and glided in casual strides to stand next to his boss. In a quiet voice, he issued a simple command to UU: "Run away."

Several of the group followed UU's lead and cleared the area, unsure of how the ground would react to the powerful charge about to be delivered. UU moved backward in what seemed a half-backward run and half dance.

Blik fired the weapon, let out a pleased grunt, and took several steps backward. Two seconds later, the grenade exploded deep in the cave. The ground shook and dust rose from the cave's mouth and the ground around it.

Blik looked at his friends. "That was a deep cave."

"We probably didn't get everyone," Mookie yelled out from above and behind the entrance.

"I'll give it a minute," Blik reasoned with a casual tone which would lend itself to a relaxing day at a beach. "Does anyone have any poison gas?" After glances were exchanged but no responses, Blik groaned with disappointment. "I've always wanted to use poison gas. It sounds like fun."

As several of the gang smiled or laughed at Blik's serene approach to killing, a roar from above caught their attention. The first laser blast caused the group to scatter, but it struck the Drebehran Armed Shuttle. Kreeg opened fire at the larger craft before restoring shields to 100-percent.

Defenseless against the ship's large cannons, the exposed eight team members knew better than to shoot with their limited firepower lest they draw the fury of the enemy.

To UU's shock and horror, he looked over his shoulder, from behind the large boulder which shielded him from sight above, and saw Blik loading another grenade into the Rojani Hyper Grenade Launcher. "What are you doing?!" he shouted.

Despite the rumble of laser explosions and roar of the hovering space craft, Blik heard the colonel's voice and gave his answer. "Shields protect against lasers, not grenades."

"It'll never destroy a ship like that!"

"I don't need to destroy it." With that, Blik stood, exposing himself to potential laser fire, and launched his rocket-propelled hyper grenade.

The explosion caused greater damage than UU had imagined. For all of his military experience, he had never seen such an attempt with a Rojani Hyper Grenade. He knew the Rojanis made outstanding weaponry, but UU failed to account for the effect provided by the ship's defensive force field. The high-energy shields were designed to keep laser fire out; but, once a projectile penetrated the shields, the opposite effect occurred. The shields kept the concussion of the blast within the force field, allowing the explosion's energy to careen around the craft and inflict more damage. Blik was right: the explosion would not destroy the small ship, but it could cause crippling damage.

The detonation sounded different compared with other grenade explosions. With energy spreading around most of the ship, jet ports which controlled the vehicle while in the atmosphere faltered. The ship listed, then completed a slow descent into the ground, two hundred meters away.

As the spaceship hit the hard ground and the outer hull screeched and groaned in protest, another blast rocked the vehicle. Blik's second shot did greater damage as cracks widened from the collision with the planet's surface. Energy from the blast—small relative to enemy spacecraft laser fire—penetrated the ship and caused extensive damage.

Blik spotted a wider opening created by the impact with the ground and fired another grenade at the ship. This time, the sound of the explosion was blunted by the hull itself. The blast took place inside the craft. He had no doubt the damage was extensive.

Fire broke out in the region of the most recent grenade burst. The craft, stuck into the ground at an odd angle, leveled out as the high side of the vehicle crashed to the ground. The lifeless ship sat, burning from within.

Blik started to celebrate but was interrupted by the opening of a hydraulic door. Intended to allow passengers to walk out on level ground, the door only opened enough to allow occupants to crawl out; with the landing gear in the "up" position, the ground impinged the door's intended capabilities.

Smoke poured out of the small opening. The observers understood the meaning of the Civics who crawled out of the craft with great haste and held their arms up in surrender: the combatants had chosen death at the hands of UU over burning alive.

•   •   •

Five Asimoni Civics stood in a line eight hundred meters from the burning attack vehicle. Kreeg had moved the gang's shuttle over a kilometer away in case the crashed craft exploded as it burned from within. For over ten minutes, UU alternated between lecturing, berating, and questioning the Civics.

At long last, he lost his patience.

Before UU could act, Geeba raced the several paces forward and stood between her beloved boss and the prisoners. "What are you going to do?"

"I'm going to kill them one-by-one until they talk."

"Untas," Geeba began. "Please. The killing doesn't bother me; they probably deserve it. But we are to bring home prisoners. We'll never get out of this quadrant as free creatures if we keep killing prisoners."

UU nodded. "I'm afraid you're correct. But if we show mercy now, eventually the Premier will find a way to use that against us. To him and those like him mercy is weakness."

Tears filled Geeba's bright blue eyes as she took a step back, out of her leader's path. She cared for him, but she did not wish to challenge him further in front of the others.

UU looked at Anthun. "You're knife, please."

Anthun reached down and pulled his large, curved knife from the sheath attached to his right leg. He stepped toward UU and handed it to him, handle first. "The Andalian sword would be more fun right now," Anthun chuckled as UU took the weapon from the Andalian's hands.

"Yes, it would," was all UU offered as he took the knife and stepped toward the Civic at the left end of the line.

"Wait!" It was the third Civic. "Let my gang be. Let them live. I am the one you want!"

UU looked at Mookie and Bill. "Bind the others. We will take them with us." He returned his gaze to the valiant, self-proclaimed leader. "And you are?"

"Weektu the Corsan."

"Asimonis and Corsans look a lot alike." UU paused and looked the opponent over. "How do I know you are really Weektu?"

"I am known throughout the quadrant. You do not recognize me?"

UU shook his head. "No. I don't. And I don't know whether I believe you."

"Then let me tell you this: your warrior, the one you call Chabdab. He escaped me." Weektu frowned as he made the announcement. "The one you call Kimbyk did not."

"What became of Kimberlina?" UU asked.

"One of my creatures enjoyed her, then killed her." Weektu looked UU in the eye. "I had him killed for such an act."

"And then what happened?"

"We used her body to frame you for the massacre on Fank."

UU nodded. "I understand. So, you are really Weektu the Corsan."

"Yes." Weektu nodded as he continued to look UU in the eye.

UU strode the final step which separated the two leaders. In one motion, the knife in his right hand dropped downward, then came upward with great force. As the tip of the blade entered the Corsan's torso, slicing flesh, muscle, and intestines, it drove upward with great power, into the chest cavity.

Weektu let out a shrill gasp which faded over the course of two seconds.

UU dropped his center of gravity and then raised up, pushing hard with his legs, to drive the knife ever farther into Weektu's body, taking advantage of the blade's shape. "This is for Kimberlina!" he shouted. After another second, the Civic's body went limp. UU held to the knife with a firm grip as he allowed the dead warrior to fall to the ground, making a loud 'thump' as it collided with the arid soil.

A meek voice was heard from off to the side. It was Alana. "We were supposed to bring him back alive."

UU eyed her for just a moment before responding. "Yeah, I forgot." He then turned his attention toward the prisoners. "I will spare them. We will go back to Abuss Onuss and give him our results: four prisoners."

The UU Gang relaxed. The cold, calculated focus their leader exhibited demonstrated why they each secretly feared him.

Bill spoke in a low tone, afraid to disturb UU. "Chabdab is alive! That's great news."

Head hanging, Geeba responded as tears filled her eyes. "I'm happy he is, but Kimberlina is not."

Still angry and in no mood to relax, UU walked to Anthun to return the knife. As he reached the Andalian he said in an even tone. "This is for betraying our hideout at Umbr." As he completed his statement, UU drove the blood-soaked Andalian knife into the weapon's owner, repeating the same deadly path just used against the Corsan.

Gasps and screams emanated from the entire gang. Shock gripped them all. Anthun dropped to his knees, then to the ground, on his back.

UU smiled through a vicious glare as he locked eyes with Anthun as the latter slipped into shock. "You betrayed us, Anthun. You are responsible for the massacre of Gigorl law enforcement."

"No," Anthun gasped as life began its escape from his large frame. "Crartrarn."

UU frowned as he struggled to understand the word.

"Crartrarn," Anthun repeated.

What sounded like garbled speech to UU was ignored as he continued his explanation for his action. "I lied to you. I told you the location would be our next hideout." UU paused and changed tone to a more sarcastic delivery. "I was testing you. I've doubted you since our early days together after the Great Exodus."

"No." Anthun attempted to muster a bold response but could not.

"After I lied to you, I reconsidered, thinking we could indeed use the hideout again." UU looked up at his gang members, then returned his focus to the dying Andalian. "As I watched from a distance, law enforcement raided the building. But they were blown into pieces. It was a trap, but a trap I did not arrange. You did." He stressed the word "you" to emphasize what the dying Andalian needed to hear before expiring. "*You!*" UU glared at Anthun and repeated.

"Crartrarn." With his last gasp, Anthun repeated the mysterious word. Part of his knife handle was visible—sticking out of his torso—covered with the red blood of a Corsan and his own Andalian blood. Eyes bulging, Anthun expired.

UU pulled the Andalian knife out of its victim. Bloodied knife in hand, UU walked away in disgust, not wanting to see the hated traitor again.

•　　•　　•

On the flight to turn over their hostages, UU explained his actions to his sullen squad of bandits-turned-bounty-hunters. His words rang hollow to his team, straining credibility even with his most ardent supporter, Geeba. With tears in her eyes, she struggled to look at him.

Away from earshot, the gang grumbled about such a cowardly act, his rash behavior, whether UU was losing touch with reality, or some combination of all of the above.

While the group, including the other Andalians, never felt close to Anthun, the shock of his death lingered for the entirety of the trip. They all understood if UU emotionally unraveled, their odds of escaping the Nova Quadrant while maintaining freedom would remain close to zero.

Chapter Twenty-Five

"I don't understand."

"You don't understand what?"

"What you mean."

Julie pursed her lips in a failed attempt to hide her emotions. "On my planet." She stopped, searching for the correct words. "We've never seen aliens before."

"Aliens?" Rick's confusion seemed genuine, which perplexed Julie more.

"Creatures from other planets. We've never had that here."

"Of course you have," Rick said, again with genuine confusion. "I told you about the Shersheen—and there may have been others."

The pair walked through a small, one-acre field behind her house not intended for cattle or wheat. A relic of prior generations and their chosen spot to enjoy time together outdoors—for badminton, croquet, and other games through the years—Julie and Rick enjoyed the smell of freshly cut grass and the cloudless night sky dominated by a three-quarter moon.

"Okay, so let me put it this way." She paused again, still fighting for words which would enlighten him and convince herself. "No one on Earth has ever been in a relationship..." She stopped herself as she noted Rick's expression change in the moonlight. "A romantic relationship, that anyone else has known about, ever in Earth's history. Not with an alien."

Rick looked around as though he could find the answer in the nearby wheat field or in the reflection of the soft white moonlight reflecting off windows on the rear elevation of Julie's house.

"What I'm trying to say is, it's really weird to think about an Earth person and an ali—a creature from another planet being a couple."

"A couple. We use that expression, too."

Julie shook her head at the irrelevant observation. "What I'm trying to say is, you're not human—I'm not—what are you again?"

"Heislerian."

"Yeah. I'm not that."

For the first time on the walk, Rick smiled. "I understand. You're uncomfortable because we're from different planets."

"Exactly!"

"And I don't look human."

"Exactly!"

"And I can expand my body by forty percent. That is a fantastic trick, just so you are aware." Rick laughed until he understood the depth of Julie's discomfort. "I'm sorry."

Julie shook her head.

"So, what would an Earth male do in this situation?" Rick asked, innocence apparent.

Julie's look of exasperation remained veiled due to the limited light. "I don't know!" Her internal conflict overcame her words and left her sounding as confused as her other-worldly friend.

Rick stopped, placed a hand on her shoulder, and smiled. His face glowed in the moonlight, happy to put her at ease. "We don't belong in the same world—I know that, you know that." He caressed her cheek with one hand. "So, let's just enjoy the time we have together and not approach our relationship in an overly serious manner."

Julie took note of what she had already grown accustomed: the complex speech patterns often employed by her friends from the other side of the galaxy. Tears escaped her eyes as she nodded.

"In my world," Rick continued. "We are not used to cross-species breeding. Some accept it, it's just rare." He paused before thinking of even another point. "Besides," Rick laughed. "I don't think you would appreciate birthing a Heislerian child."

"Why's that?"

"Let's just say they don't know how to control when to expand their size and it's challenging enough for Heislerian females, and they have wider hips."

An aghast, almost frightened smile flashed across the female earthling's face. "Oh! That doesn't sound good!"

"My mother told me the same thing—not good at all." Rick howled in laughter.

Julie pushed her elbows into her waist as she walked, as though compacting her body could protect her from the grotesque thought. "Let's change the subject."

•　　　•　　　•

No one had seen Aelo Seveen this angry in a long time—certainly not since he hatched his plan to dominate the quadrants within days of the onset of the Great Exodus. Calm, assertive, and confident, the Premier experienced the daily bout of anger, but never to this degree. Screams reached such high decibels and his white Asimoni face turned so bright red even the brown stripes on his arms and chest seemed to fade, giving way to the blood which threatened to reach the very surface of his lanky body.

Shirt in tatters, no one attempted to hand him another item of any type. Chief Aide Rocash, who usually was tasked with calming their leader, refused to approach the Premier. They stood in the large bedroom chamber; Rocash wished to take advantage of the distance he could attain.

A back-hand from the Premier sent bottles of perfume flying through the air. As the bottles crashed to the carpeted floor—a few broke but most survived the attack—another swipe at items on his dresser sent jewelry flying. Before the jewelry could hit the floor, the thunderous crack of Asimoni oak being greeted by the angry closed hand of the Premier filled the chamber. Little of the wood gave way, causing a wave of pain to envelope him, starting at his hand.

"I want UU dead! Does anyone here understand me?! I want UU dead!"

Aides and servants looked at each other. None knew how to respond. Those responsible for failing to kill the UU Gang previously, or counter the attack from UU and his team on Jermibu, were not present.

Nothing abated the Premier's rage which continued for several more minutes.

With a quick head movement and slight motion of his hand, Rocash attempted to signal the messenger that he should depart. The short, dark, black and brown Corsan looked too young to be a gang member, but at 16 Heislerian years, his young eyes had witnessed more than they should have.

"My instructions, Premier, are to get your instructions." The young messenger made it clear with his tone he had a job to do and did not wish to waste time by watching the Premier's tantrum.

The Premier stopped and glared at the Corsan.

Rocash took a step forward, then thought better of intervention. Over ten meters away, he felt a degree of safety from his boss' wrath.

The Premier raced toward the messenger, hands extended, ready to choke the one who brought news which angered him. Out of instinct and training, the messenger reached to his hip and pulled out his Corsan hunting knife which he carried at all times. In a defensive position—knees bent, feet apart, torso leaning forward ever so slightly—the Corsan called out, "Stay away."

Before either the angry despot or defensive messenger could react at this new development, a round from a hand laser struck the Corsan in the shoulder, sending him to the carpet in a heap of pain and defeat. One of the palace guards had neutralized the threat. The messenger writhed in pain, low moans replacing the sound of the laser blast.

Cockiness restored, the Premier walked toward the wounded creature, his tall frame allowing his strides to lengthen as his energy remained high, and grabbed the knife which lay centimeters from the owner's hands. In one motion, the Premier picked up the knife, dropped to one knee, and thrust the blade into the young creature's heart. Writhing and moaning ceased, but the killer's anger did not subside. The premier who would rule the quadrants rose to his feet as he looked at Rocash. "How dare a subject of mine raise a weapon at me!"

Rocash knew the messenger was not a subject of the Premier, but in the rising tyrant's mind, all of the Nova Quadrant was his and all should obey his wishes.

"Bring me someone to deliver a message," the Premier hissed. "UU killed my best warrior and he will pay!" He looked around the room at his guards and aides. "I've never killed before." His hands began to tremble. "It feels pretty good!"

The Premier had killed a wounded, defenseless boy. No one was impressed with the sociopathic ruler.

•　　　•　　　•

Blik and Bill handed over their four prisoners before being escorted by a Drebehran bureaucrat to a conference room. Though unaware of it, the pair waited for the three Board of Ten members in the same room in which Kreeg, Yane, and Alana had met the same three law officers when they set in motion the idea to work on the side of the Law.

Abuss Onuss, Bingus Jam, and Pracen entered through a side door. Before anyone spoke, Abuss Onuss stretched his hand out and motioned for the Andalian and the Ozkzokojan to take seats opposite them. As the five sat, with Abuss Onuss in the middle on his side of the table, no one spoke.

Blik and Bill took in their surroundings. A large conference room with so many empty chairs; only five creatures present. They noted the angry looks they received before Abuss Onuss broke the brief silence.

"Where is Weektu the Corsan?"

Pracen leaned forward. His light blue Zhiloan skin contrasted with his leader's. "Either you failed to capture him, which would be understandable, or UU killed him." After a pause for effect, he continued. "Which is it?"

Blik looked at Bill, then back at Pracen. "Capturing him did not work out." Blik's straight-faced delivery served to underscore his lack of concern.

Bingus Jam pounded his fist into the table. "This is why we did not trust him!"

"You blame UU?" Blik's deadpan delivery caught the three off-guard.

"Are you telling us UU did not deliver the fatal blow?" Pracen asked in his typical dramatic turn of phrase.

Bill responded before Blik could. "I don't know that we are positive who was who. We had to shoot a lot of gangsters and we found him dead."

The three officers sat silent. Bingus Jam and Pracen allowed their faces to reflect their disappointment of being unable to blame the colonel.

"UU is a sharp leader," Blik continued the ruse. "He told the prisoners to insist he killed Weektu himself. He wants the Premier to get the message."

"And what message is that?" Bingus Jam asked.

"That UU is going to kill him." Blik again delivered his message without emotion.

"If the Premier is who you say he is," Bingus Jam interjected.

"We still believe he's a hostage," Pracen added.

"We don't." Bill stated their case as succinctly as possible.

"We know better," Blik added.

"Where is UU?" Pracen's question evoked raised eyebrows from the two gang members.

"Why would you care?" Blik asked, in a tart tone.

"We have all spread out," Bill said, furthering the secrecy. "We will come together when it is time to take out the Premier."

"Or rescue him," Bingus Jam retorted in a harsh tone.

"How is it only the Board of Ten refuses to acknowledge what the Premier has achieved?" Blik's caustic tone caused tensions to rise higher.

While snarls covered the faces of the Zhiloans, Abuss Onuss advanced the conversation with appropriate haste. "On Shanj Five, be here, in this room." The Drebehran referred to the Heislerian calendar—"Five" meaning the fifth day—to avoid confusion. "UU and anyone he chooses from your organization."

"Shanj Five," Blik repeated as he and Bill stood, ready to depart.

Chapter Twenty-Six

The tall pine trees lifted upward toward the blue sky, blocking off a large percentage of the light from Lucan, Eemlurian's sun. Close enough together to hinder vehicles which tried to enter, yet far enough apart to allow foot traffic, the trees provided perfect cover for anyone wishing to hide for a short time—whether fugitive or refugee—provided a shield was employed to deceive those who scanned for life forms from above.

Only three hundred meters from their ships, the four outlaws-turned-bounty-hunters relaxed under electronic cover once the shields were set up.

With Blik and Bill delivering their recent prisoners and UU and Geeba going their separate ways for the sake of security, the remaining four members of the gang met in secrecy to discuss their concern. That concern could be summed up in the form of one warrior: Colonel Untas Ursulanus.

Alana swept her eyes from Kreeg to Yane to Mookie as she squinted, her face reflecting the tense subject at hand. "You know I like him, you know I trust him." Her words tailed off. "But I'm just concerned about him lately."

"What besides killing Anthun?" Kreeg asked.

"Isn't that enough?" Mookie could not hide his amazement. His Andalian chest heaved outward as his brief words flowed with emotion.

"No." Yane's response expressed concerns of his own. "I'm not even sure why we're here."

"Yane," Alana began, then paused as though still trying to settle on which words to speak. "I know how close you are to UU and how loyal you are. Well I'm loyal, too, but killing Anthun—"

"And how he killed him!" Mookie interjected.

"Killing Anthun was disturbing to me," Alana concluded.

Kreeg held up his hand so he could speak next and allow the conversation's pace to slow. "If you're that concerned, then why not wait until Blik and Bill are here? And where's Geeba?"

Alana pursed her thin Sanlandan lips. "You know I'm strong friends with Geeba, but she loves UU."

"She does?" Yane asked.

Yane's surprise caused Alana to turn her head with a quick snap in disbelief. "How can you not know that? It's obvious."

"Well, I know they're close," Yane struggled to find the correct words. "That doesn't mean she loves him."

"She does," was all Alana would offer.

Mookie spoke up before anyone else could. "Blik is Andalian. He just likes to kill. He'll follow UU into the volcanoes on Diln if ordered," he said as he referred to a seismically active planet in Quadrant 2.

"And Bill never says much about anything," Alana explained. "He follows the path of least resistance."

"Plus, he worships the ground UU walks on," Mookie offered.

Kreeg's patience showed cracks. "Wait. So, you didn't want to have too many voices who are pro-UU here to dilute your arguments. You are here to convince us to do something about him."

"Yes," Mookie responded.

"No," Alana countered, almost speaking over her Andalian friend. "No!" She added emphasis to her statement. "I'm not saying anything should be done with UU; I'm just concerned and I want your opinions."

Yane looked at Mookie. "But you said 'yes'."

With an embarrassed look, Mookie looked at the others. "I have serious concerns, yes."

"You're not like other Andalians," Kreeg chuckled.

Mookie shrugged, not knowing how to respond. Kreeg's observation hit its mark: most Andalians followed their leaders to a fault, even if certain death stared them in their faces. They simply enjoyed fighting and killing. But not Mookie.

Yane carried Kreeg's banner of analyzing Mookie. "You're the calmest, most peaceful Andalian I've ever seen. How did you get into a gang, Mookie?"

"I've always been an enigma to my kind, I guess." He paused, sorting through his word choices. "But I'm still Andalian. I still enjoy the thrills of battle. I just don't relish it to the same levels as my Andalian brothers."

"Okay, let's get back on track." Alana tired of the review of Mookie's temperament. "UU just killed one of our most trusted companions in front of us, with no real cause, just suspicion."

"And we should...?" Kreeg attempted to draw a conclusion out of her.

"We should discuss our concerns," she answered.

"This is not a coup?" Yane wanted clarification.

"No. Not at all." She looked at her peers before continuing. "My friends, I have yet to recover from the loss of Kimberlina. And we've lost Chabdab—he's probably dead. Rytkjmk is out of action, and now Anthun. I miss them all, but Kimberlina was a great friend."

"I don't see how we can trust UU anymore." Mookie's approach sounded blunter and firmer than Alana's.

"Then what do we do, replace him?" Kreeg laughed before allowing a more serious tone to overtake his words. "How could we go on with a group so small and no real leader? How could we go on without UU?"

"And how would we get out of this quadrant?" Yane asked, though all knew the question only served as a rhetorical point.

Alana seemed to be near tears. "I don't want to depose UU. I just want him to sound rational. He's starting to sound too irrational."

No one spoke for over 10 seconds before Yane attempted to bring focus to the discombobulated conversation. "We were all shocked by the killing of Anthun, but UU is still the great leader he was last week and the week before, so I propose we keep an eye on him but still trust him."

"Why wouldn't he bother to explain himself?" Mookie asked.

"I want us to focus on what we control," Yane answered by not answering Mookie's question. "This is about moving forward, not pedaling backward."

Alana ended the next round of 10-second silence. "I didn't come here to get rid of UU or leave. I came here to talk. I think we've talked enough."

Mookie sighed his displeasure at her statement.

"Are you two favorable to moving forward with UU?" Kreeg asked, curiosity dancing in his voice.

"Yes," Alana nodded her approval. "But I want you two to please keep your eye on him at all times."

The first genuine smile of the meeting came from Yane. "We can do that."

"I don't necessarily like it, but I'll stay." Mookie's words caused Kreeg and Yane to react with surprise. "I just don't want UU to get me killed."

"You don't sound confident, Mookie," Kreeg chastised. "We can't afford hesitation."

Mookie sighed again. "This meeting never took place."

"I agree with that," Kreeg said, a sardonic tone seeping from his speech. "If UU found out I attended a meeting that contemplated overthrowing him, he'd kill me." He looked at the others before adding. "Figuratively, of course."

"Are you sure?" Mookie asked, allowing a sting to envelop his words.

Kreeg smiled as he turned and walked deeper into the forest. Within moments, Yane joined him.

•　　•　　•

When the members of the religious order watched the unfamiliar ship drop in its slow landing pattern to the surface, they instinctively knew evil was afoot. After a quick word to Rokila, she began a frantic search for her daughter. With the search over in a matter of seconds, Kreeg's wife and daughter raced down a maze of stairways and hid from the unknown intruders.

The sect's collective hunch was confirmed when two vile-looking beasts departed the craft and without hesitation began to threaten residents with torture and death if they did not reveal the whereabouts of Kreeg's family.

The two top lieutenants to the Premier, heir apparent to the recently-deceased Weektu the Corsan, slapped and punched members of the religious order, intent on finding any weak link possible to get at the UU Gang.

Chapter Twenty-Seven

For the first time, UU, Kreeg, and Yane saw the familiar conference room filled to capacity. Geeba joined them as they took in the sight of the full Board of Ten, all of whom sat on the opposite side of the lengthy table. Other chairs were filled by advisers, a secretary who input into his computer every word spoken, and a technician on hand in case a microphone ceased to operate. Multiple cameras—built into the walls and ceiling—recorded the event.

Seated on either side of Abuss Onuss were his favorite board members: Pracen on his left and Bingus Jam on his right. The chairman ran the meeting but would cede to questions or interjections by his counterparts as necessary. Directly across from Abuss Onuss sat UU, with Kreeg and Yane on either side of him; Geeba sat next to Yane.

Ten minutes into the meeting, mostly occupied by sermonettes from three members who felt discomfort at working with UU, Abuss Onuss directed the meeting back to its original purpose. "Yane, you say you can penetrate the Asimoni shields. Our best ships and agents could not do so. How can this be?"

"I'm not one of your agents," Yane responded in a flat tone. "If I were, the shields would have been penetrated by now."

A native of Ceratofs, with his light skin and short stature, voiced his offense at Yane's bravado. "I see UU isn't the only one overflowing with arrogance."

"True. Blik is egotistical as well." Yane's expression did not change.

"Incorrigible! Completely unnecessary!" the Ceratofs board member barked.

Yane smiled as he broke the fast-rising tension. "We're on a planet in a system within a quadrant that could cease to exist at any moment. Let us not die with grim faces, minister."

"How shall we die?" the former Minister of Ceratofs' Law Enforcement asked in a mocking tone.

"Of old age in another quadrant," Yane smiled as he answered.

Laughs emanated from most of the Board of Ten. Predictably, Bingus Jam was not one of them. "What is your plan, Yane?" he asked as the brief laughter faded. "You have a tall order to get in, rescue the Premier, and get out alive."

Yane shook his head. "My plan involves getting us to the palace, then back again. UU is the mastermind behind the actions we take."

UU looked at Bingus Jam, then turned his gaze to the other officers of the law as he spoke. "The plan is a simple one. There is no brilliance to it. We rush in, kill anyone who gets in our way, and grab the Premier."

"And if he resists?" Bingus Jam asked.

"What sort of hostage defies rescue?" UU's voice boomed stronger than normal. "Then he's not a hostage. We kill him and get off the planet as fast as possible."

Ten creatures began speaking and yelling at once. Abuss Onuss tried to quiet everyone, but UU's voice performed the task instead. "You are officers of the law; you have your ways. I understand that." UU paused as the momentary cacophony of voices ended. "I was once a soldier; I had certain rules and protocols. We once lived in a civilized society; we had norms and acceptable behaviors to consider." Confident he was speaking for his gang, as well, UU glanced to either side of him before continuing. "Today we live in anarchy and therefore we eschew certain rules and protocols and behaviors. If we try to live as civilized creatures in an uncivilized time, we will surely die as those who foolishly thought they could stay and continue with their civilized lives. We cannot; we will not die fools' deaths."

"You're saying you have the right to kill the Premier if he's not a hostage?" Pracen asked, incredulity saturating every syllable.

"I am saying if he's not a hostage then he's a warlord, the ultimate warlord," UU posited, firmness dominating his speech. "To what end? What is the profit in ruling a fiefdom that is days or weeks or a year or two from being obliterated?" He paused before answering his own question. "There is no such profit. That tells me Aelo Seveen doesn't see himself as premier of Asimon, but the leader of a larger, grander society. If not here, where? In one of the other three quadrants, of course. Or *all* the quadrants."

Again a verbal commotion ensued from the opposite side of the long table. Questions peppered the gang leader, but he chose to wait until the minor roar abated.

"We cannot survive here in the Nova Quadrant," UU continued.

"I hate that term," one of the officers blurted out.

"You may hate it, but the facts remain. We are a doomed society—no one doubts that." UU's eyes narrowed as he mentally sunk his teeth into the topic of their dystopian predicament. "We either leave or die. But why have so many of us stayed? Have you considered that there are many reasons? I'm sure the ten of you all believe you have stayed for noble reasons. But have you? Do you also not believe you will be rewarded in the future with higher or more prestigious jobs in one of the other quadrants? Of course you do."

Bingus Jam started to speak but UU cut him off by continuing. "We had our reasons for staying. Most of my team wanted to become wealthy and then settle elsewhere. Along the way, we figured out we would never have homes elsewhere, not in peace, anyway, because creatures still thinking within civilized norms viewed us as outlaws." UU's pause was brief enough to not allow anyone to interrupt. "We were thinking through the logic of an uncivilized realm, but we saw how that would end and we've changed our ways; but, that doesn't mean we should apply all the civilized norms. Some, perhaps, but not all."

UU's eyes swept the Board of Ten members; he saw that they were now engrossed in his impromptu speech. "The civilized thing to do is for law enforcement to capture a law breaker; but, where there is no law, law enforcement cannot be applied judiciously. If the good creatures follow rules that are unenforceable, we will achieve nothing except our own demise." UU leaned forward, elbows on the table, hands clasped together, as though adding drama to his subsequent words. "We could burst in and announce the Premier is under arrest." He sat up straight again. "But the Premier's warriors have no fear of law—they are the law. There is no other law to them. So, if gangs are the law and law enforcement has no power, then we can only achieve a goal within the confines of what life has become, not what it was. The past is dead, at least in our quadrant. To allow the Premier to live is death for those who once loved the law."

Silence enveloped the large conference room. Heads turned and eyes darted as each member of the board wanted to comment but seemed to lack the boldness to open their mouths.

"I do not enjoy killing," UU said, though the strength of his voice dropped a little. "I will do what is necessary—sometimes you have to kill—but I don't enjoy it. We wish to restore our good names, and we will do so by either rescuing a hostage or killing a tyrant."

•　　•　　•

Rocash called the meeting to order. As was his habit, the Premier sat in silence, arms folded over his purple robe, a small, satisfied yet pompous grin etched in his face as he watched the launch of the discussions. The eight around the table—all Asimonis except the warlord Aetreph, who was Andalian—engaged in a healthy discussion about the manner and timing plans would be executed.

The Premier felt secure enough to hold his meeting in the courtyard, away from the stuffy conference rooms; outdoors, under Bellik's warm rays. At two kilometers by one kilometer in size, the capitol was the largest in the known universe. Six stories tall, by law the building was the tallest structure within a 10-kilometer radius. The heart of Roandan, its business district filled with hundreds of massive superstructures, many of which soared over 100 stories into the sky, lay just outside the capitol's height limitation zone. The river city was at once majestic and accessible to all, rich, middle class, and poor.

The capitol and palace served as a massive office building, housing much of the federal bureaucracy by day and the living quarters for the premier and family by night. Despite numerous bedrooms, by law only family members of the sitting premier could dwell in the palace. "Palace" and "Capitol" were used interchangeably; but, either way, the massive steel-framed building with the marble façade was a sight to behold.

Asimon's history books recited ongoing flirtations with autocratic rule. The culture bred a need for strong hands at the helm while demanding those same hands not choke liberty to death—a coma would do. Through the ages, numerous premiers sought more power than the usually pliable

Asimonis would accept, then found themselves either out of office or dead.

Aelo Seveen found himself in the unprecedented situation of leading through an existential crisis resolved only through mass exodus from the planet. The few thousands of Asimonis who were Remainers held not a care for how Seveen governed over an empty world. Chaos and departure became a welcome sight when he formulated his plan, and with the help of his cadre of warlords, gang members, and reprobates, anarchy proved the perfect cover for his preparations.

The final piece of the deception puzzle was his claim to being a hostage inside the plushest capitol in the quadrants. He believed the claim was the best way to avoid having his time taken away by other quadrant leaders and explaining why he was the highest-ranking government official to remain.

Now, as Rocash turned the meeting over to the Premier, the latter had the opportunity to finally reveal the logistical details of the next steps for conquering the known universe.

•　　•　　•

"You should have at least one hundred police or soldiers with you," the former Minister of Ceratofs' Law Enforcement said to UU and his three comrades.

"Too large of an operation," UU shook his head as he rendered his verdict. "But I do agree with Pracen that six is too small. My original desire was for my gang to accomplish the goal, but it's an impractical thought. We are too small now."

"Thank you," Pracen nodded, though he did not allow himself to smile.

"Please continue, Yane," Abuss Onuss ordered in a polite tone.

"Once we separate from the larger ship—civilian transport, presumably—our ship will drop into Asimon's atmosphere and the larger ship will fly away." Yane saw reticent faces staring back at him, so he continued. "Asimoni defenses will see the large ship fly away and assume the matter is done."

"But why will your ship survive the shields?" Abuss Onuss asked.

"Due to electromagnetic disturbances, which are common at the poles, the shield will be weakest there." Yane spoke every word with great confidence.

"You hope," a member of the Board interjected.

"Yes, I do. But I dealt with this in the military," Yane responded. "By the end of the Quadrant 3 Wars, I was a cybersecurity expert and I helped design and defeat shields of various types."

"But never planetary shields, correct?" Bingus Jam asked.

"No. No planet has ever even attempted to accomplish that." Yane squinted his eyes in thought before he continued. "Only the Premier has attained such a massive milestone." He paused. "I've never considered this previously, but this must have been in the works before the Great Exodus. The Premier surely planned to quarantine his planet years ago."

"How long would it have taken?" Bingus Jam inquired.

"Design. Prototype." Yane looked at the ceiling, then back to the board as he spoke. "Testing. Recalibrations, which could be many. Final testing. Production. Implementation. Years. At least ten Heislerian years." Yane nodded, comfortable with his off-the-cuff estimate.

"He's been in office for twelve Heislerian years," Abuss Onuss pointed out. "Perhaps you are correct, UU." He turned his attention from Yane to UU. "Perhaps he is not the innocent we think."

Geeba and UU exchanged glances and tried not to laugh.

•   •   •

"Why is it necessary to slaughter those who have helped us?" Aetreph asked, displaying obvious disdain for the Premier's plan.

"Because they are not essential. Anyone who knows my plans and is non-essential is a liability." The lack of emotion in the Premier's voice telegraphed his sincerity. "We will gain supporters in Quadrant 3. We will have like-minded souls gather to us from all three quadrants. Our message of prosperity through equality will resonate until we become a powerful force in the known universe." The Premier's eyes narrowed. "Through remaining here, we have acquired great wealth, unmeasurable firepower and military hardware. We already employed the greatest scientists, who formulated and deployed the planetary shield. They are safely in Quadrant 3 at this very moment." He smiled as he reached his conclusion. "We are unstoppable."

"Do you fear the authorities here?" an adviser asked.

The Premier laughed as though witnessing the most uproarious moment of his life. "Authorities? Authority over what?!" His belly laugh roared and he slapped the table with his palm in delight. "They cannot even reach the surface of our planet. They cannot protect a jewelry shop or food market, let alone protect themselves." He stopped to continue his hearty laugh. "They cannot even successfully raid an empty hideout!"

The Premier's laugh faded at his last comment. When he had heard of the failed police raid on Gigorl he did not react with contempt, rather with rage. He was unaware of the full story; he only cared that UU and his gang still survived—an unacceptable state of affairs.

The Premier eyed Aetreph. "When I elevated you after the loss of Weektu, I did not count on you being squeamish."

The observation was received by the warrior as the taunt it was intended to be. Unlike the advisers and bureaucrats, Aetreph did not fear the autocrat, which he made clear with his indignant facial expression and snarling reply. "I've killed more creatures in a Heislerian hour than you have in a lifetime, Premier. I am considering strategy, not blood."

"You leave the strategizing to me," the Premier returned the snarl. "We have more than two thousand soldiers who have gone ahead of us, preparing our next base of operations and working with scientists on another planetary shield." He glared at the newest member of his inner circle. "Seventy-five police will suffice."

"You have seventy-five police officers ready to massacre thousands?" The question from Aetreph was more shock than curiosity.

"They are substitute police—not by trade. They are more like you than police." The Premier's response resolved the matter.

"Where will we be during this event?" a bureaucrat wondered aloud.

"In the palace, of course." The Premier's face seemed to glow every time he spoke of his plan. "And we will have a dozen guards who will remain in the palace, just as a safety valve, in case a few workers get away in the chaos."

Rocash wrapped up the meeting. "We will close operations on Asimon within two Heislerian weeks. The last material shipments will take place the day we leave. We will only have loose ends to tie after those shipments of weapons and equipment."

"How many shipments have there been?" an adviser asked.

"More than five hundred cargo ships full of jewels and other valuables," Rocash reported. "We estimated the value as enough to finance our business for a Heislerian century, including, uh, sufficient salaries for us."

Chatter broke out among the other six—excluding Rocash and the Premier—seated at the table. The staggering quantity of wealth which the Premier had amassed and then shipped out of the quadrant defied comprehension.

The Premier's enjoyment of communicating the final plans had reached its end. He now wanted to turn plans into action—as soon as possible. "My dear comrades, this meeting is hereby concluded. These are exhilarating days. Let us approach them with gusto." He looked around the table. "In two days, we take the next step. In two weeks, we depart. In two Heislerian years, we will rule the known universe."

As the group chatted among themselves, the Premier flashed a hard look at Aetreph. The public challenge dominated the leader's thoughts.

•　　•　　•

"Before we conclude," Geeba spoke up for the first time. "I would like to make a request." She leaned forward and looked past Yane, at her boss. "I believe UU will not disagree with me. I would ask you to allow word to leak that we have plans to attack the Premier in a Heislerian month.”

Out of the ten, Pracen looked the most shocked. “Why would we do that? Why let anyone know an attack is coming at all?! Ever?!”

Geeba sighed—both an involuntary reaction and then for effect. “Please consider my words. Word will leak out.” By stressing “will,” she knew the sentence would cause offense. “You will tell creatures who need to know who will then tell creatures who do not.” She frowned before her concluding thought. “Our gang has experienced this far too many times not to take it seriously.”

“We will put out the word as you wish,” Abuss Onuss announced to groans on his side of the table. “And we agree you can limit your force to the eight of you and twenty officers.”

UU, Kreeg, Yane, and Geeba exchanged smiles.

“Can you have the twenty officers we select briefed and your team ready to go in two days?” the chairman asked.

“We can be ready tomorrow morning,” UU offered. “That would be preferable.”

“Then it is settled,” Abuss Onuss commanded. “The attack will commence in two days.”

UU frowned but decided to not argue.

•   •   •

The planet Drebehr had an honorable history, but its claim to fame among the quadrants was the mass production of weapons and war craft. While not on the level of Rojan, which turned out a higher quality—and more expensive—product, the Drebehrans had long ago mastered the mass production of relatively inexpensive yet effective weapons and supplies, including craft to engage in battle or transport troops. Nearly every gang member, warrior, police officer, or soldier owned at least one device or item manufactured on Drebehr.

Unlike Rojan, pre-Great-Exodus Drebehr boasted a wide-ranging economy which included manufacturing of a great variety of products, from massive cargo ships and passenger spaceliners to touristy trinkets.

What the planet rarely produced, however, were athletes or warriors—on either side of the law. Their diminutive stature, when compared to those from other planets, directed their culture to the affairs of business rather than battle. The tallest Drebehran usually stood no more than one-meter-sixty. When a Drebehran entered a room, his mere presence did not command the attention of others.

The Drebehran fighter who stood before the Premier was not an exception. The autocratic leader stood at two-meters-one—a full 41 centimeters above his informant.

"You have confirmed this, I take it?"

"I have," the Drebehran nodded. His large forehead gave the nods an exaggerated effect, as though he thrust his head forward with great force.

"If they are waiting a month, then they certainly lack the firepower now," the Premier spoke his thoughts, looking past his informant. "Then they cannot muster the force to stop us from leaving even if they know our day of departure." A small grin grew until his face could no longer contain it and he burst into a hearty laugh. "They may not even know we've gone when they get here!" He pulled away from his jovial thoughts and returned to his serious demeanor.

"What do you need from me?" the spy inquired.

"Stay here. No need to return to your planet." The Premier's calm command settled the matter, in his view.

"Aren't you in need of additional intelligence?" the Drebehran asked.

The Premier shook his head side to side. "No. In two weeks, we leave. All of us. And tomorrow is a big day, which you will learn about tomorrow." The Premier referred to the surprise action planned for those deemed "non-essential."

A sizable smile dominated the Drebehran's small face. "I am ready! This is our next glorious step!"

"Go and receive your briefing from your captain. You will play a role when we gather everyone in the city square for an explanation of our journey."

The Drebehran nodded with excitement. He no longer had to risk his life for the sake of supplying much-needed information to the Premier and his followers. As he exited the Premier's business chamber, in his mind he began telling himself about the money he would make and the lavish lifestyle he would lead.

Chapter Twenty-Eight

Colonel Untas Ursulanus stood at the bottom of the steps of the Rojani Cargo Craft and looked over his team, which included a former lawyer, an accountant, a police officer, and soldiers. Excluding Rick, who continued to convalesce on the distant planet with the odd name, the group numbered eight.

The gang felt refreshed, having taken the opportunity over the last couple of days—a needed respite from fighting—to bathe, clean their clothes, eat better, and relax. Dressed in standard camouflage army pants—matching shirts for those who were ex-military, but only because they happened to retain their uniforms—and a mish-mash of dark-colored-shirts for the others, the gang always looked a bit ragtag; but, down to such a small group, the colonel knew his gang was now just that: ragtag.

As the team talked among themselves, UU let his mind go, reflecting on when he met each of them. Blik and Geeba were former soldiers whom UU came to trust when they were under his command; Kreeg was also military, but UU had only met him a Heislerian year prior; Yane, too, was a veteran but in cybersecurity; Mookie was an experienced police officer—the 44th and final member to join the group when they named themselves the "Band of 44;" Bill, the accountant with no fighting experience, seemed to stay on the fringe of the team, possibly feeling out of place; and Alana, the lawyer who seemed to have a strategic mind cut out for military planning. Rick was also military, but UU wondered whether time out of the quadrant had made him soft. UU intended to drag Rick back from Earth if he had to—after the important business at hand was concluded.

UU continued to reflect on his friendships with each comrade until Yane interrupted his thoughts.

"UU, where are the police?"

UU responded with a wry smile at the thought of them wanting the police to arrive. He gave a head shake before answering in a calm voice, "They'll be here."

"Hey," Mookie piped up. "Why weren't we running around the quadrant in one of these?" he asked as his eyes fondled the expensive craft. "Those Rojanis know how to make war look stylish."

The others laughed until twenty police officers entered the hangar; in two columns of ten, the large beasts were an all-Andalian force. Dressed in black from head to toe, with only their large faces exposed, although a shield could be quickly lowered to protect the eyes, the force looked menacing without even a bellicose word or movement. Rifles at the ready, grasped with both hands in front of their bodies; a pistol on one hip—Drebehran laser guns—and the traditional Andalian battle knife on the other; a black bandolier from shoulder to hip across the chest and back again across their wide backs, loaded with laser cartridges; the Andalian Insertion Force did not take battle lightly.

Alana gulped before speaking. "Glad they're not after us."

"We'll know in a few seconds if they are," Bill quipped.

"Hey, Blik," Mookie called out. "How do you like that? They got the meanest species in the known universe to handle the toughest jobs." Everyone laughed, understanding Blik and Mookie were of the same race as the approaching police force.

Not far behind the marching police officers a lone creature in black followed. Considerably smaller than the others, the Mangan carried his helmet, allowing the others to see his entire head.

"That must be our pilot," Kreeg surmised. "Look, Yane. They brought a little guy like you to fly us."

"They needed to bring in the brains." Yane's smile reflected his pride—he believed his words about his own species.

Blik and Mookie laughed the hardest at Yane's comment, and they all enjoyed their first banter since the depressing demise of Anthun.

•   •   •

Briefing complete, arms loaded, the eight members of the UU Gang, twenty Special Insertion Force officers, and one pilot boarded the craft. The distinction between UU's gang and the professional police officers could not be missed. The former laughed and chatted while the latter sat in stony silence and stared, as though in mild trances.

As Yane took the co-pilot's chair, he closed the cockpit door behind him to block out the conversation a few meters away between UU and Qerl'ashp, captain of the Insertion Force.

"I see the Andalians needed your brains for this mission." Yane chuckled at his own humor.

The pilot hesitated before looking in Yane's general direction. "We are on a serious mission. We should avoid frivolities and focus on our task."

Yane stared at the creature, unsure whether to laugh or mock him. "Whatever you say." Yane shook his head as the pilot lifted the craft off the hangar floor, through the wide hangar doors, and up into Drebehr's atmosphere for the first leg of the journey. "Maybe we'll run into each other at a Nova Quadrant reunion someday," Yane quipped.

The pilot ignored the obviously sarcastic remark and aimed the vehicle into space to rendezvous with a spaceliner which sported civilian markings.

•　　•　　•

Captain Qerl'ashp sat on a bench seat next to UU, away from the others. The Rojani Cargo Craft was not a true troop transporter, but this particular model often found itself in service of various special operations forces—military and police. Because of its speed and maneuverability, insertion teams preferred the craft. It's fore and aft guns were in no way remarkable, but they sufficed when facing individual fighter craft, usually to buy time before the ship could jump to light speed to escape.

"I must warn you; I have been given orders to prevent you from killing the Premier," the captain said with no emotion in his voice.

"If he's a hostage, we will rescue him," the colonel responded.

"And if he's not?"

"Good luck." UU narrowed his eyes and allowed a haughty stare to escape through the narrow slits which helped draw up the skin around his nose and cheeks. Once he looked away from the officer, he allowed his features to again relax.

"Word throughout the systems is he's a warlord above all warlords." Qerl'ashp stared at UU until the look was returned. "Then he has earned death." He paused for his words to sink into UU's brain. "Besides, he would resist, and such resistance would probably get us killed. I'm not dying for the Premier, poor hostage or evil tyrant."

UU smiled. "I like the way you think."

"I do, too." Qerl'ashp laughed. "I do, too."

UU's smile grew. "You're a warrior I could have a drink or two with."

"Only two?" Qerl'ashp chuckled. "When this is over, I will buy your entire gang drinks and we will sit in the finest pub on Drebehr and swap stories."

"It's a deal."

"I have to warn you, though," Qerl'ashp added. "My team has the same orders I do and they will not countermand orders, ever. They are rule followers. You may be arrested if you kill the Premier."

"How can anyone stop me when I won't be with your unit?"

Qerl'ashp smiled. "I guess I shouldn't have delayed getting the final plan to Abuss Onuss until this morning. He'll probably wonder the same thing."

UU laughed at Qerl'ashp's craftiness.

"We will just have to arrest you after the fact," Qerl'ashp said with a flat tone.

"If that happens, we'll sort it out back on Drebehr." UU nodded along with the captain, a smile still dominating his Zhiloan face.

•   •   •

From the direction of the cockpit, Yane approached UU. "We are minutes away from separating from the spaceliner."

"We're already above the planet?" UU referred to Asimon.

"Yes. We will listen for the liner's captain to apologize to Asimoni Space Control for losing control of his ship—he'll say it gave them quite a scare—then we'll shut off all communication."

"Let me know if the communication doesn't go out or the liner doesn't jump to light," UU ordered.

"Yes, sir." After answering, Yane returned to the cockpit.

UU motioned toward Captain Qerl'ashp, who in turn gave a laconic bark of an order and everyone in the cargo hold found a seat and buckled straps to secure them during entry in preparation for the next phase of the assault.

Within minutes, the passengers felt the craft rock to starboard as it separated from the spaceliner with a lurch. Moments later, they felt the sensation of being in a deep dive, like on a roller coaster at an amusement park, as they shot almost straight down toward the surface. They knew they were in the Asimoni atmosphere.

As the craft leveled off, they felt the sensation of speed transferring energy into their bodies several times more powerful than the pull of the planet's gravity. The craft bumped and bounced from time to time and the sound of air as it roared past the craft left no doubt their supersonic speed brought them closer to their intended target.

Qerl'ashp stuck one of his large, hairy fingers into his left ear so he could hear through his dover. He nodded, as he answered. "Very good. Thank you." He then turned to UU and raised his voice to be heard over the noise. "As according to plan, the spaceliner referenced the warship in a communication with the Asimoni defenses. The battleship left the atmosphere to pursue, so we know we went undetected."

UU nodded with satisfaction.

•   •   •

Because of the distance they had to cover, over three Heislerian hours passed as the small craft buffeted in the Asimoni winds. Finally, the cantankerous pilot announced they had dropped to a subsonic speed. Touchdown would take place in an estimated fifteen minutes.

The minutes seemed to last hours to the insurgents. UU looked around and wondered who would not make it out alive, or if any of them would survive. The mission sounded solid in briefings, but the lack of intelligence about Asimoni defenses left them to only have the information sent by small craft which had previously scanned the surface from a distance.

UU felt the urge to go forward one compartment and look through one of the small windows, though he could not because of the rough ride they were experiencing. Instead, he remained seated until he felt the pleasant sensation of the craft completing a gentle landing—without being blown to pieces by artillery.

Chapter Twenty-Nine

All twenty members of the Andalian Special Insertion Force exited the craft, lined up in two columns of ten, and divided up—half heading southwest and the other half southeast. The plan for the two teams to approach the capitol from different directions would have been made easier if they could have been dropped off separately, but flying the small ship as little as possible seemed logical during the planning stage. Flying beneath the reach of the electronic aircraft monitors scattered about the city would prove meaningless if spotted by the Premier's minions.

To coordinate the timing of the Insertion Groups reaching their assigned targets on opposite sides of the capitol with UU's two teams achieving their separate missions, the eight left at the same time as the police but took two different paths.

Kreeg led Alana, Bill, and Mookie south of the capitol to plant bombs throughout the area in an effort to divert whatever planetary forces the mission might encounter. The large, dark-green duffel bags they carried over their shoulders weighed them down with small bombs and grenades. The only other weapons they carried were laser pistols and fighting knives; they carried reloadable magazines in the pockets of their attire—the usual quasi-military urban warfare attire they always wore.

Headed toward the north end of the massive palace, UU, Blik, Yane, and Geeba carried smaller dark-green duffel bags. They, too, carried the same equipment as their peers, but with fewer bombs and grenades.

As they made their way the ten blocks to the capitol, they were baffled by what they saw.

"I expected a nearly deserted city," UU said as he looked around without breaking his pace. "But I expected to see at least some life."

"Stop!" Geeba held out an arm as though to physically stop everyone. The group came to an immediate halt, which allowed them to hear a voice—distant and garbled. "Listen!" The sound seemed to come at them from multiple directions as the voice reverberated off the short buildings; none was higher than three stories so the palace could be seen easily from a distance.

With a head bob, UU commanded the continuation of their journey. He resumed their fast-paced walk and the others followed.

As they navigated the streets devoid of life, a small "ding" alerted Blik to an awaiting message on his wrist communicator. He stopped in order to avoid letting UU know he was breaking communication rules during the operation— interaction with someone off-planet. He looked down at his wrist and double-tapped a specific portion of the device. "Yeah?" He tried to keep his voice low. After he read the next message, he dictated a response. "Meet us in front of the palace entrance."

As Blik began to run to catch up to his small group, UU turned around and saw a teammate was lagging. "Blik, you have to keep up with us." He waved his arm to communicate to the Andalian that he needed to move faster.

"Colonel," Blik yelled. "I would feel better if we had rifles like the Insertion Force."

"Yeah, and I'd feel better if you'd keep up."

Blik smiled at UU's rudeness and continued to close the gap between himself and his friends.

UU slowed in a courtyard, concerned guards could leap out from underneath nearby tables or from behind the scattered out-buildings which, prior to the Great Exodus, had housed food vendors for tourists or small stores for sellers of local maps and trinkets. UU had no way of knowing the Premier had recently held a meeting in this very courtyard as he plotted domination of the known universe.

The four reached the north end of the palace and stood at the base of the stairs.

"How can this place be so empty?" Yane asked.

"I've been wondering the same thing," UU said.

Just as they began their ascent on the marble stairs, the loud, distant and garbled voice resumed. UU and Yane looked at each other. "Who is that?!" they both asked, nearly in unison. The voice stopped.

A sound from UU's wrist communicator signaled a message. He looked at the others. "I need to talk to him." He pushed multiple buttons on the small gadget and spoke into it. "What's the problem, Kreeg?"

"They are all out here, in the south square," the disembodied voice said. "Every last one of them. It appears the Premier is about to speak and they're all gathered in this giant courtyard to listen. One of their creatures announced the Premier's almost ready."

"Where is he?"

"He's in the palace; he'll be on a balcony here at the south end," Kreeg responded. "Should we go forward with the plan?"

UU paused before answering. "Yes. Yes, you should. Communication out." UU tapped his wrist communicator and looked at the others. "We have to get in that palace and get to the Premier before he finishes speaking and the crowd disperses."

"Maybe the Insertion Group will see this and take them out all at once." Blik sounded hopeful.

"They're police, Blik." UU scolded as he shook his head. "They don't think in the same manner we do. They stick to their orders. I'll be shocked if they fire first. Now let's go. Eyes open."

"There's no one to kill, Blik," Geeba teased as she resumed her trek forward along with the others. The Andalian growled his unhappiness.

Without further conversation, the four raced up the stairs and entered the palace through the second-floor rear entrance.

.   .   .

"Kreeg! Where is he?!" UU's voice cracked with intensity and became a snarl. "I need to know where he is."

"He's here on the south end, on a balcony," Kreeg responded, which Yane, Blik, and Geeba could hear.

"I know that! What level?"

"Sixth floor."

"We have a long way to go," UU said as he began to run. "Colonel, out."

Only seconds into their rush forward, the foursome heard a voice from behind. UU and company spun around to see an Asimoni guard jogging in hasty strides, rifle on his shoulder.

Recognizing the guard's lack of high alarm—he merely expressed confusion—UU holstered his Zhiloan laser gun as he walked, wanting to avoid raising the guard's suspicions. "We have a report we're needed at the south end," UU said in an innocent tone.

Understanding the need to overload the guard's thoughts, Geeba called out. "We're here for the Premier's safety. Don't worry."

"There's been an electrical short," Blik announced.

UU flashed a baffled look, first at Blik, then at Geeba and Yane.

"What?" Confusion became deep bewilderment. "Electrical?! For his safety?! He's safe here! Who are you?" He eyed how the visitors were dressed.

The colonel closed the gap. He reached to his belt and pulled his prized Zhiloan knife—a more compact version of the famous Zhiloan sword.

Before the guard could react, UU thrust the blade forward; it cut through the throat and exited through the base of the guard's brain. UU's strength drove the knife as deep as he could force it. Immediate death dropped the guard to the floor. UU pulled on his knife, wiped the red blood on the victim's shirt to clean off the blade, then resumed his hasty advance in the general direction of the Premier. "We need to get to the sixth floor," UU announced as though nothing had just happened.

"Electrical short?!" Geeba mocked Blik as they resumed their jog through the massive structure.

Blik looked at Geeba, then straight ahead.

After advancing for thirty seconds at a brisk jog, UU shouted, "To the stairs!" The group veered to their left and climbed the wide, carpeted stairway.

•   •   •

The Premier, decked in his purple robe, donned his tall hat which resembled that which a baker would wear rather than royalty or clergy—the intended visage the Premier wished to convey. The roar of the crowd of four thousand continued even though their leader signaled otherwise.

Aelo Seveen's plan was simple yet challenging: to plot and carry out the killing of one was easy; to plot and carry out the killing of four thousand was a herculean task when using just lasers and grenades. His plan was visually almost artistic yet ghoulish; intellectual yet sociopathic. But first, he wanted to deliver a brief message—for the sake of both the executioners and himself. That he delivered any kind of message underscored his bizarre and narcissistic mental state.

"To my friends and subjects," he began. He had never before used that particular noun when addressing a crowd, but he liked the sound of it: "subjects" carried a degree of sweetness and warmth, in his mind. "We begin the next step in our grand exit this evening, before Bellik falls below the horizon." His reference to Asimon's star was one of many instances in which he invoked the cosmos during important speeches. He did so many times as the legitimate, elected leader of his home world.

The Premier could not continue until the roar of the four thousand subsided enough. "Today will mark another triumph. The process will take two Asimoni years before we completely regroup, allow the political world to settle, then launch the next phase, but this is an important step on the way to domination."

Again the crowd roared. Again the Premier attempted to quiet the crowd with just enough effort to appear humble yet to not produce silence. He inhaled the cool breeze and soaked up the morning sunshine as he absorbed the moment.

•　　•　　•

"Isn't this too far away?" Bill asked over his wrist communicator, concern in his voice.

"No," Kreeg explained. "You forget, we are not here to annihilate the crowd but to distract."

"I'm just worried the crowd will annihilate us," Bill said with chagrin. "Why does everyone have rifles except us?"

"The Andalian Insertion Force has brought enough ammunition to deal with the matter." Kreeg sounded less patient with his response and jerked his wrist away from his mouth.

"Hey, Kreeg," Alana seemed a bit alarmed. "Where's Mookie? I haven't seen him since before we reached the courtyard."

Kreeg did not bother to look around; if Alana asked the question, she had already done so. Instead, he tilted his head down to speak into his communicator. "Mookie." He paused.

"Mookie, it's Kreeg. Respond." Another pause. "Mookie. It's Kreeg, I need to hear from you. If you're in a situation where you can't talk, key your microphone a couple of times." Kreeg put his wrist to his ear. Nothing.

"I didn't hear anything," Alana said as she pulled her ear away from her own communicator.

"I don't know. That's not like Mookie." Kreeg shook his head. "But he can take care of himself." Kreeg looked around. "He's an Andalian. He'll be fine. We have to get into position. Now."

The roar finally faded and the Premier resumed his speech.

•   •   •

UU and company jogged up the stairs with all the energy they could muster. After flights up three of the long, over-sized stairways, they rested. A long jog had preceded the stairs and UU wanted his tiny team to be prepared for hand-to-hand combat, if required.

The Premier's voice filled the palace through a network of speakers, although the voice sounded quieter, calmer, inside the massive capitol and palace.

"*After we rule Quadrant Three, we will easily engulf Quadrant Two,*" they heard him say. "*We will pick up many additional supporters and fighters and will take Quadrant One long before they can put up a coordinated defense.”*

The voice stopped. The microphones were not needed for anyone in the south end of the building to hear the crowd, even if not near windows.

“Can you believe him?” Yane marveled. “He’s just going to take over the known universe like it was nothing.” He shook his head.

“I wonder whether the Andalian police force has figured out he’s not a hostage?” Geeba said with a wry tone as she laughed.

“Let’s go kill us a tyrant,” UU ordered with a grunt as he started up the final flight of stairs required to reach their target.

• • •

The Premier ended his brief speech. He raised both hands to receive the glory emanating from the thousands of voices. At long last, as his arms grew tired, he knew his forces, small but effective, were now ready. He dropped his arms to his side—the signal for slaughter.

• • •

Just as the Premier dropped his arms, UU stuck his head out of the window in order to determine how many rooms away their target stood. After a moment of shock, UU stepped back, away from the window in the large conference room. After a slight delay, still recovering from the bizarre scene outside, he gave the order. Within a second, Yane and Geeba followed their leader as he raced toward the door of the concourse.

The sound of mayhem and murder lured the large Andalian toward the window. Blik peeked out for just a moment before deciding he should catch up with his comrades.

As Blik crossed the room, he heard shouting in the concourse. He stopped at the door and peered out. UU, Yane, and Geeba were in the midst of lowering their weapons. Blik jerked his head back into the conference room and thought for a moment. He peered out again, this time in the opposite direction, satisfying his curiosity as to whether other guards were headed in their direction.

An odd thought struck Blik and he poked his head out once again with a quick motion. One of the guards he saw was Andalian. He looked closely, down the concourse, past his three friends, and confirmed: only one aggressor carried a rifle; little time to react existed. Blik strained to hear the words spoken, but it was his eyes which brought the biggest shock: the Andalian was Mookie.

•   •   •

Alone on the balcony, the Premier continued, for a full minute, to soak in the glorious moment. He had wished to watch the wicked spectacle, but changed his mind when he determined the risk was high that he could receive the lethal debris of inadvertent shrapnel.

•   •   •

Mookie's mocking tone was inescapable. "And you thought it was Anthun who gave the information to the Premier's team."

"But I had only told Anthun of my plan—the fake plan," UU sounded baffled, his words heavy, like blocks of concrete attempting to float.

"I overheard you. I had made a quick jaunt to my ship and passed by near enough to your conversation to overhear." Mookie's evil laughed reached an exaggerated level.

"How could you do this to us, Mookie?!" Geeba demanded. "Andalians are famous for being loyal—betrayers are cowards to you!" Her indignant voice rose as she finished her sentence.

One of the Drebehran guards, laser rifle at his hip, finger on the trigger, walked with a casual stride to move the weapons away from their adversaries. "Step back!" he growled.

As UU, Yane, and Geeba each took one step backward, away from their weapons, Mookie resumed his mockery. "The Premier will celebrate when I execute you in front of him, UU."

"Answer me!" Geeba shouted, angry at her now-former friend.

The Drebehran guard bent down to pick up UU's pistol just as Geeba yelled at Mookie. Sensing increasing tensions, Blik chose from the six targets: Mookie. With the smoothness of a slithering snake, Blik slid downward, along the door casing, exposing his body as he took aim.

Before Blik could pull the trigger, UU delivered one continuous motion to dispense death. He reached down to the sheath tied to his leg, pulled out Anthun's knife, stepped forward, then shot his body upward with great force. The blade of Anthun's knife entered underneath the Drebehran guard's chin and through his brain until the tip of the knife reached the top of the skull.

While UU completed his fatal blow, Blik squeezed off a round before Mookie's hands could keep up with his eyes. Though not a bad shot from 20 meters, to his chagrin, Blik could only manage to hit his target in the shoulder. The force of the laser's impact knocked Mookie backward and onto his back.

Everyone opened fire, but the benefit of surprise helped Yane and Geeba take out one guard each as Blik's second shot struck another guard. The remaining guard, the farthest away, well over ten meters beyond Mookie, ran laterally and fired shots with rapid succession as he attempted to strike without being struck. UU picked up his hand laser and timed the creature as the latter ran from UU's left to right. One shot dropped the remaining guard.

As Blik ran to join his friends, UU turned to the group. "Make sure they're all dead. I don't want—"

A laser shot rang out. With eyes bulging, Geeba grabbed her stomach and looked at UU. She dropped to her knees, then fell to her right side.

Yane fired one round into the guilty attacker: Mookie.

"Nooo!" UU shouted as he dropped his weapon.

With Geeba now on her side, UU knelt on the carpet, dropped his laser, and grabbed his beloved friend's head and underneath her right shoulder. "Cover us!" UU screamed, his anger and sadness overcoming him.

UU's mind raced. He would have preferred to have been beheaded in front of the Premier rather than witness this horrific event. He truly loved Geeba, but the unraveling of life since his dearest wife Karesh died prevented him from feeling anything the way he had before her death. Patient and understanding, Geeba tried to draw feelings from UU. Now, all that he felt and tried to express and wished he could communicate—all of it unraveled.

Bright blue eyes open, Geeba tried to speak but could not. Tears flooded forth. Her vibrant chocolate brown skin seemed to highlight the red which overcame the whites of her eyeballs. A look of shock faded into sadness. Though unable to speak, she moved her lips and mouthed a weak "Goodbye." She looked into UU's eyes as the life drained out of her. Her body went limp.

After a full minute of tears, curses, and sobs, UU squeezed his dear Geeba one last time, bringing her shoulders to his. He then rose to his feet in a slow, deliberate climb. He looked at Yane and Blik, unable to speak. The large, tough colonel closed his eyes. Tears flowed down his rough cheeks. "We'll get her body later," he managed to mutter in a halting voice.

Yane and Blik stared for a moment; no one in the UU Gang had ever seen their leader emotional like this.

"Mookie should be dead," Yane announced, unsure how to act after losing his endearing friend.

With rage overtaking him, UU marched toward Mookie. Whether dead or alive, Mookie's body was about to receive the colonel's wrath. UU had previously killed the wrong member of his gang, and this treasonous being had robbed him of the female for whom he had a warm spot in his heart.

UU growled with rage, interrupted only by a quiet squeak from the dying Andalian. "Good!" UU roared. "You are alive! I want to be the one who puts an end to you!" His booming voice echoed through the wide concourse. The colonel did not hesitate. With both hands, he grabbed Mookie by his head and pulled upward. In one motion, UU changed the application of force from an upward trajectory to sideways in one harsh thrust. The other survivors of the fire fight—Yane and Blik—could hear vertebrae and spinal cord snap. With hands still only on Mookie's head, UU threw Mookie's lifeless body to the floor and let go of the corpse.

The fiery colonel walked with a slow gait toward his comrades. He looked as though he had just lost a battle, yet the fight in him grew.

"Grab my weapons!" UU shouted, his voice deeper than normal. He then turned and marched ahead, toward the targeted conference room. He showed no concern that his only weapon, besides the grenades located in the bag strapped to his back, was his Zhiloan knife.

Yane picked up UU and Geeba's lasers. Blik picked up Anthun's knife and the guard's rifle, looked at the red liquid which dripped to the carpet from the carcass, tilted his head, then walked to the Drebehran who had met his end from the knife. Blik wiped the blood on the dead guard's shirt, then raced to catch up to Yane.

Chapter Thirty

"What in the name of holy Shershin is happening?!" Kreeg could not believe his eyes. He spun his head with great alarm as he looked in Bill's direction, now fifty meters away. He shouted into his wrist communicator as he surveyed the scene. "Do not detonate! Everyone! Do not detonate!" He looked back and saw Alana, forty meters behind him. She nodded and thrust an arm upward, thumb extended, to signal her receipt of the urgent message.

Kreeg again shouted into his wrist communicator over the weapons firing and bombs exploding in the great square. "We cannot bring attention to ourselves! Do not detonate!"

"Understood," Bill responded.

The Premier's guards fired their rifles and vehicle-mounted weapons into the unarmed crowd of thousands. The relentless slaughter shocked hardened warriors—Andalian police and UU's Gang.

"We're going to wait, then move in to help the Andalians," Kreeg ordered. "Stay hidden."

"What do you think they'll do?" Bill asked, his lack of police or military training exposed, as his thoughts went to the Insertion Force.

"I would take advantage of the noise and move in," Alana answered over her communicator. "Leaving us to pick off those who flee." She paused. "But even though they're Andalians, they're police, so I see them as the type who would follow orders, regardless of the change in circumstances."

"Exactly!" Kreeg shouted.

The vehicle-mounted rapid-fire laser cannons continued to pour death into the crowd—one of over a dozen such killing machines. The Premier's soldiers fired on the defenseless crowd with efficiency and zeal. Spaced apart so they did not strike their allies on the opposite side of the great square, they pulverized the four thousand creatures who scrambled to stay alive to little avail.

A laser blast exploded into the chest of one of the Premier's gunmen, silencing the weapon for nearly a minute. When another fighter mounted the vehicle and prepared to fire, he was met with the same fate as his comrade.

"Bill!" Kreeg shouted into his wrist communicator. "What are you doing! You're going to draw attention to us!"

"I heard Alana say we should take advantage of the confusion and move in!" came Bill's response.

"I like it!" Alana shouted from her position, aware that Bill must have heard only part of her message. She stood up, in the open for a brief moment, and let three rounds go—the third finding its mark. "Bill!" She shouted into her wrist. "Make sure you move after you take out each enemy fighter!" She then followed her own advice.

"Got it!" Bill responded as a laser blast ricocheted off a stone pillar near him.

"Well, there went our surprise." Kreeg shook his head as he lifted enough of his head and body to find a target and fire one round into another vehicle-mounted attacker. "This is going to get interesting." He continued to mumble to himself as he ducked and ran in his crouched position, on the hunt for another place to open fire. He lifted a small pair of field glasses and scanned the scene three hundred meters away, at the far end of the massacre.

Kreeg turned, looked behind him, and saw one of the Andalian police officers, partially hidden by a small building. The former noted the latter made no effort to join in the fray—orders were orders, and the time for a full attack would come soon enough. The Insertion Force had moved into a new position, warranted by the unexpected bedlam, but stayed away from the carnage.

•　　•　　•

Breath regained, laser and Anthun's knife returned to him, UU walked through the doorway, hand laser at the ready. The large, well-furnished room lacked the presence of guards, which surprised the colonel. As Yane and Blik entered, UU spotted the figure of the Premier approaching and then passing through a thin curtain which draped the doorway of the balcony.

The Premier's key aides had been ordered to remain on the balcony one floor below to watch the gruesome proceedings and verify that all transpired as ordered, so the would-be ruler of the known universe expected to enter an empty suite. He did not.

Before the trio could get far into the room and advance toward the maniacal ruler, shouts could be heard from the hallway. Yane and Blik exited the room to investigate; UU retreated to close the door behind them. He wanted to be alone with the Premier and it appeared his wish had been granted.

When the Premier looked up as UU walked toward him, he recognized from photographs and holograms the famed colonel—famous, at least, in the Nova Quadrant. Nearly 10 meters away, the Premier rushed toward his adversary, clasped his hands together, and shouted as he ran. As he neared UU, the latter began to understand the cries and looked on as a quizzical expression dominated his face.

"Thank you! Thank you! Ooooh thank you!" the Premier cried as he fell to his knees in front of the one he deemed his savior. "You are Colonel Untas Ursulanus, are you not?! Oh! I am so grateful you are here to rescue me!" He prayed to UU only three meters away. "You are my hero, Colonel! Thank you for rescuing me from my bondage!"

Sensing no immediate danger, UU chose to lower his laser pistol to his side. As he spoke, UU glanced down at Anthun's knife, now safely nestled in his pant leg scabbard. "This is amusing."

UU's ironic tone was not lost on Aelo Seveen. "What do you mean?" he asked, concern leaking out of his mouth.

"I mean we heard your speech, Seveen. At least part of it. Enough of it." UU laughed as he stepped toward the kneeling Asimoni. UU stared at the tyrant who had employed numerous warriors in attempts to snuff out his life. "And I don't think those thousands of creatures who work for you are killing themselves." UU swept his hand in the direction of the shooting and screaming in the courtyard as he took a step away from the Premier.

"Wait!" the Premier begged. "Hear me out!" Every sentence was a shout—a plea—designed to appeal to emotions UU lacked. "I wanted to get as much as possible out of this quadrant, as you do. I admit that. I merely employed thousands while you employed a few." He crawled on his knees as he beseeched UU. "You're going to take me alive, aren't you? To stand trial." Hope rose in his voice.

UU holstered his laser.

The Premier allowed a twinge of hope to swirl in his eyes.

"Of course I'm not going to let you live, Premier!" UU laughed as he closed the small gap between the two.

The colonel grabbed the upper portion of the Premier's right arm and used his own right hand to strike his adversary in the nose with an open palm. Aelo Seveen's frame flipped backward, onto his back. Before the Premier could respond, UU delivered a brutal kick to the ribs. A high-pitched squeal rushed out of the Premier's throat.

UU stepped back and smiled—it was the smile of a hunter preparing to finish off his prey. He reached down and lifted Anthun's knife. "I don't know if it's fitting to kill you with the knife of a warrior. You don't have the courage to get your own hands bloodied."

The sound of a laser battle in the hallway proved to be but a brief distraction for the revenge-riddled warrior. As the Premier staggered to his feet, UU swept in with a quick slice with Anthun's knife, which cut into the wounded leader's side. A scream of pain concealed the laser blasts on the other side of the door for just a moment.

On his knees again, the Premier absorbed another slash of the Andalian Battle Knife and let out another cry of pain.

UU's cruel smile bordered on psychopathic; he enjoyed every second of his torturous vengeance. "You will bleed out, Premier. You are going to die slowly." Another smile covered the colonel's face. "Because of you, I've lost numerous soldiers, but you could never stop me." The smile graduated to laughter. "You will die like an Asimoni warthog in a camouflaged pit. Helpless. Squealing. Pathetic!"

The sound of a laser blast glancing off the wall near the door again distracted UU, but this time he took his mind off his prey. He trotted to the door and peered out.

Across the hall, protected by a wall which jutted into the concourse from another doorway, Yane looked up in time to see his leader. "We got this!" the Mangan called out. "There's only six of them."

A look of surprise swept over UU, who then closed the door as a red laser beam raced past where his face had been a second prior. With the door closed again, the colonel returned to the object of his rage. Upon returning to striking distance, UU reached for the Premier's left arm to yank him to his feet. At the same time, Seveen swept his right arm forward. A short-bladed Asimoni knife, not known for its combat utility, protruded from the Premier's hand. He swung and missed as UU leaped backward, sensing the counterattack. The full arc of the spin achieved, the Premier now reached his feet, though on unsteady footing.

The Premier stepped backward as Yane and Blik entered the room, lasers drawn. He then turned his gaze to UU. "Tell them to lower their weapons so one of us may die like a hero."

"You're already bleeding out, Premier," UU chuckled. The cessation of words brought another quick strike from the enraged—almost delirious—colonel. The slice ripped through clothing, flesh, and muscle in Aelo Seveen's leg. UU ensured a safe attack for himself by moving past his victim and stepping away with a deft shuffle of his feet.

"I don't know if we have time to torture him to death," Yane interjected.

Yane's comment did not awaken UU from his calm yet enraged state: inwardly, UU's emotions roared like a waterfall; outwardly, he remained focused, like a lion about to pounce on an unsuspecting prey, ready to sink his teeth into his quarry's neck. With a calm gait, UU strode to within three meters from the Premier and cocked his head, as though to ponder when his next strike should come.

"We really do need to move, UU," Yane added.

Unfazed by Yane's request, UU again addressed the beast he hated. "Aelo Seveen. Such a priestly name, and yet you—"

Before UU could finish his sentence, the small explosion from the rifle Blik had inherited from a dead foe startled the colonel. He looked at Blik, then back to the Premier. The body hit the floor, deceased before it came to a mangled end, crumpled into an odd pile as arms and head plopped down at awkward angles.

"Blik!" UU turned to face his friend, Andalian battle knife still in hand. "Why did you rob me of this?!"

In a flat voice, Blik answered. "We don't have time for this."

UU returned Anthun's knife to its resting place.

"Besides," Blik continued. "You're starting to act like an Andalian and I'm understanding why other creatures hate us."

Angry but at a loss for words, UU returned his stare to the lifeless Premier. UU could not decide whether to scream, attack Blik, or allow himself to writhe in a depressed stupor. He settled for mumbling as dozens of thoughts raced through his brain yet could not find his tongue.

Blik strolled out of the conference room with no regard for feelings. If they wanted to get out of the palace alive, they all knew they must keep moving.

As Blik exited the large room and disappeared behind a wall, Yane looked in the direction of his leader. "That was pretty funny." The Mangan's smile did not sell his conclusion to the colonel.

UU shook his head and followed Yane across the room and out the door. Side by side they walked after entering the concourse. "We don't have to bring back the body, do we?" Yane asked.

UU stared straight ahead. The absence of words and the continuation of their journey answered Yane's question.

•   •   •

With very little movement in the great square, bodies representing just about every race in the quadrants lay still. While some of the four thousand remained alive—either by hiding under the remains of like-minded friends and acquaintances or by sheer happenstance—well over 95% of the Premier's hard working minions met their end.

"Qerl'ashp!" Kreeg shouted into his wrist communicator. "Do you see where they are going?" He and his friends watched as the Premier's elite guard retreated to one central location, in the direction of the Stoon River.

"We see them," Qerl'ashp responded. "I don't know if they're going to cross the river, but we'll cut off that route and trap them."

"Copy that," Kreeg answered.

"The four of you hang back and pick off anyone who escapes," the police captain ordered, as though Kreeg was in the dark about the plan.

"Will do." Kreeg did not bother to tell Qerl'ashp that his group had already killed ten of the Premier's killers.

Plans had changed—drastically so. What started out as a pincer move from two separate teams of ten morphed into 85 combatants—65 of the Premier's guards and 20 Andalians from the Insertion Force—choked into a small area, leading to a shooting gallery for the Andalians. The plans for first contact with the enemy had been immediately discarded for a plan which proved much easier to execute.

The police force chose to take the first step of targeting the cannon operators on the vehicles. With the dangerous weapons neutralized, half the force used the high ground, from the direction of the square, to wipe out the guards as they approached the lower ground of the river. The other half of the Andalian force lay hidden closer to the bridge, in strategic spacing, eliminating the Premier's guards in a withering crossfire.

Kreeg watched as the elite corps of the Premier's faithful met their end after their retreat to a pre-determined site near the river which wound its way through the western section of the capitol area. The Premier's elite squad never expected resistance.

The sound of the second bloodbath of the hour roared through the city streets.

Kreeg raced toward the location of the battle. With everyone previously gathered in the great square, the rout was made easier. Now, instead of playing the role of diversion, he and his two compatriots spread out to terminate anyone who attempted escape. The fierce fight, with laser blasts and small explosions, combined with the screams and shouts of those annihilating and being annihilated, presented a confusing scene.

With no one else left to kill, the three members of UU's gang took cover and watched events unfold. Bill took a position behind a small troop transport at the western edge of the square. Something was off. It did not make sense. He kept his eye on one of the Insertion Force officers. The warrior wore a black jacket like the rest of the Special Insertion Force, but his shirt, only visible on his chest, flashed bright red in the Asimoni sunlight.

Then a thought struck Bill: this was a Drebehran. With a much smaller build than Andalians, if Bill could see him better he knew he would see a black jacket far too large for the slender impostor.

Bill stared at the figure as the out-of-place fighter fired toward the Premier's elite guard but nowhere near any of the combatants. After firing a few rounds in a bid to act as though he belonged, the mysterious figure glided with the stealth of a ninja in a series of lateral moves until hidden by a small building which before the Great Exodus had served as a small snack bar for tourists. Once out of sight of the battle, he turned and jogged in the direction of the palace.

"Kreeg!" Bill shouted into his communicator. "I found one who is escaping and he's in disguise. I'm going to go find him." Bill began his search for the warrior who did not belong and had just disappeared.

"Disguise? As what?" came Kreeg's voice over the small electronic device.

"He's Drebehran, wearing an Insertion Force jacket and headed toward the palace." Bill's voice became labored as he spoke and picked up his jog to a sprint.

"Okay, but check in regularly," Kreeg ordered. "This is hostile territory." After the communication ended, Kreeg continued speaking, but to himself. "And you don't have soldier instincts, so that worries me."

•   •   •

Bill had not gone far when he came upon the body of a Special Insertion Force warrior. Called Oorb, Bill recalled the creature's face upon seeing it. The lifeless Andalian looked like the other 19 police officers—minus the jacket. With his head turned to the side, Bill could see the burn mark on the back of Oorb's head. Bill paused long enough to fill in blanks in his mind, then renewed his pursuit of the mysterious Drebehran.

•   •   •

For their own protection, UU, Yane, and Blik jogged side-by-side as they traversed the long, wide hallway.

"Those stairs there," UU ordered as he pointed to a wide staircase up ahead. "We'll get on the ground floor and go out the main doors."

Up ahead and to the right, the marble-floored hallway gave way to a carpeted staircase, the flooring just as plush as the rest of the building's flooring throughout. The team veered toward the staircase and slowed. Yane did not slow as quickly and found himself slightly ahead of the others.

"Wait!" UU commanded.

Before they could stop, a blast roared past Yane's right ear. "Get down!" UU shouted as he aimed his laser pistol. Yane and Blik did not need the order to dive for cover, and they returned fire without delay as a single red flash exploded from UU's laser, down the staircase.

UU's shot found its mark. The lack of other laser blasts eased their tension. The threesome ran down the stairs, ready to fire their weapons at any moment needed.

    •   •   •

Bill slowed to a jog, unable to maintain a sprint for any meaningful length of time. As he rounded a corner of a building a block from the great square, he caught a fleeting glimpse of his quarry. The Drebehran disappeared around a massive column which served as a visual spectacle for anyone in the city square, although the column did not bear weight of the massive palace. Breathing in heavy surges, Bill slowed the pace of his jog.

"I think he may be headed to the front of the capitol," Bill spoke into his communicator, his voice evincing witness to the effort his lungs put out.

"I'll wait to hear from UU, then let him know," Kreeg said. "I'd bring you back but he's wearing that black jacket. That could cause a problem." Kreeg's concern was obvious: the unidentified warrior could put himself in a position to harm UU and his team or interfere with their plans for the Premier. "You're going to have to kill him, I'm sure."

To any other member of the group, Kreeg would not have uttered that final line, but he knew Bill had joined the gang out of zealotry more than talent. Bill was half accountant and half political radical, but not one drop of police or military blood flowed through his veins. Kreeg always found himself worrying about Bill, who had convinced himself he was now a bona fide rebel in action.

Chapter Thirty-One

The lone non-combatant who made the trip to Asimon broke the rules. He knew orders were to stay inside the shuttle unless an overwhelming need outside the craft called for his skills. Orders or not, Krun Temper caved to his desire to exit the shuttle and walk around. This was his first visit to the planet and he wanted to step outside, breathe the air, and feel the sunshine from the star Bellik.

After a couple of minutes of walking around, stretching, and enjoying his solitude, the 21st member of the Special Insertion Force wandered a few meters away from his craft. After a thought occurred to him, Krun Temper halted all movements, cupped his small Mangan hands around his ears, and tried to hear distant laser fire. Hearing none, he turned to walk back to the shuttle.

The Asimoni standing in front of Krun Temper was neither intimidating nor frightening in appearance, but the way the opponent seemed to magically materialize startled the police officer. Krun Temper's eyes shot from the fighter's eyes and face to the weapon in his right hand. With his own side arm holstered, the pilot's fate was sealed. The laser blast echoed among the buildings but, despite the decibels the weapon put out, the sound went unheard by anyone.

Krun Temper died within seconds.

"Aeshle!" Qerl'ashp snapped. "Get the force together. We are to report to the front steps of the capitol where we'll meet Colonel UU. There are numerous guards inside the palace."

"Yes, sir," Aeshle answered.

Qerl'ashp turned his attention to the lieutenant. "While the team assembles, raise Krun Temper on the radio and have him destroy this bridge. I don't want those who fled interfering with our plans."

"Yes, sir," came the response.

"And send the message to engage Albelb," Qerl'ashp ordered.

Aeshle pursed his lips and fought off a frown before giving a delayed, quiet response. "Yes, sir."

•   •   •

For the older Andalians who feared their race would weaken to the point of softness and eventual extinction, Albelb was a shining star, a true warrior, faithful to their old ways yet diplomatic enough to survive in modern times. Despite their toughness and cold attitudes, most Andalians knew how to be diplomatic. A veteran of wars and peace, the old warrior received the message to launch his final mission; he sat motionless in the pilot's seat. For a long five seconds, he allowed his mind to race in fifty different directions. Memories of battles, his now-deceased wife, his offspring, political progress on their home world, the impending end of their home world, and more battles—they all flooded his thoughts as he acknowledged the communication and steered the ancient battleship toward Asimon.

The old soldier—no one seemed to know his true age—engaged a computer program with the push of one button, then spent a few seconds terminating the ship's gravity. Strapped in for the ride, he realized he had not flown in a ship with its gravity boosters disengaged since he was a cadet so long ago.

As he pushed buttons and flipped switches, he felt a twinge of pain in his chest. Yes, the timing was good. He might not be alive in another Heislerian month, though he had three months to live according to his doctors.

With gravity disengaged, Albelb would not face the concern of blacking out from g-forces as his ship completed its pre-programmed path.

The mission was two-fold. As he approached the planet, he would shoot a high-energy electron beam, focused through a magnetic generator which magnified electromagnetic flow and increased microwave resonance, at the atmosphere. This, in theory, should envelop the atmosphere and disrupt electronic flow, which would disable the planet's defensive force field. Because no one had ever activated a planetary defense shield, no one was certain about how to deactivate it through force. Albelb had wanted to begin the Special Insertion Force mission with this tactic, but Qerl'ashp had demanded a secret insertion into the atmosphere based on Yane's plan.

His melancholy mood came about because of the second aspect of the mission: he had to take out the battle cruiser which patrolled Asimon. At times, the craft guarded the skies while other times it orbited the planet outside the atmosphere. When necessary, it chased ships away which flew too close to the planet. Outside of Asimon, scientists held multiple theories about how the battle cruiser could pierce the shield without effort, but the scientific question held no importance to Albelb—he knew the Asimoni ship had mastered the force field but law enforcement had not.

All military previously vacated the quadrant and took their equipment and weapons with them. Albelb had proposed repairing a long-ago-retired battleship which had been mothballed many years prior to the Quadrant 3 wars of the prior decade. So, without a cause or mission, on Albelb's orders, a group of Andalians repaired the craft. No one minded Albelb lacked the authority to order anyone to do anything; as a retired general, all—military and civilian—respected and listened to him.

When UU and Yane's plan met his ears, the dying Andalian once again had a purpose for living and a warship to go with it.

The tumor which grew around his heart led Albelb to concoct a plan no one liked except him. As he thought about what was about to transpire, he checked multiple cameras to ensure his cargo looked stable—he did not know what he would do if it had become unstable, but he checked, nevertheless.

Albelb's audacious yet outrageous plan would send his old warship hurtling into the Asimoni battleship, thereby detonating his cargo: 18 tons of explosives. Albelb was ready to die like a warrior.

•　　•　　•

Pinned down in a fire fight, UU shouted at Yane and Blik—both of whom were on either side of him by ten meters. In an expansive ballroom, they felt trapped in the room in which they were forced to retreat after enduring heavy fire from two guards who had held superior firing positions. Shooting their way out was the only answer. "Qerl'ashp and his force are headed our way."

"How close?" Yane hollered above the fray as flashes of laser light filled the room and the resulting small explosions which demolished chairs and tables crashed all around them.

Blik held no interest in the brief conversation. From behind a table, which provided little actual protection but did allow for concealment, he lofted a small Rojani grenade toward the doorway from which the laser fire emanated. Locking his elbow as he threw the device allowed him to use just his arm without exposing his body to the withering laser fire which would be directed his way if his location were to be discovered.

The grenade took out both Asimoni guards. Blik understood the impact of the blast when he realized the assault to his life and ears had ended. Not willing to take a chance, the Andalian crawled to a new position and attempted to look through the debris, smoke, and dust. Comfortable with the result, he rose to his feet and announced "That's over with."

UU and Yane leaped from their fragile hideouts, lasers aimed.

A light fixture dangled from the ceiling; electrical current arced and dust floated downward. Every step saw a perilous condition for keeping one's balance, with few items left fully assembled.

"Let's go," Blik barked. "I don't want to be trapped in here again."

UU smiled. "We earned our pay there."

"What pay?" Yane snapped, still shaken from the close call.

UU eyed his long-time friend. "When we get out of this quadrant and haul our booty with us, we're rich. Don't forget it."

"You think Bingus Jam and Pracen will allow us to take booty out of the quadrant?" Yane asked with cynicism lacing every word.

"They won't have a choice," UU said with confidence. "Blik's right. We have to go."

"Well, that's a big hole." For the first time, Blik saw the result of his grenade blast; he pondered their dilemma. The grenade had blown a hole in the floor, leaving the basement exposed, right where they needed to walk in order to exit the room.

UU frowned. "If that had been a hyper grenade we'd all be dead."

"It was a small grenade," Blik said with a touch of confusion covering his face, surprised by the degree of damage. He walked a few meters laterally from the door.

Still annoyed by his brief conversation with UU, Yane threw up his hands. "Now what?"

Before UU could respond, Blik opened fire at the wall with his pistol laser while he stood near the entrance. Debris bounced around the room; wood turned into shrapnel. UU and Yane dived for cover, but Blik—dangerously close to the wall, six meters away—stood firm, even as a piece of plaster bounced off his forehead, causing the Andalian to close his eyes from the dust as he fired away.

Blik finally stopped firing and turned around as he asked "Are you ready? Hey! Where did you go?"

UU and Yane rose from behind a table which lay on its side. UU shook his head. "Must you always be crazy?"

"You're fine with part-time crazy?" Blik asked with a deadpan tone.

"Maybe. It just may be best." UU again shook his head.

"Part-time crazy and we're stuck in this room or jumping into the basement." Blik smiled with a triumphant look.

"Why didn't you use the rifle?" Yane asked.

"I don't have extra ammo," Blik responded in a matter-of-fact voice. "UU had gone crazy—part-time—and I didn't have time to grab the dead fighter's spares."

After a military-styled exit through the large hole in the ballroom wall, which included covering each other and taking careful steps around corners, ready to fire, the trio entered the main concourse with the front lobby in sight. They traveled but a few meters before they found themselves under attack again. They dived for cover—what little they could find.

From behind a pillar, UU directed his friends with military hand signals. On the count of "three" from UU's fingers, Blik rolled sideways from behind a couch and coffee table, Yane climbed to his knees from behind a large piece of furniture used to store alcohol for bartenders, and UU rolled from behind his pillar. All opened fire simultaneously but hit nothing.

"Stay low!" UU ordered. With his comrades maintaining a degree of concealment, UU crawled forward, out into the open. The plan was simple: draw fire and allow his team to extinguish the antagonist. Just as he realized he had crawled too far forward, an Asimoni guard leaped out and fired at UU, then leaped back for cover.

The shot sailed over the colonel and hit the floor not far behind his feet, but the enemy's exposure was enough for Blik. The Andalian fired his captured rifle; his shot hit the combatant in the chest as he attempted to leap backward. From Yane's angle, he saw the result and called out. "You got him, Blik!"

Yane checked behind them then joined his peers as they returned to their feet, ready to exit the capitol. "I've never seen a capitol building with a bar in it."

"Maybe we should get some refreshments," Blik chuckled.

"I looked when I took cover; it's empty," Yane laughed as he shook his head.

The three remained spread out as they advanced through the concourse.

"When we get outside, take cover as soon as possible," UU instructed. "I don't want any surprises to get us."

"I vote for that," Yane said in a wry tone.

"Me, too," Blik chimed in.

•   •   •

Bill huffed and gasped until his brain finally agreed with his body and slowed his pace to a walk. Bill had learned to become a warrior, to a degree, during his time with the UU

Gang, but on-the-job training did not include conditioning classes. Currently on the south side, the east side of the massive capitol building was still over one hundred meters away. Bill had not seen his quarry in several minutes. With his energy spent, his walk slowed as he approached the next titanic pillar, which matched the other columns surrounding the building on all sides. The architecture gave the appearance of an ancient Shersheen city. The pillars announced strength and royalty to citizens of the quadrants, even if that royalty was only found in architecture.

Bill approached the pillar, ready to sit down and take a breather. Exhausted by the long, hasty chase, he prepared for a controlled collapse when he spotted a black jacket. He recognized it immediately.

With his back to the pillar and superstructure, he walked the six meters to the jacket and bent down to pick it up. He never saw the Drebehran in the red shirt.

The mysterious combatant stepped out into the open, at the foot of the great pillar.

Bill stood, jacket in hand, and allowed his mind to get lost in the moment. He looked out across the great square—the "courtyard," as it had been referred to by the Asimoni legislature before they fled their planet—and stared in wonder at the number of dead souls.

The Drebehran fired his rifle; Bill never knew what hit him.

In the distance, Bill's killer could see the advancing silhouettes of the 19 remaining Andalians of the Special

Insertion Force. He stared at the approaching police and cocked his head in thought. He fled to the east, toward the front of the great capitol, but veered away to the south to find shelter from the approaching police.

.   .   .

As planned, the Asimoni battle cruiser emerged from the atmosphere, intent on deterring the old warship from continuing its loitering. Albelb's old ship's computers included artificial intelligence only the military possessed which allowed the craft to fly the pre-programmed path yet adapt to maneuvers made by the Asimoni craft.

Albelb pulled from his jacket a flask full of Andalian rye whiskey—a difficult drink to come by these days. He sucked down a big gulp, then engaged the flight program. Unless something went wrong or a last-minute sentient decision was needed, Albelb was along for the ride.

The old ship, which he named Cleelah only thirty seconds prior, raced toward the Asimoni battleship. As Cleelah's computer detected a laser about to be discharged on the opposing craft, Albelb watched as his craft executed a 45-degree turn to port followed by an immediate thrust straight up, away from the planet. Within seconds, Cleelah's computers calculated the battle cruiser's lack of corrective actions; the Asimoni captain undoubtedly watched the speedy movements in confusion and would rather destroy it from a distance. Two quick laser bursts missed again as Cleelah reacted again.

Albelb took another quick swig from his flask and smiled. "I see what you're doing Cleelah." Just as the final syllable escaped Albelb's mouth, the ship performed as he expected. Cleelah ignited afterburners and the large, lumbering relic from another era blasted forward, straight into the battle cruiser. The high-speed collision, with a boost from 18 tons of explosives, obliterated both craft.

On the opposite side of the planet from the battles being fought in the once-beautiful Asimoni capital of Roandan, debris from two obliterated military spaceships rained down on the surface for over 20 minutes. The theory proved true; the planetary defense shield ceased to exist. And so did Albelb.

Chapter Thirty-Two

Lagging over 200 meters behind, Kreeg and Alana followed the 19 police officers. Like the members of the Insertion Force, they, too, had seen the body of the Andalian called Oorb. Besides protecting the rear flank for the officers, Kreeg and Alana spent their trek discussing the unknown locations of Mookie and Bill, including what radio silence from both of them meant.

"I agree Bill is probably dead," Alana responded to Kreeg's latest comment. "He was a civilian his whole life. But not Mookie."

"I'm hoping we'll find Bill when we reach UU." He continued the identical progression of motions he performed every 10-12 seconds: he looked behind them; to his left and right; up in the air lest someone attack by roof or air; and aimed his hand laser in the same direction his eyes looked with each movement. "As far as Mookie, I cannot imagine he survived—we should have heard from him by now."

"Why don't you reach him on the communicator?" Alana asked.

"Because UU, Qerl'ashp, and I agreed we would communicate only when necessary," Kreeg explained. "It's really important for UU because he's inside the palace. We don't want to get him killed if he needs the silence."

"Stop!" Alana stopped in her tracks and held out her right arm, causing Kreeg to come to a halt. "Look!" She pointed ahead. "They've found something." Alana referred to the 19 Andalians, all of whom were gathered close to one of the pillars, though many looked in various directions for their own safety. "Something's wrong."

Kreeg stared straight ahead as the duo resumed then picked up their pace. "I'll bet it's Bill. I'll bet they found him."

"Or the one he was pursuing." Alana's attempt at optimism fell flat as she considered the odds.

The two rushed forward until they caught up to the police team. Qerl'ashp spoke first. "Kreeg, I believe this is your comrade."

With Alana by his side, Kreeg looked down at their lifeless colleague. "Yes, he's ours."

•　　•　　•

As the Insertion Force approached, UU, Yane, and Blik wandered out into the open lawn in front of the capitol and palace. The front lawn extended the length of the two-kilometer front elevation of the building and extended nearly eight hundred meters away from the spectacular structure. A few outbuildings littered the lawn, as well as gigantic boulders meant to give the appearance of one of Shershin's great cities—at least how a famous ancient painting depicted the great civilization's capitol.

Within minutes, UU and Qerl'ashp met in the open, only 40 meters from the sidewalk which encircled the entire structure and led visitors to the "Great Steps," as they were known, to be climbed to enter the lobby. In UU's case, he had walked down the same stairs minutes before.

When the two leaders met again, they felt mutual admiration based on their common battle. They both extended right hands, but UU grabbed the Insertion captain's right forearm, allowing Qerl'ashp to do the same with UU, in a traditional Andalian warrior greeting.

"You survived," UU said with genuine pleasure.

"You have as well," Qerl'ashp responded.

"I lost Geeba," UU's countenance dropped as he spoke the words. "She was special to me."

"I lost Oorb, although I doubt you know who he is."

UU shook his head. Rather than continue with the distraction of memories, UU pointed upward, toward the palace. "I am certain we did not kill everyone. I'm sure there are some we didn't see. We just wanted out alive."

"I don't see the Premier." Qerl'ashp looked around as he spoke.

"Did you expect to?"

Qerl'ashp laughed. "No, not after hearing that speech of his." The two paused their conversation as they watched Yane and Blik speak with one of Qerl'ashp's police officers. On the sidewalk, the trio carried on an animated conversation, which UU assumed was about the demise of the Premier. He also noticed, not far away, a red-shirted Drebehran speaking to another member of the Insertion Force.

"This is the part of the plan that troubled me," the captain confessed as he brought his attention to the subject at hand. "I've got to guard every exit of a building larger than a spaceliner. We probably shouldn't remain in the open. I only sent a team of four officers inside the building. That's not enough."

UU's eyes narrowed. "Who is that Drebehran walking toward our three comrades?" He pointed first at the unknown beast who walked with purpose, then to Yane, Blik, and their conversant. "He doesn't look like he belongs," UU added as he studied the creature's apparel.

"Why is he here?" Qerl'ashp could not hide his surprise. "That's Crartrarn. He works for Abuss Onuss. He should have no business here." The captain's tone reflected a deep skepticism.

"Crartrarn?" UU asked. His mind leaped backward. He saw himself, while standing over the dying Anthun, listening as the latter spoke his final words.

"You betrayed us, Anthun. You are responsible for the massacre of Gigorl law enforcement."

"No," Anthun gasped as life began its escape from his large frame. "Crartrarn."

UU frowned as he struggled to understand the word.

"Crartrarn," Anthun repeated.

UU bolted. He ran as hard as he could in his bid to erase the sixty-meter separation. He did not think about his wrist communicator—only stopping Crartrarn mattered. UU had no way of knowing this same Drebehran had killed Bill, but he did understand what was about to transpire. Crartrarn worked for the Board of Ten and the Premier. He was a double agent—there could be no other explanation for his presence.

UU's wrist communicator finally came to mind. "Yane! Blik! Get down!"

Crartrarn drew his weapon—a common hand laser much like what each member of the UU Gang carried.

"Kill that Drebehran!" UU shouted at the top of his lungs. Laser in hand, the colonel fired three rounds while sprinting. The red balls of death sailed over Crartrarn's head.

Undeterred by laser rounds whizzing by, Crartrarn took aim.

Yane, Blik, and the Insertion officer looked toward the shouting colonel, not yet grasping the threat.

Crartrarn fired one round into the large target of Blik's chest. As Blik fell to the sidewalk in a heap, the Drebehran fired his second shot, which grazed Yane's hip.

Only a few meters from the adversary, UU slid into the grass, bringing himself to a quick stop to attain an agreeable firing position. He let loose with two quick volleys as his body came to a stop. The second round struck Crartrarn in the right arm and spun him around. Before the attacker could recover, UU fired another round, into the Drebehran's neck, severing the spine and separating the head from the body. Crartrarn's carcass fell onto the bottom steps of the great palace. His head bounced off a stair, then dribbled down four steps and onto the sidewalk.

With such a large opening created by the decapitation, the laser round did not cauterize the wound as most laser blasts tended to do. Instead of a bloodless death, the thick, red liquid flowed down the bottom four steps as if to reunite with the head.

UU ran to Blik and dropped to his knees. "Come on, friend!" He placed his ear to Blik's mouth to listen for breathing. Feeling and hearing nothing, he placed two fingers on the Andalian's neck. Nothing. Still on his knees, the colonel lifted his head away from the body. He lacked the words to convey his emotions so he simply stared beyond Blik's body, into nothingness. Energy drained out of him. The day's highs could not overcome the lows.

Yane climbed to his feet, although he rocked to and fro as he tried to regain his balance. The Andalian officer grabbed him to stabilize him.

As Kreeg and Alana ran up, they began to offer the pieces of the puzzle they knew. They realized that, as they accepted reality, they were now a band of four.

Leaving no time to recover from the murderous chain of events surrounding Blik's demise and Yane's injury, all eyes looked upward at the sound of numerous windows shattering high above.

The battle at the palace had yet to reach its conclusion.

Chapter Thirty-Three

The UU Gang—what was left of it—raced the few paces to the capitol steps in order to avoid the barrage of laser fire from above. Their leader eyed the situation as Qerl'ashp raced to find cover and three members of the Insertion Force returned fire. Within seconds, the barrage ended, although the gang lacked the knowledge whether the snipers were dead or had fled.

"Kreeg, stay with Yane," UU ordered. "Alana and I will find cover out there and help Qerl'ashp. We need to add to their firepower." He pointed toward the expansive lawn.

Kreeg nodded then turned his attention to the top of the steps, hopeful an enemy would not appear; Kreeg lacked concealment or cover for Yane and himself.

"Kreeg," Yane said with surprising strength. "I'm fine. I'm in a lot of pain but I can function."

Kreeg frowned as he looked around. "We're easy targets here."

"We have to move."

"I cannot disagree." With that Kreeg picked up his friend by an arm and attempted to act as an extra pair of legs for the wounded warrior. He carried Blik's captured rifle in his opposite hand.

Within a handful of steps, Yane shed his living crutch. "I'm hurting, but I can walk." After two steps he slowed, let out a quiet yet sharp yelp of pain, then glared at Kreeg. "Don't slow down," he ordered as the two lumbered into the open of the front lawn.

From behind a boulder, UU watched as Kreeg and Yane hid behind another of the massive decorative rocks. When his attention returned to the windows on the sixth floor, to his horror he saw the barrel of an Andalian laser cannon rolling into position. A small anti-aircraft weapon, it found common use on the backs of large land-based vehicles and could shoot down shuttles or fighter craft.

Sensing impending doom, a simultaneous assault began from three of the Insertion Force officers who were all positioned to UU and Alana's left. Qerl'ashp, who hid behind a small shack behind and off to UU's right, also participated in the barrage. The shack was built to house a vendor. One blast from the cannon and it and everyone near it would be vaporized by the massive laser round.

Within a second, all eight fighters fired at and near the laser's one-meter-wide barrel.

"We can't survive that cannon!" UU shouted at Alana. He paused his attack and made a brief mental survey of the area.

An explosion inside the building, signifying that someone on the ground had made a positive contribution to the counterattack, caused the large barrel to lurch to UU's left. "Alana," UU shouted as he pointed to his right. "We need to —

" Before he could finish his sentence, the incredible roar from the laser cannon startled every combatant involved in the battle. The ground shook. Trees rustled. Dirt, grass, wood, stone, and flesh rocketed 50 meters into the air. When the debris fell back to solid ground, through the dust and dirt UU could see the crater which marked the location of where the Andalian law enforcement officers had stood before they met their instantaneous demise.

"We have to get out of here!" Alana shouted. Three steps into flight away from the building, small arms laser fire sizzled over her head and exploded into the ground beyond her. She brought her body to an immediate stop and returned to cover with UU.

"We can't stay here," UU said. Again Alana turned to run, this time with UU following. After four steps, she froze and looked up and behind the position they wished to vacate.

UU joined her in shock at the armed shuttle craft which settled toward the ground, floating like a balloon losing its helium. Instinctively, UU shot a glance back toward the palace. The barrel swung slowly into place, preparing for its next target—either UU and Alana's position or the descending craft. He turned to the spaceship one more time before the sense of urgency overcame him. He opened his mouth to inform Alana of impending death when a series of blasts emanated from the shuttle craft's guns just as the laser cannon pounded out another shot.

"We have to get away from that ship!" UU finally shouted, but his words failed to be heard, muted by the tremendous eruption inside the building. His concerns about the craft proved warranted, but not for the reason he thought. In the confusion, UU saw the shuttle as an enemy; he was slow to consider it had just fired on the wicked cannon in the building.

Unfortunately for the pilot of the spaceship, destruction of the cannon came a split second after the ship absorbed a round.

Debris from the exploding laser cannon shot in all directions, even though the combatants on the ground were only aware of the damage caused outside the building.

A sick, grinding, metallic sound from metals of various types which made up the ship's outer hull and inner shell echoed across the lawn as the ship staggered. The laser cannon's final shot had been a direct hit. The small craft suffered an internal blast as one of the engines exploded, which in turn rocked the vehicle and debris shot out the rear of the craft. With one sharp lurch, the shuttle tilted at a 30-degree angle toward the palace and crashed the final 10 meters to the ground. The sound of the collision signaled possible serious injury—or worse—for the inhabitants.

A side door lifted upward. Rick and Julie forced their way through the truncated opening as the ship's damage did not allow the door to fully open.

"Rytkjmk!" Alana shouted as she saw her friend stumble out of the craft, Julie in tow. As Alana sprinted the forty meters to the craft, she slowed for a moment, gripped in horror. "Rytkjmk!"

Rick collapsed to the ground as Julie fought to keep him on his feet. Burned across his head, a piece of smoking metal protruding through his right ribs and out his back, the Heislerian's fate was evident to all.

"Rick!" Julie shouted as she dropped to her knees to clutch his face. "Rick!" Tears fell onto his face as Julie drew her face nearer, panic in her voice, face, and heart. "Rick!" she shouted one more time.

Alana raced to Julie's side and dropped to her knees just as Rick expired. Despite lacking knowledge about Julie's identity, Alana grabbed Julie's far shoulder and pulled in her fellow mourner. They dropped their heads onto each other's left shoulders and wept together.

Meters shy of the scene, UU stopped to survey the side of the capitol. The building appeared free of warriors, so he continued to his fallen comrade.

Alana stepped away as Julie continued with a quiet sob and Kreeg and Yane reached the location.

Qerl'ashp joined the group and looked at UU. "One of yours, I see."

UU could only nod.

"We were doomed without those blasts from the shuttle," the captain added.

Losing one of his soldiers always proved depressing, but only the night in the Zhiloan caves proved a worse day for UU as a leader—military officer or outlaw, in war or post-Exodus skirmishes. On that night on Zhilo he lost six soldiers—compared to this day's loss of five, counting the traitorous Mookie—but the loss of Geeba and Blik tore at his heart like the brutal bite of an Andalian screeching scorpion. He hated losing the six in the diamond mines, but now his mind was foggy and heart heavy because of the personal connections. The agony and emptiness proved too deep to ponder yet too painful to forget.

An explosion a kilometer away caused the startled group of mourners to jump in place. Even Qerl'ashp, who understood the meaning of the explosion, jerked his body in a moment of alarm. "My team found a cache of explosives and blew up the bridge so the rebels on the other side cannot cross there. They'll have to go farther down if they want to cross."

"It's amazing to me they don't have flying craft at the ready," UU said, incredulous at the thought the Premier's forces were stymied by a river. The two leaders, UU and Qerl'ashp, did not know only a handful of fighters lay across the bridge and would later surrender at the news of Aelo Seveen's death.

"You were in the briefing," Qerl'ashp said with a flat tone, knowing UU was not surprised.

"Had they not gotten everything off the planet so quickly," UU mused. "We would've had to bring in an entire army."

"That should buy us time to get out of here, then," the Insertion Group captain added, referring to the exploded bridge. "Because to get out of here, we're going to have to borrow one of the Premier's craft—if we can find one."

"What happened to yours?" UU inquired.

"I don't know. Maybe it's fine, but we lost contact with our shuttle pilot. We assume he's dead." Qerl'ashp shook his head in recognition of the costly, bloody day.

A brief silence settled on the group. Julie stood as the others joined her; they stared at Rick's body as though they could will him back to life.

•   •   •

The relative quiet which hung over the victors like a cloud of industrial pollution reflected their unhappiness despite the battle's outcome. The Special Insertion Force had achieved its goal of providing support for UU and his gang of outlaws-turned-heroes. Too many deaths haunted the two leaders as they watched the fire in the building subside. The resulting explosions and fire had eaten away a 300-meter section of the façade and untold steel framing, destroying everything from roof to ground. Large granite slabs, which began the day as parts of the great building's exterior lay around the perimeter, strewn as though kicked by a monstrous but unseen foot.

As Qerl'ashp prepared to finalize his plans for launching a search for a suitable spaceship to carry them away from the planet, his impending order was interrupted by a shout.

"That looks like a Drebehran craft!" Yane cried out as he pointed above them.

"It's Abuss Onus," UU said as he observed the ship.

•   •   •

As the Drebehran craft settled to the ground, a thought struck UU. He turned to Julie, only steps away, as the latter continued to stare at the corpse of her extraterrestrial sweetheart.

"Julie, what are you doing here?"

"I convinced Rick to take me with him, through the portal," she explained. "We found a shuttle—he stole it—and we were headed to a secret base of yours, but he reached Blik who told him to come here."

Before UU could contemplate the explanation, a door opened on the craft which had just landed over 100 meters away. "I have to go. Stay close to Kreeg or Alana, please," he ordered Julie but made it sound as though it were a request. With that, he walked, then jogged, toward the craft as Abuss Onuss, Pracen, and Bingus Jam emerged one after the other.

Alana eyed Julie. "Your skin is so soft. Where are you from, female?"

Kreeg and Yane chuckled with the realization that UU's tight-lipped approach to living as an outlaw led to members of their group not having important information.

Julie's eyes flitted between the questioner and the source of the soft laughter. "I'm the person at the other end of the portal."

Alana's features crinkled into a confused look. "*Person?*"

"That's what we said, Alana," the wounded Yane responded.

"I'm from the planet Earth."

"Er—where's that?" Alana's voice rose as she reached 'that.' "I've never heard of that planet."

"It's on the other side of Quadrant One," Kreeg teased.

"Oh, it is not!" Alana tried to laugh as she defended herself from her remaining friends.

"How do you know it's not?" Yane challenged her.

"Because you said it was," Alana said with a flat response until she could no longer hold in her smile.

"My house is one of UU's hideaways. I've been nursing Rick back to health."

Alana shook her head. "I've never heard that nickname for Rytkjmk before." She smiled as she looked at her new friend. "Where is that planet of yours?"

"From here? I have no idea." Julie's face reflected her inability to answer the question.

"It's that way," Kreeg pointed upward.

Alana smiled and shook her head.

•   •   •

"What happened to Rocash?" Bingus Jam demanded. Already angry at the news about the Premier's demise, he searched for additional answers.

"Who is that?" UU asked.

"He was supposed to be captive along with the Premier. We mentioned him in the briefing!" Bingus Jam's old ways returned.

"Oh, I didn't pay attention to all that," UU waved both hands toward Bingus Jam, as though the wind created by his fingers could push the annoying bureaucrat away from him.

"Bingus Jam," Abuss Onuss started. "It's over. You tried. They were criminals."

The fat Zhiloan's body relaxed; he turned to Pracen. "I don't understand how the Premier was the evil one and the colonel is the good one."

Pracen frowned. "It's not as we had hoped."

Bingus Jam shook his head. "No. Not at all."

UU's smile radiated bright enough they could almost see a glow. "But I am the good one, so please remember that." He turned to the leader of the Board of Ten. "Abuss Onuss, let's get out of here before any of the survivors attack."

Abuss Onuss patted UU on the shoulder. "You are a good one."

UU's smile did not abate.

"I never doubted you, UU," Abuss Onuss lied.

"We didn't either," Bingus Jam chimed in as he suppressed a smile.

The explosive laugh which started in UU's belly and roared out of his throat proved infectious as the four embraced the lie. After UU finally gained control of his reaction, he blurted, "And I have always appreciated you."

The laughter continued as onlookers, out of earshot, eyed the small group with befuddled expressions.

UU's expression changed. "I have to go back in and retrieve Geeba's body." Laughter faded quickly once Geeba's fate returned to UU's mind.

The three law enforcement leaders frowned. It was Pracen who spoke first. "We did not know. We are sorry to hear it."

"If you would like," Abuss Onuss offered. "Our officers can take care of the corpse when they document the dead."

UU shook his head. "No. I will do it."

Chapter Thirty-Four

The pub in downtown Ersch had been the city's epicenter for the Drebehran capital's nightlife, but those days now were nothing more than ethereal memories. Without the celebrations of the victorious combatants, fewer than a dozen patrons would inhabit the establishment.

The bar's owner, with his stereotypically small Drebehran frame and large forehead, refused to identify his source of alcohol. UU tried and failed several times to gain the information before he settled down to an evening of quiet drinking with the Insertion Force police captain.

The other battle survivors, 21 in all including their leaders and Julie, shared drinks, enjoyed the background music, and played various table games available for their amusement.

Moments after the two leaders sat, Abuss Onuss, Pracen, and Bingus Jam entered the bar and found their way to UU and Qerl'ashp. After a stilted start to the conversation, the three Board of Ten members relaxed and filled in blanks for the two leaders' knowledge.

"Crartrarn was not law enforcement," Abuss Onuss explained. "But we thought he was. We have learned his true identity—and that he blamed you for his brother's death not long after the Great Exodus."

"Where?" UU asked, curiosity taking over.

"In a diamond mine, apparently," Bingus Jam interjected.

"I don't recall seeing Drebehrans in the Zhiloan mine," UU responded before his expression changed when a thought hit him. "You trusted him even after that?"

"We kept him away from you," Bingus Jam explained. "He professed a hatred for the Premier and said he was a criminal. We assumed Crartrarn could be objective because he hated you both—or so we thought."

UU shook his head and held back his anger. He opted for another shot of the Eemlurian whiskey. Their miscalculation cost the lives of one Insertion Force officer and two members of UU's gang.

"Since we have returned from Asimon," Abuss Onuss tried to make amends. "We learned he was the informant, working for the Premier all along."

UU frowned as his annoyed gaze floated from creature to creature. The burning question in his mind was Anthun's relationship to the vile thug. *Did Anthun tell Crartrarn about the hideout because he trusted him? Because he thought it would help Abuss Onuss? How did they know each other?* His brain raced with theories about the Anthun-Crartrarn connection, but UU did not wish to turn the conversation to how Anthun died.

"We're very sorry," Pracen said, referring to the damage caused by Crartrarn.

"Yes," Bingus Jam answered.

"Yes," Abuss Onuss added.

UU looked at Qerl'ashp and shrugged. "Crartrarn is dead. What's done is done."

"It appears every traitorous law enforcement officer was not really law enforcement before the Great Exodus," Abuss Onuss explained. "We had many volunteers come forward so they could wear the veil of Law for the sake of information and power."

"Unfortunately, Blik is dead, as well," the Andalian captain said with sorrow. "He was greatly respected by my team. He had a stellar reputation as a warrior; he always acted with great courage."

"Just don't make him mad enough to want to kill you," UU chortled.

"But something I don't understand is Mookie." Qerl'ashp's puzzled expression conveyed his sincere confusion. "Andalians don't turn; we don't shy away from battle. We are a courageous race."

"Yane and I discussed this," UU answered as he flashed a glance across the pub toward his Mangan friend who continued his card game with several of the Andalians. "When we left a Zhiloan diamond mine." He paused with a nervous glance toward Abuss Onuss, as though the law enforcement leader did not know of UU's prior banditry. "Mookie fled the planet by going straight up, leaving the planet immediately. That should have been certain death and it's why the rest of us flew around Zhilo and left from unpredictable locations, where a mothership would not be waiting for us."

"I see," Qerl'ashp said as he nodded.

"Then when they sent us to Ceratofs," UU motioned toward the three members of the Board of Ten. "Mookie ran out into the open and did not draw fire—all of us drew fire except him. But we forgot about those two incidents." He took another drink. "Had we taken time to consider his actions, we would have scrutinized him more than we did."

"My race's history is full of courageous heroes, not cowards like Mookie." Qerl'ashp set his glass down as he considered his own words. "Not something I would have predicted."

"Heroes like Albelb," UU added.

"Indeed!" Qerl'ashp's exhortation came out just under a shout. "The old warrior probably saved all our lives." He picked up his glass and clanked it on UU's glass.

"You Andalians with the reputation of being violent and crude were the heroes saving the known universe from a tyrant," UU said with gusto, intending his words to be complimentary. He showed a small sign of relief when the captain roared with laughter.

"We do have reputations, don't we?!" Qerl'ashp continued his laugh.

"What happened to Anthun?" Pracen inquired, the question seemed like an interruption to the two warriors. "I never heard how he died."

With a straight face, UU responded. "He met an ignominious end not suitable for an Andalian." The colonel dropped his head, which discouraged further questions.

Qerl'ashp took another sip of his Heislerian whiskey. He looked into his glass and back up to UU. "I don't understand where he gets all these great drinks!"

"It's beyond my comprehension," UU answered. He paused, then turned from the captain and looked at the other three with him. "I still don't understand Crartrarn and how he could move about so easily."

"He was a bitter soul," Bingus Jam said. "Vengeful. Filled with hatred."

UU's thoughts raced as he stared across the room, not focused on any particular creature or object. He chose to ignore Bingus Jam's obvious dodge of the posed concern.

"I've made the arrangements, UU." Abuss Onuss wanted to keep the subject off of Crartrarn. "You can take out as much loot as you would like, as can your gang, that you can get out in one trip."

UU smiled. "That's a lot."

"I'm sure it is." Abuss Onuss understood the large amount of booty UU surely had stored away somewhere—or multiple somewheres.

"My team—what's left of them—we're all leaving soon," UU added. "We all have a little personal business here and there, but we'll be out soon."

"We're leaving, too," Pracen said. "All law enforcement is pulling out within the next Heislerian month. Anyone who stays will have no help but themselves." None of the three Board members felt the need to inform UU or Qerl'ashp of the identities of a few of the rebels found dead in or around the capitol palace. The two soldiers did not recognize the names of Rocash or Aetreph outside of the pre-raid briefing, and with their hasty exit, leaving clean-up to the Board of Ten's officers, they surely missed the names of other aides or warlords. And right now, neither UU nor Qerl'ashp cared about the identities of the dead; they were simply pleased the goons met their deaths.

"Now scientists are saying we have less than a Heislerian year before Kirkzen goes supernova," Bingus Jam added.

"Supernova? Nova?" Qerl'ashp expressed a lack of discernment about the two words.

"It's literally a 'supernova,' but no one says that, for some reason," Bingus Jam said.

Pracen stared at Julie, who sat at another table, alone with Alana. That the two females carried on an intensely deep and personal conversation could not be missed. "Where is that one from? She looks odd."

UU laughed. "She's a mutant Rojani. An albino, sort of." UU kept a straight face. "No scales. No webbed digits. An outcast among her own kind."

"Where did you find her?" Pracen's curiosity did not abate.

"Oh, a long way away." UU flashed a smile which sent a message the subject was closed by his new topic of interest. "I'm sure Kreeg will leave today. The rest of us will sleep off tonight's drinks." He lifted his glass for a moment.

UU glanced toward Alana and Julie. Laughter and smiles evaded the two. They drank, but not in victory.

"Before that star explodes, the UU Gang—or at least what's left of it—will settle in the other Quadrants." The colonel spoke as he stared, unaware to whom he was speaking or even whether anyone listened. "We will decide later, but I'm sure we'll disband. Our day has come and gone. There's no need to look back at these days as glorious." He paused in thought. "We've lost too much to celebrate. We've done some things we'll regret when we're alone or trying to sleep. The ghosts will haunt us forever." UU snapped out of his mini-trance and looked at each occupant at his table—first at his newfound friend and captain of the Andalian Insertion Force, then at the leader of the Board of Ten, whom he had begrudgingly learned to trust, then at the two officials he struggled to tolerate. "We will leave this quadrant victors and losers, saviors and killers. But, we'll walk away with our heads high, until some random creature decides he wants infamy by killing one of the heroes who fought in the final days of the Nova Quadrant."

Qerl'ashp lifted his small glass and clanked it against UU's, who reciprocated their second toast. "To the Nova Quadrant!" Qerl'ashp called out. The five lifted their glasses upward and repeated in unison, "To the Nova Quadrant!"

UU smiled and added one final thought before taking another drink. "And may it disappear from the galaxy with a bang!"

. . .

Kreeg's fighter craft landed on Rojan's second moon as his wife and daughter, Rokila and Rekil, rushed toward the ship to greet him. Kreeg would learn on the uncomfortable flight to the transport station—uncomfortable because the fighter craft was not built for a family of three—just how close he had come to losing them when Weektu's enforcers nearly discovered them. If not for the tenacious commitment to protect innocent life exhibited by the adherents to the peculiar religious order, Kreeg's small family would not have survived.

. . .

Julie followed close behind as UU led the way up the stairs to her main basement. With the lights off, Julie stepped around the colonel and instinctively found a switch. She sighed, thrust her hands in her jeans, and announced with a nervous voice, "Well, I guess this is it."

"This is what?" UU looked puzzled, unfamiliar with the expression.

"This is goodbye, silly." She laughed as she stepped forward.

"It is," UU nodded.

Julie thrust her arms around UU as far as she could. His size made a complete hug impossible. "Goodbye, Untas Ursulanus." She giggled. "See, I even remembered your name."

UU smiled. "Goodbye, my Earth friend."

They both laughed at UU's ability to remember the planet's name.

"Will I ever see you again?" She stepped back to receive his answer.

"No." UU shook his head. "Once the nova explodes, either the portal will seal or you will step into a void and die in the vacuum of deep space. The radiation from the nova will be around for eons, and you would step into nothingness either way."

Julie nodded her head. "Okay. Then I'll make sure not to go back."

"Oh! No! Don't do that." UU smiled before adding. "I go now."

A tear slid down Julie's right check. "I will miss you." She paused. "And Rick."

UU smiled, turned, and disappeared into the second basement. The thought to turn around and give one last look to his friend never occurred to him.

Julie did not move for over a minute, when she was sure the large creature from another part of the galaxy had returned home, to his world—his "known universe." She broke down and cried as she found a chair to sit on.

After several minutes of crying, she looked up to see something on the floor, near the entrance to the second basement. She walked over, picked it off the floor, and understood. Without her seeing it, UU had dropped Rick's red headband, leaving a memento for the earthling to cherish forever.

Acknowledgments

Brothers Mick and Jamie Buttress, my cousins whom I have known since I was four years old, have been a tremendous help to me, including reading this story before it was released. Their knowledge and opinions were very helpful in ensuring this became a quality novel.

Brandie "Bren" Postell did a great job editing my novel and I appreciated her meticulous approach. Any errors in this book are mine.

Artist and painter Melinda Patrick continues making me look good, having created every book cover of mine. I am forever in her debt as she continues to host my website, create my covers, and help me to get my novels published.

There's a song which says 'don't fall in love with a dreamer,' but Mindy did. I spend a lot of my time dragging those dreams and ideas out of my head and into a computer. Her patience is amazing.

Mick, you wanted a series — this is Book One of a sci-fi series.

About the Author

Sci-fi and psychological thriller author Brian W. Peterson loves a good story and interesting, complex characters. No matter the genre, Brian is interested in entertaining his readers, nothing more. Born in Kansas City, his characters often reflect Midwestern sensibilities based on people he has known and people we all have known at some points in our lives.

You can follow Brian on social media or email him. As you read this, he is working on the next novel, also set in The Nova Quadrant.

Website   : WrittenByBWP.com

Twitter   : @WrittenByBWP

Facebook   : Facebook.com/WrittenByBWP

Email   : WrittenByBWP@gmail.com